W9-ABE-347

SOJOURN IN A STRANGE LAND

SOJOURN IN A STRANGE LAND

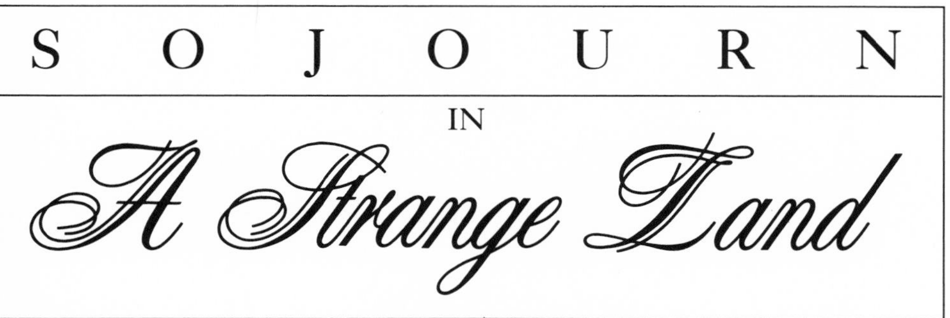

BY STUART HALPINE

First Edition

DESIRE BOOKS, NEW MILFORD, CONNECTICUT 06776

DESIRE BOOKS
New Milford, Connecticut 06776

Designed by Kathleen Hohl-Phillips

Manufactured in the United States of America

Library of Congress catalog Card Number 94-72708

Stuart Halpine
Sojourn In a Strange Land

Publisher's Cataloging in Publication
(Prepared by Quality Books Inc.)

Halpine, Stuart.
Sojourn in a strange land / Stuart Halpine.
p. cm.
ISBN 0-9642452-0-5

1. New England – History – Fiction. I. Title.
PS3558.A3775S65 1994 813.54
QBI94-1558

First Edition 1994

ISBN 0-9642452-0-5

To Mimi

In prayer you call upon a Father who judges each one justly, on the basis of his actions. Since this is true, conduct yourselves reverently during your sojourn in a strange land.

FROM THE FIRST LETTER OF PETER, 1/17–21

CHAPTER ONE

1818

AS BRENDAN MCCAULEY turned off of East Broadway into the squalor of the Five Points district, his late afternoon reveries were blasted by a gang of young toughs who suddenly swarmed over him. Before he knew what was happening, they struck him in the face, on the head, and all over his body even as he struggled to comprehend what was going on. As they beat him, they hurled insults at him.

Your mother is a whore, your sister is a whore.

The words cut into his head as sorely as their fists. Brendan fought back ferociously. He smashed his left fist into the nose of the closest taunter and saw the crimson spurt.

The blows and slashing words stepped up. You bastard, you pretend you're better'n us, you with your fairy airs.

He staggered the attacker who said it with a right to the jaw, but the onslaught only grew fiercer.

You're shit; you're the son of a whore and brother of a whore.

The new insult goaded Brendan. He kicked the lad who said it in the groin with all the force he could muster. But even as this youth dropped from the ranks of the attackers, the rest pressed him even harder. The insults came faster than he could possibly respond with his fists and feet.

All your larnin makes no nevermind; you're still the son of a whore.

You're the lowest shit in Five Points because you and your family are fakes.

Even as the terrible words registered, the tempo of hardened fists striking his face and head stepped up. Others pumped repeatedly into his belly. One youth hit him again and again over the shoulders and in the back with a club. In a short time his face was streaming blood, his jacket and shirt ripped nearly away.

We are going to beat your ass until you admit you're the son of a whore.

Brendan had fought this neighborhood gang many times and had always managed to either beat them off or escape. But this afternoon their fury and numbers exceeded that of any time before. The taunts about his mother and his sister were new; they spewed out of the mouths of the attackers like battle cries that pumped them into an unparalleled frenzy. Before long they knocked Brendan to the ground. They rained kicks and blows from the club on him in spite of his struggles to evade them and regain his feet. They spat on him and jeered as he tried to strike out or seize the nearest foot.

Finally as he sunk, defenseless, into a huddled shape, unable to resist or evade the torrent of blows, a police whistle sounded. A policeman with a high helmet ran to the scene, brandishing his billy. Within seconds the hoodlums ceased the attack and ran, all in different directions, and disappeared into the stinking alleys on all sides.

Brendan slowly rose to his knees and shook his head groggily. The policeman helped him rise unsteadily to his feet.

Mighty glad to see you, Officer Torrance.

Brendan! Are you all right? That spawn of hell was certainly working you over. Still got all of your teeth? Anything broken? What started it this time?

Brendan tried to smile through the blood. Nothing wrong that a good soaking and a night's sleep won't cure. I don't know what got into them. They caught me by surprise just as I started up Anthony Street. I didn't even see them coming.

Officer Torrance saw a lot of incidents like these. No one expected him to make a big thing of it as long as nobody was seriously injured.

Get home and clean yourself up, he said. Next time remember it's no sin to run when that many comes after you.

Brendan nodded, picked up his battered books, and resumed his way on Anthony Street.

The odors marked the boundary of Five Points more clearly than the ramshackle buildings, the prevalence of illegal drinking establishments, the shabbiness and hopeless faces of the inhabitants. The smells of decaying wood, urine and feces, rotting food, the dregs from stale beer and spilled whiskey, the pheremones from unwashed bodies, told Brendan he was almost home. The stink was his welcome each evening when he returned from his classes in the better part of the city. He was aware he lived in a slum, but it didn't bother him; he had lived there all the sixteen years of his life. The stench was the subconscious signal for him to put aside his thoughts about Latin conjugations, French verbs, logarithms and algebraic equations which had occupied him since early morning, and to harbor pleasant thoughts about food, contacts with his friends and conversations with his mother and sister. Because he was a conscientious student, he would study for at least two hours after supper. He usually fell asleep on his bed in his nightshirt, reading his next day assignments. He recalled that there had been some hubub in the kitchen last night as he was dropping off, too tired to ask about the strange voices he dimly heard.

He walked west on to Anthony Street and continued to the subdivided wooden frame house which in more prosperous times, forty or more years before, had been the home of a merchant. He walked around to the door of the back apartment on the ground floor. As he entered, the wood stove in the kitchen provided welcome warmth from the spring chill outside and an oil lamp cast a soft light against the evening gloom. It felt good, as his cuts and bruises had begun to pain him. He dropped his books in a chair.

Usually he called out *Bon soir, chère Maman. Bon soir, chère Agnes*, but tonight it wouldn't come out. Instead he said, not very loudly, Hello Mom.

Normally he liked to use snatches of French with his mother and sister to show how he was progressing in fluency. His mother, who spoke the language, humored him, but his sister, who had studied it only in passing, disliked hearing it. She thought wrongly that it was an affectation. Now there was no response from either.

Brendan made the wide chestnut boards creak as he opened the door and passed into the tiny room beyond, which served both as a sitting room and dining space. The original walls still showed varnished, if marred and chipped, wainscoating. The other walls that had created the later, smaller rooms were of ordinary pine boards which the carpenter had not devoted many pains to installing. The house was one of dozens that had been bought and divided into apartments after the Revolution by John R. Livingston, brother of Robert R. Livingston, a signer of the Declaration of Independence. John Livingston bought so much property on lower Manhattan that he was one of the city's leading landlords. One who was not fussy about who lived in his properties as long as they produced a good return.

His mother, Catherine, and sister, Agnes, were intent on a conversation and had not heard him enter. When they finally saw him, they gasped and sprang to their feet.

Oh Brendan! Oh my God, what has happened to you. Oh,

my poor boy, are you hurt badly?

He's covered with blood, his sister exclaimed. Look at his clothes.

I'm not hurt badly, Brendan said. Just sore from the bruises. Let me wash up and I won't look so badly.

As his mother led him to the kitchen, he explained to her what had happened. It was the usual gang. Then proudly, I took out a couple of them but they were too many for me. Then Officer Torrance came up and drove them away.

Those hellions should be put away. They are a menace to all civilized persons. Torrance must know who they are, why doesn't he take action against them? What brought it up this time?

I don't know. They surprised me as I turned off of East Broadway. They were shouting awful things about you and Agnes.

Why am I talking like this when you're in this condition? Take off those bloody clothes and come over to the sink so I can wash you. She pumped some water into a basin and took a wash cloth to wipe away the blood on his face.

Then she resumed her questioning. What awful things were they saying about us?

It's best unsaid.

His mother faltered. You better tell me. I should know.

He was too tired to argue. They said you and Agnes were whores. Immediately Brendan was horrified that he had said it.

Agnes froze. The mother turned deadly pale, but looked steadily at Brendan for a long moment. It was bound to come out, she said softly. We knew we would have to tell you. We should have told you before you ran into it on the street. Poor Brendan. What the hoodlums shouted at you is true.

No, it can't be. Then it sunk in. So that's why you are all dolled up. So that's why I heard all that shuffling around out here last night. Oh, mother, how could you? And Agnes?

Agnes clutched her handkerchief and tears formed in her eyes.

The mother with difficulty retained her composure.

I can't believe it, Brendan continued. How could you do such a thing? That's so out of character for you both. What would poor Father say?

This struck a spark in the mother. Lad, let me tell you a few facts about this life on earth. And these are not going to be facts that your father would tell you even if he was alive. You must know that we've never had much money. Why would we live in such a benighted place as Five Points if we had a choice? Your father never had anything. After the way the affair in '98 turned out, it took the heart right out of him. He couldn't get over the thought of poor Wolfe Tone bleeding to death in his cell, and all his friends that died. To say nothing of our beloved Ireland still ground under the English boot after all that suffering. Actually I think he was ashamed he was alive. When he got to this country he couldn't cope. He was admitted to the New York Bar after a bit but his practice was very limited. He just barely eked out a living for us tutoring. There were no savings when he died. You know Agnes and I tried to make a living sewing. That was a joke; every delicate young thing, every genteel widow was trying to do the same thing. What else was there? There are no jobs for women in this city, not even in this country. We tried. We did indeed, both Agnes and I.

Brendan was righteous and spouted his religious training. That's no excuse. What you're doing is against the Sixth Commandment. It's a mortal sin every time you fornicate with a man. You both have always been practicing Catholics. You will lose your immortal souls. How can you do such a thing, over and over again.

Agnes sneered. You're still a virgin. What do you know

about it?

The mother intervened. Don't hurt him, Agnes. He's a good lad. Then she turned back to Brendan. Poor people starve to death every day, right in this city. I don't want anyone in my family to be among them. If you want to talk about commandments, let me tell you this city, perhaps most of this world, is controlled by men who constantly violate the Tenth Commandment. They not only covet the goods of others, but they scheme to get them, they refuse to pay women enough for honest work so that they can live decently. When Mary Williams lost her husband, both she and her daughter had to do exactly what Agnes and I are doing. There's many of us turning to this way of life among the people who have recently arrived in this country. Agnes and I can earn five dollars a night with the men. The women who work as maids and cleaners are lucky if they get forty cents a day. Because Agnes was a virgin she earned ten dollars with her first man, and even two or three times after that. When you reflect that she would have to work a year to earn thirty-five dollars as a chambermaid, who would not give up the maidenhead for the money? As for the church, we who grew up in the old country know very well that kings, the nobility and the rich openly flaunt their mistresses, have children by them, and no pope, no cardinal, no bishop ever deigns to raise a voice against it. The mistresses of Louis XIV are still famous in Europe. Who there hasn't heard of Louise de la Vallière, or Madame de Montespan or the Marquise de Maintenon? Louis XV had Madame du Barry. Charles II had Louise de Keroualle. We're just as Catholic as those noble tarts, let me tell you. And Brendan lad, you might as well know, not only are Agnes and I feeding you, but you couldn't continue your classes without us. Yes, we're whoring, if you like. How else do we eat?

Brendan was crushed. He tried to speak, but he was too shaken. Finally he said: This hurts more than the beating.

His mother took pity on him and moved to put an arm around him.

I know this is a a terrible shock for you. I would have done anything to spare you this, and Agnes too. The way of the world is hard, hard, hard for those of us without money. If we are going to exist, the alternatives are indeed limited. You are our only hope. You must continue with your schooling and become a lawyer like your father. Only then can we live as all our instincts and our faith tell us we should. Will you do that for us lad?

Brendan, as he felt the touch of his mother's arm, made an effort of the will not to shrink from her. With how many men each night did she falsely touch?

I don't know, mom. I can't say now. It's so overwhelming. I don't know what I think. Please give me some time. I know you and Agnes are trying to sacrifice yourselves for me. You shouldn't have to do this. I must seem selfish. But it seems so monstruous. Let me go.

* * *

Brendan arose even earlier than usual the next morning. He had thought he wouldn't sleep but after a couple of hours of fitful turning, he had dropped off. Within a few seconds of waking, the terrible session with his mother and Agnes came back to him. Then he realized how sore he was from the beating. He winced with every move. But he knew the soreness would soon leave his young body; he would be left with the other hurt. The only other similar wrench he had ever experienced had been his father's death the year before. But then the family had been united in its sorrow. He had not been confronted with a choice, it had simply been a matter of enduring and letting the grief ebb away, day by day.

Now he had to make a choice. He could stay as his mother asked and let her and his sister lay with men to support him and further his education, or he could go away, go anywhere. All his feeling rejected staying even though rationally it made a good deal of sense. It was too callous to be an accessory to an immoral and reprehensible way of life. Yet he knew his mother and his sister were not evil, they were both good women. He knew that they would have to continue to prostitute themselves to earn their own livings, but at least the responsibility would not be his. If he remained here, he would be, in effect, a kept child, trying constantly to overlook the procession of rank and fetid males into the little rooms next to his. Even if he worked, the income would be derisory. What could he, a lad of sixteen, earn? He with no trade and his unfinished schooling. He couldn't stay.

But where to go? He had never been anywhere outside of the Manhattan suburbs, really only on picnic excursions up above Washington Square. He had never been on a ship and had unfavorable impressions of them from the tales his parents had told of their transatlantic crossing. He knew some men who had gone to the west, to the wilds of Ohio and Indiana, but the solitary life of a small wilderness farmer had no appeal for him. He recalled that his mother had a brother in another state with an Indian name, Connecticut, as he remembered. As nearly as he could recall, the settlement was called Danbury. He had never met the man and had not heard of him in recent years, but it seemed like a possibility. Perhaps this uncle could help him find a job. He was sixteen, taller than most boys, even if somewhat slim. He was in good health and had a better education than most of the lads he knew, certainly much better than any of the Five Points boys, whose learning tended to be concentrated on street skills.

He sat at the kitchen table and, in the faint morning light coming through the window, penciled a note to his mother.

Dearest Mom,

I think you know I have to go. I want to stay with you

and Agnes very much, but I'm not able to do it. I wish I could complete my education and take care of you both. Sometime in the future I hope I can. Meanwhile I hope God will bless and protect you both. All my love.

Brendan

CHAPTER TWO

EARLY IN THE AFERNOON on the fourth day since his departure from Five Points, Brendan saw Danbury before him. He was on a knoll on the west side of the town with the sun at his back, so he could see its features clearly. What appeared to be a main street ran north and south through the settlement, intersected by several lateral ways including the one on which he was walking. In Ridgefield, where he had spent the night before in a barn in back of a tavern, a stable hand told him Danbury was a large town; he said it had nearly four-thousand people. Compared with New York, it was insignificant; it didn't even have as many people as Five Points. Neither did it come up to Norwalk where he had stayed two nights ago, but then Norwalk was a port and he knew the coastal strip was more thickly settled because of the ease of marine travel. He mused what life in Danbury might be like. It must be healthier than New York with its slums like Five Points, but it could be a lot duller. He suspected that he might miss the hubbub of the city and the diversity it offered. He knew he did miss his mother and his sister. His thoughts turned to them often as he swung along the dirt roads; he wished he had someone to talk to about them. Never in his life had he spent so many hours without another human being to exchange words with.

He walked downhill toward the center. There were now other people on the street and there were more as he neared the center. On his right were white two-story homes with windows up and down symetrically balanced on both sides of the central doorway. One of them had a small shop alongside to make hats. Another had a tannery in the rear. A third had a small scale fuller's shop to spin wool and flax and weave it into fabric. On the other side of the street was a merchant's house, a tavern housed in a substantial brick building, a cobbler's shop, a brick store, a saddlemaker's, and another tavern.

The people looked busy and preoccupied; no one paid any attention to him. He wandered along the main street, observing the people and the activity. There was a silversmith and a carriage shop. Down a sidestreet to the east he spotted a livery stable. He headed for it. He had found them a helpful refuge during his days on the road. Not only was a stable a good place to sleep, he had also been offered bread and salt pork.

He headed for a man seated on an empty keg alongside the barn door. Howdy, he said.

The sitter looked him up and down, spat a stream of tobacco juice in the dirt. Where you from?

I just came up from Norwalk. I'm going to visit my uncle here.

You don't talk like a feller from around here. You don't even sound like Norwalk. I been there. Who's your uncle?

Peter O'Brien. Do you know where he lives?

Say, you're Irish ain't you. I thought you sounded queer. We don't take much to foreigners around here. Why did you leave your own country? What the hell are you doing around here?

Brendan walked away. No sense in getting in a scrape the first thing. Nevertheless the anger seethed within him.

He doubled back to the main street and walked along until he cooled. He came to a general store. He decided to try again.

He mounted the wooden stoop and went up to a clerk behind the counter.

A loaf of bread, please.

The clerk glanced at him, then reached for a loaf nearby. That'll be five cents.

Brendan paid him, then asked if he knew where Peter O'Brien lived.

Hell, we've only got one Irishman in town that I know of. That must be him. Another older man behind the counter agreed. Ayah, that's him.

Well, he lives out on Stony Hill. He has quite a palace out there. He and the other man behind the counter laughed. Just go out White Street and keep going on the road to Newtown. It's probably four or five miles out there. You can't miss it. The two men looked at each other and laughed again.

Brendan headed out the door. The clerk turned to the older man. Looks like we got two Irishmen in town now.

What could he expect? Plainly attitudes here were not like Five Points. No one cared there where anyone else came from. No one even cared what color a person was. African-Americans mingled with French, Dutch, German and English stock, both in daily contact and in the whorehouses at night. He remembered that his father had told him that a man named Jackson had brought three thousand women, half white and half black, from Britain and the West Indies at the time of the Revolution and set them up as prostitutes on the north side of the city. They were called Jackson Whites and Jackson Blacks. Not much chance of anything like that happening in this Yankee town. Thinking of this made him smile. Feeling a little better, he sought out White Street.

A mile out of town he found a dry spot, sat down and slowly ate a chunk of the bread. It was stale. The clerk had seen him coming. He continued on the Newtown Road to the east. He wondered how he would find Peter's house.

He needn't have concerned himself. An hour further along as he headed up a small hill, he saw a structure in the distance. It's nature wasn't clear at first. It seemed to thrust itself out of the ground like an irregular rock formation. When he got closer it appeared to be one with its stony surroundings. But it was man-made, constructed of stones, clay, sod, tree limbs and weathered boards. Its most distinctive feature was a barrel sitting on the roof. Brendan knew at once that it was his uncle's home. Now he knew why the men in the store had laughed when they called it a palace. He was terribly depressed. Had his uncle come all the way from New York to live in a hovel like this?

He turned off the road and approached the hut. At first he thought that perhaps he had been mistaken, there seemed to be no one around, perhaps it wasn't really a habitation. But as his heavy shoes ground against the small stones underfoot, a face appeared in a gap in the wall. It wasn't Peter, it wasn't a man. It was a woman in a poke bonnet. She smiled and beckoned for him to advance.

You looking for Pete?

Yes, is he in? He studied the smiling face. It hit him that she was simple.

Come right in. He's over at the next farm helping out. But he will be back in an hour or so. If you've walked all the way here from town to see him, you might just as well come along in and wait for him. Her voice had an indistinct quality just as that of the men back in the general store; the vowels and consonants were not sharp and clear. Worse, there was an annoying whine to it.

Brendan couldn't think what else to do; besides that the woman was so energetically ingratiating. He walked up the path, through the rough doorway.

Inside he glanced around. The interior was a single room

with a dirt floor. Under the barrel was a raised stone platform, hollow in the center, where coals still glowed from a fire. Iron pots and pans sat on the stone edge. So, he thought, the barrel is a chimney. Elsewhere in the room were two chairs and a table, all made from sections of oak saplings and old boards. There was a homemade set of shelves and three beds, also made of poles and saplings with criscrossed ropes holding up mattresses.

Brendan approached the woman and held out his hand. I'm Brendan McCauley. Peter is my uncle, my mother's brother.

She took his hand in her own, hard and work-worn as a man's. Land A'mighty. You don't mean it. Pete will be more than pleased to see you. I'm Pete's wife, Thankful. Here, sit down. She moved a chair to accommodate him.

The chair was surprisingly comfortable. He settled back. I haven't sat in a chair for four days, he said. It sure seems good.

Where are you coming from?

New York City. I was born there. I lived in the Five Points with my mother and my sister. My Dad died about a year ago.

Oh you poor thing. How hard it must be for the three of you. How did you come? Did you take the stage? Don't tell me you walked all that way. She saw his affirmative nod. That's a terrible long way. You must be worn out. I bet you haven't had much to eat in all that time, either. Let me get you something to hold you until supper.

Thankful moved to the fire. She peeled a potato, cut it up into a frying pan, and threw in a chunk of salt pork. She added some sticks of firewood from a stack near the fire and set the frying pan on top of them.

While these are heating up, why don't you lay down on that bed over there and rest yourself. I'll give you a quilt. It's getting on to warm outside but the sun don't get inside here much.

Brendan stretched out on one of the beds and was surprised how comfortable the mattress stuffed with corn shucks was.

Within five minutes he was asleep. Thankful shrugged, took the frying pan off the fire.

When he awoke, he was confused momentarily where he was. He was aware of the subdued hum of a whispered conversation. It was dusk. He was warm and comfortable for the first time since he had left Five Points. He luxuriated in the feeling for a few moments, then realized where he was. He sat up and swung his feet on to the bare dirt.

Mother of God. Himself is awake now. What a fine broth of a lad he is. The words came from a lanky man standing near the fire.

Brendan knew this must be his Uncle Peter. He rose and Peter threw his arms around him. Oh lad, you don't know how glad I am to see you. The last time I saw you, you were a little bugger only halfway up my leg. Now you're taller than I am and at least an axe handle through the shoulders. I've been looking at these mutton faced Yankees so long, I can't tell you how good it is to see a real Irish face. God be praised, it's good to see you. I'm sorry about your poor father, God rest his soul. How is your mother doing, and your angel sister?

This was the first time Brendan had to face this question. Quickly he answered that they were hard pressed, but getting by. They were in good health. He had decided to strike out on his own so as not to be a burden to them with his schooling and he hoped to be able before long to help them a little.

You're right, lad. It's a dreadful burden that they have. It's almighty hard for a woman to sustain a household on her own. But you've come in the wrong direction. People have been leaving Connecticut, all of New England in fact, for years. Folks are going west to get a fresh start. What's more, these Yankees don't like foreigners. Grubbing a living from these hills is so hard, they don't want anyone else coming in to take some of their share. They do their best to run you out. A foreigner can't even own land in Connecticut without permission of the General Court. I would have left if they'd been nice to me, but as it is, I'm too stubborn an old bastard to let them get the best of me. I would never have made it this far if it weren't for Thankful. Her family thought she had surely gone to the devil when she married an Irish Catholic. Which is pretty comical when you realize I haven't seen the inside of a church in years. I don't know if there is a Catholic church in all of Connecticut. As far as I know, I'm the only one of the Faith in western Connecticut.

Thankful placed three earthen dishes on the table, moved one chair next to it. Bring your chairs on over here and have a little supper, she said. The men did as they were bidden and Thankful served them fried potatoes and salt pork. Brendan put the remainder of his loaf of bread on the table.

This is a little stale, but if you don't mind, help yourself.

We'll put a little grease from the spider on it, and it'll go down good, Peter said. We don't waste nothing around here. Thankful makes our bread, but we can have that for dessert. We can give you a little spring water to clear that salt out of your system.

Ten minutes later, Thankful cleared off the table and disappeared outside.

Peter went to a shelf and pulled down a brown ceramic jug with a corn cob for a stopper. I was just teasing you about drinking water, he said. I don't want to lead you astray, but it strikes me that anybody who can walk here from Five Points in four days can relish a drop or two of the house speciality. It's made from our own corn. He poured two generous slugs into two earthen cups.

The two settled back in the chairs. Tell me about your schooling, Peter demanded.

I finished primary school in the city. Then my father sent me to a tutor. I studied Latin, French, English literature, world history and geography, and mathematics, including algebra and geometry. I would have continued with trigonometry, calculus and Greek but the money was running out. Dad wanted me to go to the university and be a lawyer.

So he would. You know, of course that he himself went to Trinity College and was called to the Dublin bar. Then he got involved in the struggle with the United Irishmen, right from the beginning in November, 1791. But I suppose he told you all about it many a time.

No, he never wanted to talk about Ireland. Tell me about it.

I only got as far as you are now in my studies. Then I joined the Defenders because I liked the idea of bringing back the Stuarts. For me they had romance. The Defenders weren't quite as theoretical as the Society of United Irishmen, but at the end there wasn't much difference; we were all in it together. But then my youth was gone and it was too late to think about Trinity. Your father, though, was a close associate of Wolfe Tone, one of the founders of the United Irishmen, who was also a lawyer out of Trinity. He was captivated by Tone, who was not only brilliant and clever, but had a sunny personality and a wonderful sense of humor. That's not to say he was not a very tough lad, and completely dedicated to the revolution. For it was a revolution, you know, one that drew much of its inspiration from the one over here just a few years before. Then the wars on the continent speeded up the tempo and all of Ireland, even in the north and among the Protestant Ascendency, knew something had to be done. Pitt in England wanted to emancipate the Catholics but crazy old George III would have none of it.

As in this country, the Revolutionary movement was largely middle-class. The main movers were from the professional and business class, men who felt deeply that the English and the Ascendency were marginalizing not only them, but the major productive forces in the country.

We were from Mayo and Catholics, but Tone was a Protestant, or maybe a Deist. He tried to keep religion in the background because he thought Catholicism was a dying superstition that would disappear with education. In spite of this, he was organizing secretary of the Catholic Committee, a forerunner of the United Irishmen, in 1791. That was a year after he wrote his first pamphlet. It was also the year your father met my sister. You could see from the start that they were heading for the altar; both families liked the match. You can imagine how frenzied life was for your father as he courted Catherine, worked at his law practice, and helped Tone to plan a revolution.

What were you and my mother doing in Dublin?

I had planned to go to the university there, and in any case it was where the opportunities were, including marital. There was nothing in Mayo for anyone who didn't want to be a farmer. So what am I now? He winced.

Peter rose and poured from the jug into both of their glasses again. This will guarantee that you sleep well tonight just in case walking twenty miles wouldn't do it for you, he said. Then he put the jug back on the shelf, sat down, and resumed his narrative.

Tone had some successes. The movement grew all over Ireland. Spurred by this, the Irish parliament in 1793 gave the franchise to Catholics. But Tone was not satisfied and entered into negotiations with the French Directory. The English found out about this and Tone fled to the United States and from here went back to France. He persuaded the French to undertake an invasion of Ireland in December, 1796, with Tone himself as adjutant general. Storms off the Irish coast frustrated a landing, sank many ships, and forced the surviving vessels to return to France. This was the golden opportunity which was lost. If the landing at Bantry Bay had been accomplished, there would have been 15,000 battle tested French troops opposed by only 11,000 militia defenders. What's more, it's certain that the Irish people would have risen to aid Tone and the French.

Peter paused and stared at the fire a few moments, then he went on.

Meanwhile, the United Irishmen reorganized and became ever more militant. The Defenders were right with them but in Ulster the Orange Order developed and drew off the people who were devoted to the Ascendency. Habeas corpus was suspended in October of 1796 and tension grew.

In May, 1798 a spontaneous revolt broke out on a diagonal axis stretching from Wexford and Wicklow in the east to Sligo and Mayo in the northwest. The rebels, your father and I among them, took Enniscorthy, the capital of Wexford, and started for Dublin. British troops intercepted us and routed our force at Vinegar Hill in June. There were terrible atrocities on both sides. Awful to see; I still have nightmares about that time twenty years later. Thirty-thousand men died in that and subsequent fighting. Those that could, fled, and I could. Your father was captured.

In August, another, smaller French expedition set out with Tone and attempted a landing but was defeated and Tone captured. He escaped the noose by cutting his own throat right in his cell. More rebels were slaughtered in County Longford and the British were mopping up until 1801.

Catherine and I managed to get a ship to France in July. Your father faced one of the many courts martial which tried more than 600 persons. He was one of the lucky ones who were acquitted or not prosecuted. But 231 were executed and twelve, only a dozen, were imprisoned.

Your father and mother were married in France and came to this country in 1800. You were born two years later. That was the end of our family's involvement in Ireland, but I understand that even today there is an organized underground there, especially among the country people. Some of the old United Irishmen are still keeping their organization together. God knows when it will all end.

Peter noticed that Brendan was beginning to nod. I'm sorry I talked so long. That's what happens when you get an Irishman going. Tomorrow we'll face what you're going to do. For now, see if you can make it to that bed over there. And a good night to you. May you have pleasant dreams.

CHAPTER THREE

BRENDAN TOOK THANKFUL'S HANDS in his own and thanked her for all of her kindnesses. I'm happy my uncle has such a good wife, he said. Then Peter walked out the door with him and down to the main road.

I know this kind of a house must have been a shock to you, Peter said. But I'm here for the long haul. When I build a real house it's going to be on land I can call my own. Some day I hope you and, who knows, your young wife, can spend some time with us in that kind of house.

Brendan was moved. He tried to shake his uncle's hand in farewell, but Peter dodged the hand and threw his arms around Brendan in a tight hug.

May God bless you, lad. It's been good to see you, so damned good. You've got a lot of guts to take off on your own like this. Remember not to take any shit from these Yankees. God didn't give this country to them, even though they think He did. We look forward to seeing you on your way back.

Brendan nodded. Thank you for taking me in for so many days. Nothing makes you appreciate family like a few days on the road. I'll see you on the way back.

He headed down the knoll to the road and turned east, away from Danbury. He inhaled deeply several times and tried not to think about about his uncle's primitive existence, his mother and sister back in Five Points, or his future. He felt strong and rested, he no longer felt the bruises from his beating, and he was more confident than when he set out from New York. The sun was shining; each day was becoming warmer. He could see the countryside responding to the spring.

A couple of miles further along, he turned left off the Newtown road which continued to the right. Peter had told him this was the road to Brookfield Center. The road gradually climbed diagonally up a ridge running north and south. As the elevation increased, Brendan was able to look to his left over a wide alluvial plain to the west. It's main feature was the Still River, geologically ancient, a meandering stream running mainly northward, but full of ox-bows, loops and turns. On each side of it for miles were bogs and swamps. He could see herds of white tail deer browsing among the brush and other small game as he went along. Overhead were varieties of birds he had never seen before. The area seemed to be teeming with wildlife. But unlike his earlier route to Danbury, he saw few people. During the first two hours, in fact, he saw no other traveler on the road; the only people he saw were residents of farm houses every half mile or so. In areas with frequent outcroppings of ledge where the fields were strewn with boulders, rocks or had cobbley soil, there were no farmhouses, no human presence. As he passed the infrequent farmsteads, occasionally a dog would charge furiously at him, growling and barking. In his first days on the road he had learned that a stout stick picked up along the way was an effective defense. Most dogs ran when he brandished it; a few needed a clout on the head before they skulked off. Sometimes a farmer or his son would sic the dog on him. He was angry at first but then realized they were afraid of him. Since the trade embargo during the war, the roads were trodden by many hungry, jobless men, sometimes desperate, who knew the farmers were eking out borderline existences, but always had food on the premises. So he just swung his stick and moved onward.

About noon he reached Brookfield Center. It was just a cluster of the usual post-and-beam, clapboarded structures he had seen in lower Fairfield County. Here, as in other villages, the two or three best homes belonged to the Congregational minister, the richest merchant and perhaps a lawyer or leading official. Most were plain and solid, a few had dentils under the eaves and other fancy touches. He stopped at the general store in the center and bought another loaf of bread. He rested nearby where the south face of a large rock formation was warmed by the midday sun. No one spoke to him, but he could see people in the store and nearby houses keeping an eye on him.

In the early afternoon he headed north on what he learned was Long Meadow Hill. Before long the houses became as widely distant as they had on leaving Stony Hill. Now instead of Still River to the west which was obscured by the intervening foothills, he could occasionally catch a glimpse of the Housatonic River and its much narrower valley to the east. The temperature rose steadily as the day wore on and he became fascinated with the scenery. Red maples still held clusters of maroon flowers, although fragments of these were being carried off by the breeze. The buds of sugar maples were bursting open, revealing the most delicate of green traceries formed by the still immature new leaves. The emerging buds of the oaks had a touch of red and resembled squirrel ears. The buds of hickories, beeches, and black cherries were shedding the hard shells that had protected them through the winter. Most entrancing of all were wisps of white on angular small trees and bushes, the flowers of the shadblow. Interspersed among these were the white pines and hemlocks whose needles had provided the only touch of arboreal color during the long season of dormancy of the hardwoods. Brendan was entranced by the spectacle. There had been no trees in Five Points and few in the remainder of lower Manhattan. He had never before contemplated trees as he was doing now, nor had he ever had any occasion to realize their beauty.

In time he reached an intersection with a crude sign reading Ironworks along with an arrow to the west. Peter had told him that Brookfield had several hamlets, none of them containing more than a few inhabitants. This was the first that indicated anything more than farming was being conducted. He continued northward along the dirt road which hugged the top of the ridge between the two valleys. The rolling meadows were more and more giving way to sharper features and rocky outcroppings. The slope to the right towards the Housatonic became steeper and more rugged. In late afternoon he became aware of other persons on the road ahead of him and others behind him, all like him, headed north. He saw that they were coming from the farms and lanes along the route. Eventually, a youth coming out of the dooryard of a farmhouse joined him on the road. They greeted each other laconically.

You headed up to the cove? the newcomer asked.

No, what's at the cove?

The newcomer looked at Brendan more carefully. You're not from around here, are you? The cove is on the Housatonic just below the Leap. This is the time of year when the shad come up the river. The cove is the best place around to catch them. Folks come with their nets and haul them in by the dozens. If you know how to bone them, they're good eating, otherwise you might as well try to eat a porcupine. You can eat 'em fresh or salt 'em and put them away. There's so many, folks give 'em away. I want to pick up a mess to take back to the house.

Can just anyone do this?

Well, actually the Hawley family leased it to different parties in Newtown, New Fairfield and New Milford who are supposed to have the rights to fishing there but nobody pays too much attention to that. Lots of people net shad there every day during the run and even more at night. I never saw any constable or anyone else ever try to stop anyone. There's even Injuns come there to catch shad. The Injuns also catch eels at the falls north of the Leap. The eels attach themselves to the rocks under the falls. The Injuns use torches to find 'em. They use poles with hooks on the end to grab them off the rocks through the sheet of water coming over the falls. Not many white folks bother with the eels though.

The Injuns ever attack the whites?

Naw, they wouldn't dare. There's only a few of them and they're a pretty grubby looking bunch.

I'd like to see one. Never had a chance before. Could you show me the way? My name's Brendan.

Joe Ruggles, said the other. Glad to. Probably most of these fellows you see on the road are bound there. The Brookfield-New Milford town line is just ahead. It's only a couple of miles after that. The shad only run for a couple of weeks. Taste good after a winter of salt pork.

The road was still damp from the thaw, but most of the puddles from the melting snow and frost were gone. Brendan walked in one track worn by wagon wheels, Joe in the other. In the center were tufts of grass just beginning to grow along with emerging weeds. They made good time along Punkin Hill Road, through a wood thick with hemlocks at least a yard in diameter. The road dipped and rose as it wandered northward. After a bit, they could see the Still River valley off to the west again.

That's Lanesville t'other side of Still River, Joe said. Some of the fellows there work at the Iron Works.

Brendan didn't pay much attention because he had his mind on the Indians. In Five Points were people of most of the countries of Europe, blacks from God knows where, Jews and

Lebanese from the middle east and even a few Chinese. But he had never seen an Indian, although people there often talked of them. He didn't say anything more about them to Joe because he didn't want to appear too innocent.

A few hundred yards further on, they crossed a covered bridge over the Housatonic. It had a couple of windows in each side so you could look down at the falls below. The level was still high from the spring freshet, so that the water boiled over the boulders in great arcs of white, twisting and dropping in constantly changing patterns. There was an incessant roar as the wider stream from upriver was squeezed through the narrow gorge, which culminated in the legendary Leap of the Lovers further downstream.

Joe recounted the fable of the Indian princess and her white lover who had plunged to their deaths from a rock outcropping two hundred yards downstream. My dad says its a lot of bullshit, said Joe. There's even different versions like one where only the girl jumps because the white guy is going off in a canoe. Me, I ain't ever seen an Injun girl I would jump over a puddle for.

The men in Lanesville built the first bridge before I was born, but it went out in a flood about five years later. Then the town built this one. All out of twelve-by-twelve oak and chestnut beams the men cut and dressed by hand in the woods near here. The town's had a lot of trouble with bridges. Most of them spanned the river up near the center of town. The original one was the first over the river from Long Island Sound on up. But it was only three years before a spring freshet hit it. The town had so many knocked down they finally had a toll company build one. That's the one that crosses west of the center this very day. Well, let's get on.

They crossed to the east bank and turned up a narrow dirt road up through more giant hemlocks to a point where the Leap was visible. It was a rock outcropping that formed a sort of platform from which one could precariously look down to the roaring torrent nearly a hundred feet below.

You'd have to be pretty damn lovesick to jump off here, Joe said. Brendan fervently agreed and backed away off the rock.

Then they continued down the road which took a sharp turn to the east and which had thank-you-ma'ms every few feet to the bottom so that rain water would not wash out the gravel. Thin wooden poles were nailed to the trees along the outside, not a futile attempt to keep travellers from crashing down to the river below, but to show them the limits of the road.

At the bottom, a narrow valley with a brook in its bed led toward the Housatonic. The brook flowed into a placid pool sheltered by the base of the Leap from the main current of the river. The air was wonderfully fragrant with the essences from shadblow, black birch,and wild cherry.

This is the cove, Joe said.

Already there were several dozen men around. There were teams of horses harnessed to sturdy wagons, a few buggies and saddle horses. But most of the men had come on foot. They had nets with poles on each end and either baskets or gunny sacks in which to carry the shad. No one seemed to be in charge, nor were any constables in evidence. A few bottles of whiskey could be seen, but so far the men were methodical and sober.

In the cold water up to their waists, two men were steadily edging their way to shore, holding the poles on opposite ends of twenty feet of sturdy netting. As they pulled it in, it bowed in the middle with the weight of struggling and tumbling shad. As they reached solid ground, other men filled baskets with the slippery fish. When the men rolled up their net on one of the poles, another pair took over, but this time one of the men pushed a small rowboat into the cove waters and manipulated one end of the net from the boat while his partner held the other pole fast in the sand at the edge of the water. Joe told

Brendan that the ice had broken up in the river and flowed downstream only in the third week of March. This water was only slightly above 40 degrees. So only the pairs without access to a boat or the showoffs waded in the cold water.

Laughing and boisterous, the men who had emerged from the river went back of the crowd, took off their wet clothes, rubbed themselves with towels and put on dry clothing. Then they sat on the back of a wagon and took long pulls from a bottle of whiskey. Others who already had their catch soon joined them.

The others waited their turn and helped with each mess of fish as it was dragged to the shore of the cove. They all knew each other and the community effort not only made the work easier and got it done more expeditiously, but gave a festive air to the effort. Brendan enjoyed the spectacle; he had never seen people cooperate to get a job done like this in the city. He and Joe helped pick the fish out of the nets as the others had done. Some of the teams gave Joe a few of the shad but they looked through Brendan as if he were not there.

I'll give you some afterward, Joe said.

I could use one, Brendan responded, but I couldn't carry more than that.

It was getting dark now, and increasingly difficult to see. As more and more of the men finished their stint with the net, the group of rollickers around the wagons grew and got noisier. Joe and Brendan drew closer to enjoy the repartee. One sturdy youth in their midst began to eye Brendan. He obviously was feeling his liquor.

Who the fuck is this guy? he finally blurted out. Who told you you could come here? What are you doing around here?

Easy, Josh, someone said.

He came with me, Joe said.

I don't give a damn who he came with. He doesn't belong

around here and I'm going to make sure he gits. Josh started toward Brendan, starting to make fists of his work-hardened hands.

The blood rushed to Brendan's head. He was getting sick of Yankees telling him he didn't belong and was not wanted. Josh came on at a rush, head down, fists pumping.

This was a threat Brendan knew how to meet. It wasn't for nothing that he had taken his lumps early on in Five Points from hoodlums who specialized in beating up other boys who went to school. He stepped slightly to the right, brought around his left fist and smashed it into Josh's nose. Blood spurted immediately, but Josh hardly noticed, and charged in the new direction. He was a very strong lad, accustomed to battering his opponents to the ground with these wild charges. Brendan shifted his body again and brought up his right with all the power he could command right on the point of Josh's jaw. Josh sagged, but did not fall. Brendan shifted his feet and delivered a hard kick with his heavy boot right into Josh's testicles. This time Josh folded over with a moan, head first into the wet ground. The fight was clearly over.

If you want to give me that fish, I'm getting out of here right away, Brendan said to Joe. Joe gave him a twenty-inch shad.

You're a pretty good scrapper, he said. Next time hang around a little longer and you'll get to see the Injuns.

No one in the crowd moved as Brendan took the fish with thanks to Joe and headed back up the Leap on the way to New Milford. It had been a long day, he reflected.

CHAPTER FOUR

IT WAS RAINING when Brendan awoke the next morning. When he heard the shower on the roof, he was pleased he was under cover. He wasn't on the road, wet and chilled as he might well have been. When he had arrived in the center of New Milford the evening before, he had walked around and chosen the less prosperous looking of two taverns he spotted. The man behind the counter had agreed to give him a place to sleep and supper in exchange for the shad. The supper turned out to be a small piece of the shad, fried potatos and a piece of pie. A lot better than bread alone. The place to sleep was unfinished space under the eaves on the third floor furnished with a cot and blankets. At least as good as corn shucks and he could have slept on the bare floor. One thing about walking the countryside all day; there was never any problem about getting to sleep.

When he descended to the lobby, the same man was still behind the counter.

If you like you can have a bite before you set out, he said.

He sat at a table where a young girl brought him a portion of hash and a glass of hard cider. The hash was heavy on potatos but not bad. He had never drank hard cider before. He found the taste harsh but drank it down.

Much obliged to you, he said to the man. He buttoned his jacket and walked out the door.

In the daylight, he had a better idea of how the town was laid out. Essentially, it consisted of two dirt streets both facing a common some two hundred yards long, sloping gently from the north to the south. As in Danbury, the frame houses were mixed with businesses. In front of the latter, hitching rails rested on heavy posts set in the earth at intervals. Because of the rain, water draining off the high hill to the north rushed in a torrent through an irregular gully gaping in the common, which eventually emptied into a brook on the south side of the village. Pigs were wallowing in the mud of the common and geese pecked away at the weeds and brambles which grew rankly along its full extent. Two cows were tethered to stakes driven into the damp ground.

Not exactly City Hall Park, Brendan thought.

Even the more comfortable houses were marred by the remains of winter firewood piles, either stacked against the clapboards or outside the property fence almost in the street. Irregular paths were worn from one house to another and to the stores in between. A store on the north end bore the sign "Hine and Lockwood, General Store". Also on the west side, were two more stores, which similar signs indicated were operated by McMahon and Mygatt, and Samuel Canfield. A half dozen horses were at the hitching rails.

Brendan was struck by the name McMahon. He entered the store and asked for Mr. McMahon. He pronounced the name MicMahn.

A clerk seemed puzzled. You mean Deacon McMahon? Only he pronounced it Mackman, with the accent on the first syllable.

It was Brendan's turn to be baffled. Deacon? An awful thought crossed his mind. Isn't Mr.–uh–Deacon McMahon Irish?

Naw. The clerk was disgusted. The family came from New

Jersey, he said. We ain't got no Irish around here. Thank God for that.

What do you want? He stared suspiciously at Brendan.

Nothing. I thank you. I just wanted to talk to him. He fled out the door.

Outside on the path, Brendan walked south. To his left on the common were two churches. Neither had a cross on top. One was Congregational, the established state religion of Connecticut, and the other Episcopalian. The only other churches in New Milford, much farther out of town, belonged to the Methodists, the Baptists and the Quakers.

So, Brendan mused, if his uncle was the only Irishman in Danbury, he himself must be the only one in this town. He didn't especially relish the thought.

He walked north on the east side of the common. From the Keeler home, only houses lined the street. The last one was more pretentious than the others, with a Grecian pediment and classical pillars supporting it. Just north of it, another dirt road led off to the east from the common. Across the street, high on a knoll was another house, but of a different style from all the rest he had seen in this town. It was built of red brick with white limestone lintels and with several chimneys, usually an index of some luxury. The narrower end, still as great a span as the longer side of most houses here, faced the street, unlike the other houses whose broad side and central doorways was oriented toward the public. The large, rectangular building looked new and it looked expensive.

As he stared at the house, a buggy with a smart appearing horse stopped and a heavyset man looked at him intently.

Good morning, he said. Can I help you with something?

Brendan was startled. I was just admiring the house.

That's good. It cost me a lot of money. You're newly arrived in town, aren't you? What are your plans?

Brendan realized he didn't have any plans. On the spur of the moment he blurted out a response. I'm looking for work.

Get in. The man moved over in the seat to make way for Brendan. He drove up the driveway, handed the reins to a waiting stablehand, and rather awkwardly got down from the buggy.

Come in with me, he said.

Together they passed through the rear door and the man took a key from a chain and unlocked the door off the main hallway in the back of the house. No one else appeared.

This is my office, the man said. Please come in and have a seat.

The room was sparsely furnished with a desk, swivel chair, bookshelves filled with law books, accounts ledgers, pamphlets. Other books, papers, newspapers were thrown haphazardly on a large table. There was a horsehair sofa and large upholstered chairs arranged so several occupants could converse easily. The plentiful windows gave on a small house to the west and downhill from that, the upper end of the common.

My name is Perry Smith. I know how you feel as a newcomer because I myself was one not too long ago. I came here from the Judea Parish section of what was Woodbury when I was born, but is now the town of Washington. I was young and restless, and didn't have any money, although my family was well enough off. I started as a storekeeper on the road to Kent just at the foot of upper Merryall. That's a district in the northern part of this town. That was in 1806. Eight years later I built this house which is supposed to be on the site of a house built by Colonel John Read. Colonel Read was one of the original proprietors of the land which became New Milford and he claimed title to more than 20,000 acres of land. He was an interesting man, trained at Harvard College, a candidate for the ministry in my home town, and also here, where he preached the first sermon in town. He was also a lawyer who later attained emminence in Boston in that profession. But Read, who was from Stratford, didn't make out too well on his land claim here. He, and others from Stratford, in 1708 sued a group of Milford people whom they alleged had trespassed on their claim by laying out lots in what is now the town center. The suit dragged on until 1711; Read won fifteen decisions in court but lost the sixteenth time and gave up his claim. He left his home here after that.

Brendan was listening intently, trying to absorb all this information even as he watched Smith closely. He felt more than a little uneasy that this obviously rich, decisive lawyer was confiding all these facts to him.

He seemed to grasp Brendan's puzzlement. You may wonder why I'm telling you all this.

Brendan tried to smile, and nodded his head affirmatively.

Well, I just wanted you to know that you're not the first one to come here with almost nothing. Some, like myself, have made out pretty well and others, like Colonel Read, have not. But maybe it was a blessing in disguise for him, because he was a much more important man in Boston than he ever could have been here.

He abruptly changed the subject. Tell me what your plans are, what do you hope to do? I know from your speech that you have some education, how far have you gotten along?

Brendan was taken aback. He realized he didn't really have fixed objectives. He responded as best he could. My father wanted me to be a lawyer, as he was. I've finished in the public school in New York and have been taking classes along with other boys from a tutor. I haven't finished all the courses I would need to enter college. I want to work so that I can finish my education. I'm only sixteen, so I have some time yet.

Time is only valuable if you use it well. But do you want to be a lawyer? I gather your father is deceased so the important thing now is whether you want to be or not. Smith put the emphasis on the word you.

Brendan faltered. I don't really know. I don't know enough about it.

Smith nodded. I can understand that. Until I tried to eke out a living among people who didn't have much money in an isolated rural area, sometimes only earning a few cents a day, I didn't know either. But need can improve your powers of concentration wonderfully. That's why I became a lawyer. I went to the Tapping Reeve Law School in Litchfield, passed the bar and began practicing here in 1807. You might consider it. I couldn't have built this house if I were still behind a counter up in Merryall. Again he switched the topic suddenly. Are you an American citizen?

I was born in New York. My father became a citizen and was admitted to the bar in New York. He felt vaguely defensive.

I don't mean to pry. But you said you were looking for work and I was wondering what you can do or what you want to do. I know you are handy with your fists, but you can't earn much in that line around here. We do it for the sheer fun of it.

Brendan was surprised. He showed it.

This is not like New York. Here everyone knows everyone else's business. News like your encounter with young Josh Sherwood gets around pretty rapidly. We don't have much else to talk about. Entertainment is limited here.

Brendan faced the question. I'm not trained to do anything. Only recently I learned my mother doesn't have the resources I thought she did and I decided not to be a burden to her and to make my way as best I can.

Connecticut is on the threshold of great change, Smith said. It appears that we are to have a new constitution. Orange Merwin from this town will be a delegate to a constitutional convention which will take place in Hartford in October. A single political party, the Federalists, has ruled this state from the beginnings of this country. This is going to change. Even a member of the ruling class in New Milford, Elijah Boardman, is now a Democrat, or at least he professes to be. Merwin is a Democrat, so am I. Of course most of the people are still Federalists at heart. Farmers are very conservative; these farmers have to work harder than you can belive to grasp a living from these rocky hills. So these farmers are more conservative even than the norm. It will take a very, very long time to change them. But there will be change anyhow, and when there's change there is money to be made-- if you are alert. All of this may not mean much to you at the moment, but think about it.

Brendan couldn't think of a thing to say. He probably knew more about political forces in Ireland than he did the United States. A few weeks ago he had barely heard of Connecticut, let alone have any thoughs about its political dynamics.

I can see I'm premature in telling you these things, Smith said. Let's begin with the basics. You need a job. I will give you one. It will not be a great thing, but it will allow you to eat and keep a roof over your head. If you keep your eyes open it might lead to better things.

Thank you, sir. I'm very grateful. What will I do?

Don't thank me until you try it. I can assure you I will get my money's worth or the arrangement will not last. I have personal plans that will require that I have someone I can trust, someone who has some brains and is not afraid of long hours. I would hope that we can find a way to continue your education as well. I will pay you fifty cents a day, which you may not know is a munificent salary around here. You will find a place to live, preferably not in that wretched tavern where you spent last night, and arrange for your own meals. Many of your duties will be quite menial until I figure out how to better employ you. It may be that Mrs. Smith will call upon you as well. I will now give you one dollar as an advance on your first week's pay. You should spend the rest of the day finding a home where you can board. I shall expect to see you here at eight o'clock tomorrow morning.

Brendan realized he was being dismissed. Thank you, sir. I shall be here tomorrow at eight.

As he walked down the hill toward the common, he ran Smith's words through his head again. He found it hard to realize he now had a job, had it before he had even started looking. Even after such a short exposure to Smith, he realized the lawyer was an intelligent, forceful individual who would be a demanding boss. He wondered how a man who, by his own admission had no money when he started as a storekeeper in an impoverished farm community like Merryall in 1806, just a dozen years ago, was now involved in town affairs and had the newest and most impressive home in the center of town. He thought about these matters all day as he searched for a place to live.

CHAPTER FIVE

THE FOURTH OF JULY hadn't been a big part of Brendan's life in Five Points but he could see that people in New Milford took it very seriously. Perry Smith had given him the day off, the first one, except for Sundays, that he had had since he went to work for him in the third week of April. When he awoke that morning, at dawn as usual, he pondered how to spend the day. He could hear Mrs. Gunn downstairs, moving around at her morning chores. He could see no point in lying abed on a beautiful summer morning. There were few enough good days in Connecticut at any time of year what with the easterly winds that kept even inland locations well watered with the moisture picked up over the Atlantic.

Mrs. Gunn – he would not dream of calling her Mary – greeted him affectionately as usual. He paid her only a dollar a week with the understanding he would help her with such household tasks as sawing and splitting the firewood she bought from a local farmer. He kept her woodbox in the kitchen full, carried her groceries home from Mygatt's store or wherever else she found better bargains, did minor repairs on the house, and helped out in any way she asked him to or that he could think of on his own. He liked his situation in her home because he had the entire second floor, which was unfinished and had limited headroom but was lighted by two windows. Perry had given him some castoff clothes which he hung on nails driven in the rafters. He had little else.

When he returned from the outhouse, he asked her how the town celebrated the Fourth.

Oh, it's a grand time. Her eyes lit up. When Abner was alive, he marched with all the men in a parade around the green to the cemetery. The marshal is usually Elisha Bostwick -- I should call him colonel, I suppose. People like Elijah Boardman and the selectmen review the parade from a stand near the church. When Mrs. Gunn said the church, like most people in town she meant the Congregational Church.

Mr. Elliot will give an invocation and perhaps Mr. Benham will give a benediction, because Mr. Boardman goes to the Episcopal Church more often that to our church just to hear Mr. Benham. I suspect Mr. Boardman doesn't like Mr. Elliot's New Light doctrines that have brought so many people back into the fold since Mr. Griswold left. Then she was apologetic. Oh, I'm sorry. I always forget that you don't care about our churches. You're such a good lad that it's hard for me to remember you're a Papist.

How many veterans of the Revolution will march? Brendan was uncomfortable talking about religion with her.

Some of them are getting on in years, but there will probably be at least twenty-five or thirty. Quite a number of them have gone west. You know Mr. Boardman is always encouraging people to move to Ohio, especially around Boardman. Isn't it nice that they have named a town after our most illustrious citizen?

Perry had spoken enough of Elijah Boardman for Brendan not to share in Mrs. Gunn's warm feeling about him. The aristocracy will have its monuments, he said.

Oh, don't say that, she exclaimed. Mr. Boardman and his

family have done a lot for the town. His grandfather was our first minister and they tell me he really held this town together. His father, Sherman, was highly respected and his wife, Sarai, was a living history book for our community. His brother, Major Daniel, was a war hero, too, and then one of our leading merchants before he moved to New York.

They seem to have been handsomely remunerated, judging from the way they live.

They are all hardworking, God-fearing people and God has recognized this by rewarding them with the goods of this world. You should follow their example.

He laughed. If I got rich I couldn't fill up your wood box anymore. If you don't have anything for me to do after breakfast, I will go to town and witness this glittering spectacle. Meanwhile just let me say how grateful I am for the griddle cakes and sausage. That is a real holiday treat.

As he headed up Grove Street toward the center he could hear band instruments tuning in the distance. Groups of small boys skipped around excitedly, obviously stimulated by the holiday atmosphere. As he neared the center, he saw that some of the more well-to-do families had hung American flags facing the street. Older men with seamed and rugged faces bore rosettes on their arms to show they were Revolutionary veterans. They searched out friends, they grasped their hands with extra warmth and exhanged little jokes. One could see that the War of 1812 had been no more popular in New Milford than in the rest of New England. No one, it appeared, was claiming credit for serving in that war on this day.

Today Brendan felt the lack of friends his own age. He knew a few youths his age but saw them infrequently and had little contact with them. Because Perry had taught him how to do title searches in the Town Hall, he did know Sam Bostwick, son of Town Clerk Elisha Bostwick, who had served in the job since

1777. Elisha was kind and helpful to him and the son seemed friendly but shy, even though he was three years older. He had seen George Boardman, son of the exalted Elijah, who was the same age as Sam, and Caroline Maria, who was his own age, but he had had no contact with either one. He had casually met a dozen other lads his age, but had no occasion to get to know them better. Perry had held out the prospect of furthering his education, but it turned out that there was no school beyond the primary level in the town. A former Yale Professor, Nehemiah Strong, had conducted a school for young men in earlier years, but had moved to Bridgeport. Families like the Boardmans could afford to hire tutors; those with lesser resources sent their sons to Litchfield or other towns where private academies were available at the secondary level. Several dozen young men prepared in this way had gone on to graduate from Yale, but this was not a possibility for Brendan. If he wanted to complete his education, he would have to leave New Milford. He was thinking about it but was reluctant to uproot himself again so soon after arriving here.

He roamed around the common. It had dried considerably since his first day in town back in April, but the rivulet still ran through the middle of it. It was no holiday for the swine and geese; there was a new crop of weeds and briars for them to pick at and root in. As he watched the adults circulating sedately and the children darting about, he noticed a well dressed man, resplendent in white pantaloons, crossing the green toward the reviewing platform. He appeared to be trying to catch up with a friend on the west side and was quickly picking his way among the obstructions, domestic animals and bog areas. As he hurried ahead, he frightened a large boar hog who suddenly charged him. The man fell over on the hog which carried him a few feet until he fell off among the bogs and mire. He slowly rose, amidst the cat calls and laughter of delighted onlookers. He looked with dismay at the sticky mud which covered his face and arms as well as the front of his clothing, especially the white pantaloons.

Which one is the hog? a raucus voice sung out. The soiled holiday celebrant slunk off.

Most of the people milling about were dressed in homespun, which was spun from either fleece or flax grown on each farm and then sewn into clothing by each wife. But in front of the Lyman Keeler home on the east side of the common, a small group of young ladies were dressed in frocks of light colored patterns and figures whose silks had come from a textile mill, very likely imported from Britain by none other than the town's leading merchant, Elijah Boardman. They talked and postured animatedly, aware that they were the focus of many stares, either admiring or envious. Brendan moved closer to get a better look at the group. He was not the only young man to do this. The girls studiously refrained from eye contact with anyone not in their group, but they covertly examined the youths as best they could. Of these, Brendan was far taller than most and his wide shoulders showed to good advantage. The whiteness of his skin combined with his black, wavy hair contrasted with the farm boys around him, with their tanned, weatherbeaten faces, white foreheads, and light brown or blond hair.

Colonel Bostwick and his aides began to line up the elements of the parade a little before ten. There was considerable confusion as each group sought to marshal its ranks. The band tootled more loudly as its great moment of the year approached, school children from some of the nearer school districts of the twenty-one in the town milled around, deliberately loud and boisterous. Other less fortunate children could not attend because the Fourth of July was traditionally the day when rye, cradled a day or so earlier, was now dry enough to be bound into sheaves and stored in mows for later threshing. Children could do this work as well if not better than their elders.

Finally, the colonel moved on his horse to Beebe Hine's United States Hotel on the west side of the green and moved out at the head of the parade. Suddenly the band was playing a march and wheeled into line behind Colonel Bostwick and his mounted escort. They moved smartly down the green southward past the point where the hog had ruined the holiday outfit, turned to the east on the road that led down the river to the bridge over the Housatonic, doubled back to the north the other side of the Episcopal and Congregational churches in the center of the green. The parade passed the old Roger Sherman house, swung by the group in front of Lyman Keeler's, on up by the old Boardman house to the Taylor house on the corner. By this time the full complement of marchers was filing along. Behind the band were the Revolutionary veterans, initiallty making some pretense of maintaining cadence to the band's beat, but before long simply striding along at their regular farmer's gait, joking among themselves and calling out to friends and family they passed along the route. Behind them were the school children lined up according to their districts, and two militia companies fancily attired in outlandish uniforms. Bringing up the rear were young men mounted on beautifully groomed saddle horses. These were not farm boys but young bloods whose families had the money for this display of horseflesh and the elegant English saddles. Some of the horses were trained to dance to the music, all pranced and arched their necks. Spectators oohed and ahed, impressed as the horsemen had hoped.

At the head of the green, the parade turned to the east. Some people straggled off at this point, others followed along. Brendan, one of these, could see Perry and his wife, the former Anne Comstock, standing on the front porch of their home with some friends. They waved to the marchers. Where Park Lane started to the east, the procession entered the cemetery and stopped at a point where the slope down to Great Brook leveled off enough to allow marchers and spectators to cluster around the speakers.

As the bodies packed together in the small area, Brendan unexpectedly found himself next to the bevy of radiant young women whom he had seen earlier in front of Keeler's. The one nearest him was Caroline Maria Boardman. He had never been this close to any girl in New Milford before. Trying not to stare, he noted that she had the grave good looks of her father. Then she turned and greeted him courteously.

You must be the young man who is working for Perry Smith. I hope you are not disappointed in our small town. It must be very dull after New York. When she smiled, the gravity in her face was replaced by a pixie air, almost flirtatious.

I've been too busy to miss New York. New Milford possesses beauties New York would envy. He could tell he she liked his response.

Some of the young people are meeting on the meadow down beside the river this afternoon after three, she said. Why don't you join us?

Before he could answer, there was a ruffle of drums to mark the beginning of the program. He tried to make himself heard. Thank you. I'll try to be there.

As Mrs. Gunn had predicted, Mr. Elliot gave the invocation, pronouncing each word with the exaggerated punctiliousness of clerical speech. Then Brendan was disappointed to see Caroline Maria and her friends move off in another direction. Captain Elizur Warner delivered what was intended to be the main oration. Brendan tried to listen but he could think of nothing but his recent encounter. Captain Warner paid the anticipated tribute to the heroism of the patriots of 1776 but he dwelled longer than might have been expected on how civilian committees in New Milford had been formed to support the men doing the fighting. He listed committees for inspection, correspondence, supply procurement, clothing procurement, and inspection of provisions. It was all lost on Brendan. He was not the only one who was not paying attention. The restlessness of the crowd grew until Captain Warner mercifully terminated after twenty minutes.

The school children didn't even notice for they were beyond the control of their teachers by now. A squad of veterans fired off their muskets as a salute, and the children immediately quieted. A bugle sounded taps. Mrs. Gunn was right again; Mr. Benham gave a benediction. Then Colonel Bostwick thanked everyone for coming and that was the end. Children and riders charged out of the cemetery on to Park Lane. The rest of the marchers and onlookers, even the mustered out militia and the dignitaries, were not far behind.

Brendan asked a youth beside him: Is that all?

What did you want, a hanging? You can go swimming in the river if you want something to do.

Brendan numbly drifted back to the center. Only a few individuals remained of the throng that had been there an hour before. He thought of Five Points. He wondered what his mother and Agnes were doing today. He wondered what Caroline Maria would think of them. Suddenly this was very important to him.

He continued on to Grove Street, but Mrs. Gunn was not home; she had probably gone visiting after the parade. He made himself a snack with some bread and cheese, went outside and lay down in the grass. He pondered whether he should accept Caroline Maria's invitation. He certainly wanted to but was not so innocent as not to realize that he might be out of place with his thick boots, the only footwear he had, and his rustic clothing. Well, she knew that when she invited him. Let the others say what they might. He would go. The decision made, he napped in the sunshine.

Around three he roused himself. He went to the pump and

washed his face and hands in the stream of water. He combed his hair in a tin mirror, got a knife from the kitchen and cut a half dozen of the wild roses growing in the yard. Then he set off.

The streets in the center were even quieter than usual. He crossed by the foot of the green, walked up on the west side and headed down the slope to the west on the drift-way leading to the Housatonic. All of the back yards of the original lots had led to the river and for the most part they were still open meadows. Hay had recently been cut on the lots so it was easy to walk through the stubble. He could see a group of people under the shade of a huge sycamore tree along the river's edge further up. Although his father had called such trees in New York plane trees, he had heard them called buttonballs here. He headed for the group.

When he drew close, Caroline Maria approached him. He held out his handful of wild roses. I was going to give you these, he said, but they wilted before I could get here. He threw them in the grass disconsolately.

She laughed. Silly! You didn't have to bring anything. It's just a picnic. Come meet my mother.

Mary Anna Whiting Boardman observed Brendan quizzically. Elijah Boardman had brought her as his bride from Great Barrington, Massachusetts, when that town was little more than a frontier settlement. She knew poverty firsthand even though she had certainly not been marked by it since she entered the wealthy Boardman family. She greeted Brendan kindly if a bit condescendingly. Her children were not accustomed to associating with the lower orders. Her church made a particular point of seating members in rank order according to the amount of money they had as reflected in the taxes they paid. When Mr. Griswold arrived in town in 1802 he had immediately reassigned pews according to the "dignity" of the members. With an income of $1,505, Elijah was already in the first rank. By 1815 he had risen to third place with $3,001. His father, Deacon Sherman, was in first place, with $4,212. So Mrs. Boardman felt she had a duty to recognize where people stood in the world, but that did not prevent her from recognizing an individual's innate worth. After all, in the fulness of time, God might reward their good qualities and their "dignity" would be reassessed by the elect.

I wish you every success in your duties with Mr. Smith. Please don't be offended if I suggest you should make every effort to continue your education, she said.

Caroline Maria introduced Brendan to her brothers, William, Henry and George, and her cousin, Homer. All were sleek young aristocrats and solemn as bishops. William, a Yale graduate and already an attorney in New Haven, was visiting for the holiday, Henry was soon to go to Boardman, Ohio, to assist in the management of his father's land holdings there and George, rather feminine and frail looking, would die young. Their reception of Brendan was decidedly perfunctory. The Honorable Elijah was nowhere to be seen.

Brendan got on better with the brothers, Normand and Oliver Baldwin, and their cousin Almon. These were essentially farm boys, hearty and earthy, devoid of any airs. He liked Isaac Beech, who was his own age, and Daniel Beers. Then there were Charley Bostwick, Seymour Buck, Harmon Buckingham, and David Bronson; it seemed as if most of the old families had names beginning with B. He wondered what alphabetical process had selected them.

Mainly they talked about farm life and the difficulties of getting grain and barrels of salt pork to market in New York by wagon. Charley complained that his family got only six cents a pound for veal; Seymour's folks had to sell salt pork for eight cents. Potatos brought only 50 cents a bushel, according to

Harmon.

Well, at least we get to live in God's fresh air and we'll never starve, said David. It's better than living in a foul city like New York. He looked at Brendan. No offense meant, he added.

None taken. I agree with you. That's why I'm here.

The best feature of the gathering as far as Brendan was concerned was the food. Servants had brought a wagon load of laden dishes direct from the Boardman kitchen and the women saw to it that they were laid out attractively on a long table. At six, Mrs. Boardman invited all to partake. This was the first opportunity for the men and women to mingle. Up to then they had kept apart, discussing their separate interests. He headed for Caroline Maria's side; so did Elisha Cogswell and David Ferris.

Elisha got in the first licks. Caroline, may I assume you have a hand in fixin' all this scrumptious repast?

Caroline giggled. You may assume I had no hand in any of the work. But I did help Mother with the planning.

Brendan jumped in. The best thing about living in the country is that everything is fresh and tastes so good, he said. He sensed that coming from New York gave him some advantage. He mentally thanked God Caroline Maria had never seen Five Points. He shuddered at the mere thought.

Elisha wanted to know if Caroline's father intended to continue in politics if a new state constitution was enacted. He was worried about tht disestablishment of the Congregational Church.

Surely, why not? Caroline responded breezily. He runs on the Democratic ticket, not the Congregational. We go to the Episcopal Church as much as the Congregational. My brother Bill has actually joined the Episcopal Church. I think it's a good thing to separate religion and politics.

I understand that a town in Ohio bears your father's name. That's quite an honor, Brendan opined.

He bought it. He can name it anything he wants. He named two others as well; one is Palmyra and the other is Medina. I think those are strange names for an American town. Imagine, Medina is an Arabian city and also the name for the native quarters of North African cities. There certainly aren't any palm trees in Ohio, either. When I complained to Father, he told me he would have named a town after me if two states didn't already bear my name. Ever since I was born he has spent at least three months of every year out there. I think he just wants to get away from us.

Brendan responded fervently. I can't believe he would want to be away from you.

Caroline smiled. You men keep after that food. I don't want to see any left. I've got to help out now. She swept off.

Brendan didn't get another chance to be near her. He dutifully circulated among the other young men and tried to make himself as amiable as he knew how. He got along well with most of them. Perry had told him it was important for him to cultivate good relations with the townspeople. Perry did it constantly; he was obviously a rising man in the community, right behind Elijah Boardman and Orange Merwin. Brendan found he enjoyed it, too, and so far had lost few opportunities to ingratiate himself with townspeople. He knew that he would always be somewhat apart as an Irish Catholic, but he didn't want to cut himself off from people as his Uncle Peter was doing in Danbury.

A little before nine, as it began to grow dark, the guests began to leave. Brendan thanked Mrs. Boardman, sincerely complimenting her on the food. He shook hands with the Boardman young men and feelingly thanked Caroline Maria for inviting him.

You have been extremely kind to a poor waif, he said.

Some waif, she responded. When you get to be six-foot-three

you forfeit your waif status. But I was happy we could get some potato salad and beef into you so you won't be so thin. Otherwise I would worry about you.

As he started away across the stubble, she called after him. Thank you, Brendan, for the roses. That was a very sweet thought.

Brendan floated up the hillside through the drift-way to the center. He couldn't believe that this attractive, wealthy young woman had treated him so hospitably. From now on, he would not think of leaving New Milford and wandering on to some other part of the country. He was hooked.

CHAPTER SIX

TODAY IS A NEW ERA in Connecticut, Perry said. We have a new state constitution. The Royal Charter of 1662 is only a memory and the Revolutionary period is behind us. The Congregational Church is no longer established. And in New Milford hardly anyone knows about it and few of those who do, care. So runs the course of history.

Now and then you do get some news out of *The Connecticut Courant*, Brendan said. Maybe its worth the money after all.

He sat in Perry's office waiting for his daily assignments. His original awe of his boss had moderated to the point where he felt he could gently twit him. How many days did it take to get here? he asked.

What difference does it make, are you in a hurry? But look, this was a close run thing; it only passed by some two-thousand votes. It didn't even pass in Hartford County. And of course it didn't pass in those two rural bastions of the 18th century, Tolland and Litchfield counties. Get this, though. It passed in New Milford; for once I am proud of my town. Only two other towns in the county approved ditching a pre-Revolutionary system of government, Colebrook and Salisbury. Litchfield, that Federalist stronghold, turned it down 252 to 282. In our town it won 219 to 196. Ratification by the convention was just two days ago. Orange Merwin and his friends did the job, and well. But it will take some time before we see the full effect. Right now you Papists can come out from underground.

Perry knew very well that Brendan had not even seen another Catholic in months and that there was not even a priest in the state; his last comment was just banter. Their relationship had eased on both sides. At the same time, since this was the first news he had heard about enactment of the new constitution, he found it hard to share Perry's enthusiasm.

Now that we have a State Senate with well defined powers, I imagine that Elijah will want to sit in it, Perry continued. He outgrew the dry goods business in 1812; now that he's becoming wealthy developing Ohio land, he may be feeling too big for anything in Hartford, but he can set the stage for going to Washington with a couple of years in the State Senate. I might like to go out to the General Assembly myself. It might be possible to get something done now.

Do you have any title searches for me?

The door to the office abruptly opened and a young woman leading a toddler by the hand entered.

Say "Hello Daddy. Excuse us for interrupting you," the woman said to the child. The child saw Brendan and immediately buried her face in her mother's skirt.

Smith smiled fondly at the pair. Hello, darling. Hello Elvira. Elvira, come sit with Daddy. Anne, I don't believe you've met Brendan McCauley. Brendan, this is my wife and our little daughter.

How do you do, Mrs. Smith. You have a beautiful little girl.

The child was charming. She was dressed identically as her mother in a white gown with small embroidered white stars set at intervals. As the mother, she had a blue sash around the waist. The blonde hair of both, with a slight natural wave, fell just to the shoulder The mother had a lively, kindly face with a wide mouth and prominent cheek bones.

Oh, Mr. McCauley, it's a pleasure to meet you. Mr. Smith has spoken of you so often.

She turned to her husband. Mrs. Brinsmade of Judea Parish is driving over in her rig to show Elvira and me some of the fall folliage. We will lunch at her house and she will bring us back this afternoon. She says she doesn't want to lose contacts with the Smith family.

Fine, my dear. The outing will do you both good. Please give my regards to Mrs. Brinsmade.

The little girl and the mother both kissed Perry on the cheek and left.

Ah, the joys of domestic life, Perry said lightly to show he relished getting back to business. You were asking about your assignments for today. No, there are no searches pending. I've got some property lines I'd like to have you walk. Nothing official, just some pieces I'm interested in. You know, I've got to hand it to Elijah. He doesn't mess around with just little properties around here. It took a lot of gumption to get up $60,000 to buy a big chunk of the Western Reserve when Connecticut sold it in 1795. Of course he had six other fellows in it with him, but he was the moving spirit. He's practically forcing young Henry to go out there and manage it for him so he can sell it for what he calls "most advantageous terms."

Perry didn't have his mind on Brendan's chores; he was on a higher plane. He went on. The state – and the country – need more people like Elijah. People have been leaving the rural areas around here since the Revolution. My old town of Woodbury dropped from 2,662 in 1790 to 1,963 in the last census and by now its down to a little over 1,800. Of course, the loss of Judea Parish is partly responsible for that decline, but the trend is there. Watertown dropped from 3,170 to 1,714 in just 20 years. Up in Cornwall, Dudleyville just disappeared. New Milford and

Danbury have gone up only slightly. Most of those missing bodies have headed west. It's mainly the folks with git-up-and-go that have left. Ambition and initiative have been drained off. This makes the small towns overly conservative. Small towns may not necessarily produce mediocre men, but they sure make it hard for genius to flourish. We need more people like you, Brendan, more Irish, more Germans, more French, more Swedes, more whatever, to shake this place up.

Thanks for the compliment. I must say that I haven't found the welcome overwhelming, with some notable exceptions.

That's because people fear change. It's uncomfortable to have to climb out of the slough.

Perry, the climate is terrible, the soil is not fertile, the working day is long, the people are miserly.

But the women are enchanting, is that it? Did Caroline Maria bewitch you?

You know my weakness. How can one hide anything from you lawyers? But you know I have no illusions. I hardly ever even see her, let alone talk to her.

That's healthy. You must realize she was just exercizing her newly found powers as a woman.

Give me something to do so I can get to work.

In the center see what you can find out about a canal project. Orange Merwin is the main mover. Is it feasible? Are people disposed to invest in it? What would the route be? Also, are people in general paying any attention to the temperance movement that Reverend Beecher from Litchfield is promoting? Don't ask direct questions, be discreet. You should get some exercise, too, so please take a scythe and trim some of the brush that grew around the property during the summer. Try and make the place look as nice as the Boardmans'.

Tell me please something about the temperance movement. I gather there is a group advocating that hard liquor be banned.

Surely Mr. Beecher is aware of the numerous references to alcoholic drinks in the Bible; he knows that Jesus drank wine regularly.

I'm confident that Mr. Beecher is at least as familiar with the Bible as you. He is concerned with the class of men who drink up most of their wages in saloons and leave their wives and children without money for food, clothing, and even shelter. He initiated the movement in Connecticut six years ago with a famous speech at the General Association of Congregational Churches. It's a small thing so far. But all social movements begin modestly.

Certainly, Perry, I'll look into it. It's just that, given the way people in New Milford appreciate their grog, the idea at first blush seems fantastic. Every working man or farmer that I know believes that to get hard work done, you've got to consume alcoholic drinks. There isn't a farmer in this town that doesn't put up at least four barrels of hard cider every fall and a lot of them have as many as twenty.

Your observations are accurate and your opinion was shared even by most of the Congregational ministers who attended the session I mentioned. They took the view that preaching is hard work, too, and that a man of the cloth is entitled to slake his thirst with something more satisfying than water after speaking for more than an hour. Reverend Thomas Robbins was a minister in Danbury before he moved to South Windsor, and a very conservative man, a conscientious Federalist. Mr. Robbins spends ten to fifteen dollars a year on his cellar. He regrets it, too, but not because he is contrite about drinking good brandies, but because they cost so much. But Federalists like Mr. Robbins will soon be a phenomenon of the past, I'm pleased to say.

Good. I know more about what you have in mind. I'm getting a practical education if not a formal one. I'm off. I'll pass around the center and see what I can learn. Beebe Hine can usually be found either in his hotel or out on the street. Then I can stop in and see Anan Hine in his store. Either one of them will talk until it's time to eat. You'd never know they weren't related.

As he walked toward the center, Brendan mused about Perry's new attitude toward Elijah Boardman, who always earlier he had chacterized as a crypto-Federalist. Now that his own land holdings were expanding, he obviously felt closer to Elijah. In various other ways, Brendan was becoming aware that Perry, for all his talk about a new era in Connecticut politics, invariably tailored his political positions to his own interests. Perhaps everyone did that, he didn't know. There had never been any political discussions in his own home or nor had anyone he had ever known in New York taken an interest in such things. He was beginning to find it intriguing. He smiled at his inadvertent pun.

He was also becoming less enchanted with Perry's promises. Perry certainly knew there was no tutor in New Milford when he held out to him the possibility of furthering his education. In talking with various men in town Brendan had learned that there was no mandatory educational level for candidates for the bar, although it was generally accepted that higher educational attainments of one kind or another were preferred. He now knew that Perry had as recently as the year before taken David Sanford of Bridgewater Neck into his office to study law even though he had only studied in an academy a year or so. For reasons unknown to Brendan and his informants, Sanford had only stayed a short while and was now studying law in Litchfield with Seth Beers. Brendan knew his case wasn't to be compared with that of David Sanford; young Sanford's father, Joel, was a prosperous merchant. Even so, it rankled.

As he though of these matters, Brendan recalled a

conversation with Mrs. Gunn. Mrs. Gunn was usually careful to say nothing ill against anyone short of George III, but she had warned him at one point that Perry was "a rather devious young man."

CHAPTER SEVEN

April - July 1819

BRENDAN AND SAM BOSTWICK took a break from their election day duties in mid-afternoon and strolled down the driftway into the meadows overlooking the Housatonic. They squatted in a dry area under the brow of the slope; the spring sun was just beginning to green the bases of last year's grass clumps. Other herbaceous plants were beginning to send out shoots as well. The willows along the edge of the river were covered by what appeared to be a soft green haze, the tiny leaves just emerging from their buds.

Brendan chewed one of the cured straws from last year's growth. I never thought I'd be helping out with an election when I came here a year ago. It was just about this time, the shadblow was out and the shad were running in the river. I didn't even intend to stay here. I just wanted to see a little bit of the country.

Now that you've settled in, are you sorry?

I don't know. It's pleasant enough here. But it's damned dull. And not much of a future. I've lost all chance of getting on with my schooling.

Work a few years and you'll have a stake so you can buy a piece of land and start a home. That's what my dad did, and my grandfather, Major John, who came here with his father in 1708.

The first white child born in New Milford was my grandfather's brother, Dan.

Hell, I don't even know what my grandpa's name was, on either side. I suppose it's a satisfaction to stay put and have a family like your's. I can't see myself as a patriarch though.

You never know. Some girl will get a holt of you and you won't think it's so dull.

Aint no girl that would have me that I would have. No family, no money.

That's just an excuse. Old Corny McMahon came here with nothing and he married a doctor's daughter. His son married a general's daughter.

Brendan was interested. Where did he come from anyhow?

My dad says he was born in County Clare, Ireland, but he lived in Nova Scotia and New Jersey before he came here.

He did? Brendan was surprised. Is he the deacon?

Sam laughed. No, that's his son. Why?

I didn't figure that anyone born in Ireland could be a deacon in the Congregational Church.

What church was he supposed to belong to? There isn't any Papist church around here. There's probably not even one in all of Connecticut.

Well, you've got Methodists and Baptists, why can't you have a Catholic church?

Baptists, that's a good one. Let me tell you a story about a Baptist preacher, a woman one at that.

A woman preacher? Never heard of such a thing.

Well this one was a woman all right. Her name was Jemima Wilkinson. She was born a Quaker in Rhode Island back in the middle of the last century. When she was a young lass she was dreadfully sick, so sick they thought at one point she had died. But she recovered and said she had been to heaven. She said she was really Jesus Christ and that his spirit was in her. She set herself up as a preacher and was mighty good at it. Nothing came out of her mouth, she said, but what was a revelation from on high. As the embodiment of Christ's spirit, she was perfection incarnate.

They put up with a lot in Rhode Island, but this was too much for even the people there, so they kind of nudged her over the state line. She taught and preached for a while in Eastern Connecticut, but eventually worked her way westward. By and by she got to New Milford. It was 1782, a year before the first peace treaty with England.

She preached in a number of places around town, but she was especially well received in Northville. For a time she held meetings in the home of Esek Wheaton, a little piece north of the burying ground up there. She carried on like this for several years, winning more and more supporters over time. Abraham Dayton was so taken with her that he deeded a piece of land to three trustees, Asahel and Ben Stone and Jonathan Botsford, for the use of the Universal Friend. The Universal Friend, of course, was Jemima. Dayton said the estate trust was to build a meeting house. This meeting house was built right north of the burying ground and Jemima preached there for some five years.

My Dad remembers her. He says she was a very good looking woman, voluptuous as Judith in the Old Testament. She was plenty smart, too, but her enemies said she was full of low cunning. You remember that the original Jesus had enemies, so it probably isn't surprising that this reincarnation of him did, too. Also there was another reason for this. Jemima received visits from angels, pretty much every night. She gave orders to her hired girl and the man in the barn that they were never to question these angels or even try to get too close to them, else they be smote by the arm of the Lord. Naturally, no one wants to try the Lord's patience, but even Lot's wife turned around, and eventually so did the hired girl, even though she was at some distance. She said Ben Stone and Amos Hallock must be very close to God because the angels sent by Him to visit Jemima bore a strong resemblance to them. You can understand how some of the wives in Northville would have been upset by the idea that their husbands looked like angels, especially if the angels were on that kind of a mission. They thought that the friend was getting to be a touch too universal.

Jemima set off an uproar right here in town one time. She let it be known that she was going to hold a service down by the side of the river, right below us here, and that she was going to cross over to the old Indian burying ground by walking on the waters of the river. As you might imagine, that attracted quite a bit of attention. People walk across the river up at the Rocky River ford, but here it's quite a few feet deeper. She got more people to show up at her service than old Reverend Taylor ever saw inside his meeting house up on the common. She preached a long sermon, then put on some particularly fine slippers to walk on the water with. Then she asked the members of the Congregation:

Do you truly believe that I have the supernatural power to walk across this river on the water?

Aye, we believe it, they roared in unison.

She asked them the same question twice more and each time, their fervor increased as they responded, Aye, we believe it.

Jemima stood before them, an imperious presence. It pleases God that you have faith, she said. If you believe, there is no need to try my powers in this fashion.

After five years at her Northville mission, Jemima revealed that the Lord had commanded her to move with all her congregation to the Genesee Valley. The decision caused quite a commotion, because several husbands left their wives and children to follow her. Some wives, too, left their husbands to join the caravan. One woman even left an infant behind. Some young women were persuaded that their destiny lay with Jemima. Dad says there was some uproar because of all the broken homes, but off they went, and none ever returned.

Ben Stone went with them as the captain of the train. His wife said she didn't care if he came back or not. He was a Revolutionary War veteran and was supposed to know how to carry out a trek of this kind, but a lot of folks thought he just wanted to be an angel every night with Jemima without worrying about competition from Amos. He eventually drifted back to town with a whole slew of cock and bull stories. He claimed that an Oneida Indian chief had forbade him and his train to cross his land. They debated the point for some time until the chief challenged Ben to wrestle with him for the privilege. Ben was an old hand at wrestling, as Jemima knew, so he went right at the Indian and pinned him just as if he had been a maiden. Then the chief said Ben would have to drink with him to seal the deal. Ben knew how to do that, too, as anybody in Northville could have told the chief. First they both "drank a thumb," then a couple of thumbs and some fingers too and it wasn't long and that noble red man didn't have any whiskey left. The wagon train rolled on and when it got to its destination Ben decided he would come back to Northville after all.

Jemima in a short while moved again, this time to what became Penn Yan, New York. Her colony thrived and she became highly respected. Some of her followers have kept up a correspondence with people in New Milford to this day. Just lately they wrote that Jemima had recently died.

That's a fine story, Brendan said. I suppose up yonder she has all the angels to wrestle with that she could ever want. I wish she were still around here; I would love to wrestle with her.

Now don't go getting horny. We better go back to the meeting house. Dad will need us to finish up the chores of the election. You can watch them count and announce the winners.

Winners! Orange Merwin has been going to Hartford since 1816. Aint nobody going to push him aside. Eli Todd will go with him because it was a done deal to have one Federalist and one Democrat.

You're gittin plenty savvy. But you forgot about Elijah Boardman. There's two chambers of the state legislature and Elijah is running for a seat in the new State Senate. He served for years in the lower house and until recently he was in the old upper house, which was quite different from the new Senate. Now that you are catching on to how things work around here, you might just as well stick around and put it all to use.

Sam winked and pulled Brendan to his feet.

* * *

The July morning was warm, so warm that Brendan had to be careful not to let the sweat from his arm drip on the copy of the legal document he was making in Perry's office. He had not seen Perry that morning but Perry didn't always come in; sometimes he had appointments with clients elsewhere or was with one of the town officials on some business.

Copying documents was one of the duller tasks that Perry imposed on him; the trick was to keep his mind on what he was doing so that he didn't write words that were in his mind rather than in the notes or original he was copying. Even so, sometimes as he worked, he drifted into a consideration of the legal profession. There was no doubt that the town government, and probably that of the county, the state, and on up to the federal system was largely controlled by lawyers. This is what made it such a powerful profession. But still, much of the work lawyers did was either pedestrian in its importance or dealt with seamier aspects of life. Representing petty criminals in court was one thing, but how about representing and doing the bidding of men who in their private affairs were comsuming the substance of the poor, the foolish, or the unwary? Clearly, not all lawyers did this, but some did. Brendan had the uneasy feeling that Perry sometimes did. He had certainly enriched himself fairly rapidly after he left the Merryall store and finished his training at Tapping Reeves' school in Litchfield. The bits and pieces of property that Perry accumulated in representing farmers who had no cash to pay a fee had certainly helped him pay for this sumptuous home in which he was now working. But, he mused, this was not his concern. Perry had always been more than generous and helpful with him.

A little after 11:30, one of the maids came to tell him that he was to leave and close up the office immediately. Mr. Smith was with his wife who was in a bad way. She was giving birth but there was a problem. Dr. Williams had been called because matters had gotten beyond the midwife. There was not much hope for the infant, a boy; everyone hoped Dr. Williams could save Anne. Brendan sadly left. He knew a high percentage of the babies born here died; in some families less than half lived to be adults. Many mothers died in childbirth, too. It was not uncommon for a man to have two or three wives because of this mortality rate. It was particularly distressing to think of Anne, who had always seemed so vital and kind to everyone, in these straits.

That afternoon in the center, Brendan learned that the baby boy had died shortly after birth. There was hope for Anne, but she was still very weak.

The next morning Brendan went to the brief religious ceremony at the Burying Ground. Only a few of Perry's associates were on hand, and some of the Comstock family. He expressed his sympathy to Perry, who told him that Anne seemed to be getting her strength back. As he walked away from the cemetery, he recalled how he had met Caroline Maria here only a year ago. He wondered if she would have to go through this ordeal some day.

CHAPTER EIGHT

1820

A WHILE BACK WE DISCUSSED the people who are against drinking, or the temperance movement as they call it. Now I keep hearing about another subject that seems to have come up only recently, abolition of slavery. What's going on? Brendan posed the question to Perry during one of their morning sessions.

You're right that people are beginning to talk about it, but it's been a national problem since the drafting of the Constitution. The southerners didn't want the black slaves counted as people, the north did. They eventually compromised on counting two-thirds of them. Now, with people streaming into the new lands of the west, it's again a problem. At the moment, it appears that Henry Clay, a Congressman from Kentucky, has come up with a compromise which will allow Maine to enter the Union as a free state and Missouri as a slave state. All Louisiana Purchase territory south of a line westward from Missouri's southern border could come into the Union as slave states, that north of it as free states. That seems fair enough to me, but meanwhile a movement has grown up which would free all the slaves. These people call themselves abolitionists. Most of them are in Massachusetts, but there is a scattering of them in all of the northern states, and a famous one, named Cassius Clay, even in Kentucky.

Freeing the slaves sounds like a good idea to me. If I understand you rightly, under the Constitution each slave is held to be two-thirds of a person. I never heard anything more ridiculous. In any event, there aren't any around here, are there?

No, I don't believe there are more than a few, certainly not more than half a dozen, remaining in New Milford, although there were several dozen in earlier times. There can't be many more than forty in the entire state now, from what I have read. But don't be hasty in advocating abolition. Remember that slaves are property, and property is protected by law. Furthermore negros are inferior to white people and the Bible has sanctioned this mark upon the descendants of Cain. Slavery has existed since time immemorial, including in this hemisphere, in this country, in this state and, as I have said, in New Milford.

You say the negros are inferior, but you can't prove any such thing. Either you're afraid of them, or you don't like them. Or maybe you don't like them because you're afraid. When people are afraid, they do cruel things. I heard of one school in town where the little negro boy has to sit on a bench by himself. Except when a white boy is naughty, then the teacher makes him sit on the same bench with the black boy. This is wrong and slavery's wrong. William Wilberforce even convinced the British it's wrong and God knows they don't draw too fine a distinction in dealing with other peoples, for example, the Irish. But who in New Milford owned slaves?

The founding family, for one. John Noble, Jr., who came here with his father, kept a slave named Robbin at his farm just south of Gallows Hill. Rev. Daniel Boardman, Elijah's grandfather, baptized him in 1737. Captain Sherman Boardman freed his slave, Nehemiah, in 1780 as did John Treat his slave Mingo in 1781. These actions are all a matter of record.

A woman named Mary Roburds freed her slave, Dan, in

1757. She said she did it because of the goodwill and respect she had for him, but he had to pay her more than three pounds a year for the rest of her life for his freedom.

Partridge Thatcher, the first lawyer in New Milford, owned many slaves. He lived right down the street on the east side of the common. Partridge freed his slaves, too, but over a period of time. He freed his servant Sibyl on the day of her marriage to a freeman named Amos in 1773. Seven years later he freed his slaves, Heber and Peleg, but Peleg had to wait two years until he was 25 for the emancipation to take effect. In 1781 Thatcher freed the father and mother of Heber and Peleg, Jacob Gratis, and his wife, Dinah. In return, Jacob and Dinah had to care for a two-year-old slave boy named Cyrus until he was five, at which time he was to be returned to Partridge. But Partridge died in 1786, so he didn't get too much service out of Cyrus. Partridge bought Jacob and Dinah from a slaver captain in Norwich in 1749, when they were both children and had been in this country only six weeks.

Little Cyrus turned out to be the patriarch of a colony of freed negros. He married Hopeful Freeman of Litchfield in 1811. They had three children. There are records of at least seventy-five freed slaves living in New Milford from just before the Revolutonary War up to the present. Most of them were married in the church and were hard workers. One of them, Javan Wilson, received a pension as a veteran of the Revolutionary War. At least two of them drowned in the river, including a two-year-old boy, Terah, who was playing near Partridge Thatcher's sawmill in Rocky River.

The Boardmans called their large estate two and a half miles north of the center Maryland, after a favorite slave who was originally from that state.

Some say that people in Connecticut only freed their slaves because it did not pay to keep them. In the case of Heber and

Peleg, I would point out that young slaves like them could have brought up to five-hundred dollars each in the market. Their labor each year should have fetched a hundred dollars if Partridge had let them out. Freeing them was not an empty gesture.

Perry, how do you know about all these things? You weren't born here anymore than I was. I know most people here don't like abolitionists but I think I've been here long enough to know that they probably never cottoned to slave holders very much, either.

Don't let your ideals interfere with your judgment. Only the wealthy can afford that. Perry's eyes narrowed; his protégé was beginning to exasperate him.

Brendan laughed. You must be glad there aren't more Irishmen around here to plague you.

Irishmen don't bother me. Youths with half formed opinions, I admit, I sometimes find irritating.

Perry, my opinions may be half formed, but only because I never really understood about slavery before. For one human being to enslave another and then try to justify it on economic grounds or by saying the slave is inferior is evil, it's an enormous perversion of values. The fact that the ancient Greeks or biblical figures did it doesn't make it right.

At one time you said you wanted to be a lawyer, but how could that have been if you make emotional declarations without weighing the merits of a case? Just a few minutes ago you told me you didn't know anything about slavery and now you are taking a very strong position on the basis of just a few facts that I have outlined for you. This is not rational conduct.

The blood rushed to Brendan's head. In his heat he gave words to a resentment he had harbored for months. I dare say I would make as good a lawyer as David Sanford. My education matches the few terms he studied in the academy. I know right from wrong, whether the matter is slavery or selection of law clerks.

Have a care, sir. Perry's voice was icy. You are on dangerous ground. You are not a law clerk, you are a day laborer. If you are unhappy with your situation, feel free to leave this minute.

Brendan tried to slow the blood throbbing in his temples. He thought about trudging along strange roads with little to eat and no one to talk to. He took a deep breath and wanted to swallow, but his mouth was too dry.

After what seemed a long time, he finally managed to speak. I'm sorry, he said. I didn't mean to be impertinent. Please overlook it. Just give me something to do. Put me to work.

In the state you're in, I doubt if you're fit to concentrate on office tasks. You had better go outside and buck up some of those logs in the pile into fireplace lengths. That should keep you busy for a while. After that, we'll see.

Brendan did as he was told. He took the old bucksaw from the barn, removed the rusty blade, and with a file sharpened the corroded teeth. He replaced the blade in the H-frame, then placed an eight foot oak log a foot in diameter on the sawbuck. In his two years in New Milford, he had filled out considerably; now he used the powerful new muscles in his arms and shoulders to push and pull the saw back and forth through the oak. He sawed all morning, cutting up the first log, and many after it, into two-foot lengths that would fit in the many fireplaces in Perry's home. He stopped briefly to eat a lunch in the kitchen that the cook prepared for him. Then he resumed sawing, relishing the work and the way it cleared his head. He didn't actually pretend the teeth were cutting Perry's flesh instead of the oak, but the effect was the same. He sawed steadily until dark, then went home to Mrs. Gunn's, tired, sore and at peace with himself.

CHAPTER NINE

1821 - 1822

WORD CAME FROM HARTFORD in February that Elijah Boardman, the wealthy scion of the town's leading family, had been selected by the General Assembly to be the next United States Senator. Boardman had previously served several terms in the House of the legislature as well as one in the upper chamber before 1818. He was a member of the State Senate, newly established under the new state constitution, at the time of his election to the U. S. Senate.

Not many people in New Milford were aware of it, but Elijah had been bitten by the Washington bug even earlier. In 1818, after he had been first elected to the State Senate, he had been nominated as one of seven contenders to replace that old Federalist, Dave Daggett, in the U.S. Senate. In the voting in the House, the chamber that made the selection, Elijah did pretty well on the first ballot. But he dropped off in the second, and was low man in the third and final tally. Even so, they remembered him two years later and he was elected.

No one in New Milford was particularly excited by Boardman's selection; Uriah Tracy of Litchfield had served in the Senate from 1796 to 1807. New Milford, although less populous than Litchfield, was regarded as its chief rival even though it could not match Litchfield's political and cultural status. But the feeling was that a major town in one of the state's eight counties was entitled to a senatorial appointment; after thirty-one years, it was time. Elijah Boardman fulfilled all the requirements; his family had been part of the ruling class in New England since his great-great grandfather, Samuel, had arrived in Ipswich, Massachusetts, in 1637. Samuel was Deputy from Wethersfield to the General Court, the forerunner of the legislature, for seven sessions and filled other important offices. His son, Daniel, was a landholder in Litchfield and New Milford; his son-in-law, John Griswold, set up the first gristmill in New Milford. Daniel's son, also named Daniel, was a Yale graduate, who served as the first pastor of the Congregational Church in the town from 1716 to 1744. His son, Captain Sherman, father of Elijah, was a member of the town's Committee of Correspondence during the Revolutionary War. Sherman was also a deacon of the church and in 1802 he was the leading taxpayer in town, with an income of $3,515 according to the church's seating plan for that year.

When the news arrived in New Milford, Perry had an evaluation for Brendan. He will be graceful and decorative but hardly effective, he said. He will be true to his aristocratic heritage, but don't expect him to do anything. He never did in Hartford.

Brendan thought of this as he labored at his newest task from Perry, to gauge sentiment in town on various transportation propositions, mainly toll roads. He had already talked to at least two dozen persons in past weeks as he casually made his way up and down both sides of the main street, in and out any store or office that he could find any excuse to enter. Usually the response he elicited when he eventually steered the conversation around to toll roads was uniformly negative. He was continually aware of how the ultra conservative character of the society retarded the development of the town and the state. The first legislative session of the new General Assembly had cut an already frugal budget by more than ten thousand dollars. Needs like education and transportation were ignored.

As he mulled the matter, he recalled his conversation with the Beecher brothers. The brothers, identical twins who had wed sisters, looked alike and even acted alike. When Brendan asked Deacon John what he thought of Isaac Hawley's proposal to "raise the bottom" of the Housatonic River, he twisted his neck, looked fixedly at the top of a nearby tree.

Why don't you ask Eleazer? he asked.

Elder Eleazer, how does Isaac Hawley's idea strike you? Brendan asked.

Eleazer twisted his neck in the same fashion as his brother, seemed to be uncomfortably looking at the same tree. I don't know that even Isaac be man enough to do that, he said.

At least they didn't say they were against it, Brendan said to himself.

The idea to dredge the Housatonic went back to 1761, when William Tanner and Jehiel Hawley, among others, were named by the General Assembly to conduct a study of the river to see if it could be rendered navigable and a lottery authorized to raise three-hundred and sixty pounds to fund the work. After a considerable amount was raised, Tanner died and Hawley suddenly moved from New Milford. Despite the Assembly's best efforts, the money was never recovered and the work never done.

Brendan decided to see Eli Todd at his tavern on Park Lane. Captain Eli had recently been revealed to be one one of the town's major taxpayers when the new seating arrangement was posted at the Congregational Church. He was worth $2,643, in ninth place, more than comfortable. He had been elected with Orange Merwin to go to the General Assembly in 1818 and again two years later.

Brendan enjoyed going to the taverns. It was not that he drank a lot, although he enjoyed a glass now and then with his friends. But there was always a cheerful atmosphere, the men there had plenty of time to talk, and they were the best places to find out what was going on and what was on people's minds. They smelled good, too; aside from the aromas from ale and spirits, there was usually the smell of hearty country cooking and, in cool weather, a comfortable wood fire. Todd had a store alongside, but all of the taverns sold at least a little tea, indigo, and other notions for the convenience of travellers. There were two on Main Street and others in different sections of town.

After a long conversation over Elijah's election to the Senate, the state of the world as seen in Hartford, and several items of local gossip, Brendan asked him what he heard about the plan to build a turnpike from the center of town westerly through Patterson, N. Y., to a town called Cold Spring Landing on the Hudson River.

Folks are agin it. I've talked to dozens of people and I haven't found one yet who thinks it's a good idea.

Brendan baited him a bit. Why not? It would open up a new transportation route to New York City. Farmers would be able to send salt pork and grain over there by wagon and ship it to the city by boat. It should mean a better price for the products we grow around here.

That's just a specious argument. Don't you know that the town would have to buy all the land for the route? We'd have to pay for a good share of the construction on our section and bridges---bridges is the mean part. Do you know how many bridges we'd have to build across every little shitty-assed brook along the way? The voters won't stand for it, they know the tax rate would go sky high.

Maybe the town could authorize a study, have an engineer go over the route, see how many bridges would be necessary, the amount of land to be acquired, and compute the cost.

Captain Eli sniffed. What do you expect it would cost the

town to hire such a fellow? Even then he'd probably come in with a low estimate to get us started on the work, and then remember some expenses he had conveniently overlooked in his first calculations. We're on to those kind of tricks and we're not going to get involved in such a thing.

The toll road from here to Roxbury and then on to Southbury passed at a town meeting just a few years ago though. That turned out pretty fair for the town didn't it? Even though there was an organized group here to work against it.

A road to a nearby town makes more sense than burrowing through the hills to New York State. One thing I learned in the legislature is that there is always some fellow who can come up with an idea that looks good at first glance but what's going to cost the rate payers a lot of money. These turnpike developers are not exactly disinterested fellows you know. They got a new idea every week how to make money for theyselves. A while back they wanted to go through Hawley's bridge, through Bridgewater Society, on through Washington to Litchfield. We come down hard on that one. Now every year they keep pushing in the legislature to make New Preston Society a separate town. The town has hired Abel Merwin and Beebe Hine to fight that one. Beebe's been out there a good many years. He knows his way around.

New Preston's part of Washington, why do you care if it's a separate town?

New Milford's the biggest town in the state. If they start splitting up towns, we got the most to lose. You're new around here. I can see you think we are against every new idea. But let me tell you, there's one turnpike I would support. That's to Sherman.

Brendan laughed. Sherman's only five or six miles away.

All right, I favor a pike to Litchfield, too. Makes sense to connect with the county seat. Some time down the line I can see pushing one down to Saugatuck.

There's more there than meets the eye, isn't there? Brendan asked.

Eli nodded his head and winked sagely. You ought to talk to Orange Merwin. He thinks that if you got the right of way for a pike you might be able to use it for a canal, too.

A canal? Brendan was incredulous.

Now who's thinking small? Eli was triumphant. You talk about getting pork barrels to New York. This would be a lot more direct than building toll roads for the Yorkers. The idea is still in its early stages, but Orange is on to it. He'll worry the idea until he gets it set up proper.

Eli knew what he was talking about. In March delegates from several towns meeting in New Milford approved a committee to secure funds for building a canal to extend from tidewater in Derby to Canaan on the Massachusetts state line. At first the proposal moved along swiftly; in April a town meeting in New Milford approved a petition to the next General Assembly asking incorporation of a company to establish navigation on the Housatonic River by means of a canal. In their usual usurious mood, the voters stipulated that nothing in the agreement could be construed as subjecting the town to any expenditures for purchase of land.

Subsequently, an engineering study estimated that the sixty-six mile project would cost $389,400. This figure included aqueducts, culverts, bridges, excavations and embankments, but not the construction of the sixty locks which would be needed to facilitate transit of the ascent of more than 600 feet. Each lock would cost an average of $3,500, thus bringing the total cost of the canal project to nearly $600,000.

By June, arrangements for a $500,000 stock subscription were made. Investors were invited to sign up at meetings at taverns in Canaan Falls, Kent, New Milford, Southbury and Derby

Landing on consecutive days from July 1 through the fourth. A five-percent down payment was required of each subscriber.

Orange Merwin was the chairman of commissioners for Ousatonic Canal Company. He was the principal drafter of a public statement on the project which revealed that the extension of the project into Massachusetts was already contemplated. This terminus at Stockbridge would be some thirty-five miles from Albany. The river valley at some points was so narrow that it barely left enough room for the canal and the road alongside it. The route was marked by three principal falls, in Canaan, in Kent, and in New Milford. Blasting by Cornelius McMahon to accommodate a gristmill had reduced the falls in New Milford considerably.

Merwin's committee expected the Ousatonic Canal to transport lime, marble, iron ore, cast and wrought iron, building stone, brick, clay, timber, posts, rails and finished lumber including barrel staves. Craft using the waterway would also carry such farm commodities as wheat, rye, oats, corn, potatoes, milled flour, cider, hay, beef, pork, butter, and cheese. The report noted that quarries, both for stone and for making white lime existed in every town above tidewater along the route. Stone from the area had already been used in construction of the City Hall in New York. At one point twenty-three saw mills cut marble for building use.

The legislative committee to which the project was assigned, chaired by Frederick Wolcott, issued a favorable report, but the canal never moved forward for reasons which are not entirely clear. What is clear, is that it gave Orange Merwin additional impetus in his career of public service.

Brendan followed the progress of the proposed canal and its eventual demise closely. He was at Booth's Tavern in New Milford on July 3 when several New Milford businessmen came forward to subscribe funds.

CHAPTER TEN

April 1822

IN APRIL OF 1822 Perry Smith was elected one of New Milford's representatives to the General Assembly. Samuel Canfield was elected with him to the other seat.

Campaigning was always low-key; there were few speeches, no billboards, no advertising (or newspapers in which to publish them). But there was intense behind-the-scenes activity as candidates made every effort to enlist the support of leading men in the town who had much influence with the voters. Perry made much of how he would cut spending once in Hartford, he spoke out against proponents of additional toll roads, and against the demoralized Federalists, whom he characterized as lovers of monarchy and aristocracy. He sneered at the abolitionists who were against property rights and were, he said, nigger lovers.

Perry touched the right notes: he outpolled his running mate, Canfield by a respectable margin, even though Canfield had one of the oldest names in the community and was well liked and respected in his own right.

Perry was properly humble at the meeting house when the results of the ballot counting were announced. He made a few short remarks in which he thanked the men present for the honor they had vested in him and promised to work untiringly on behalf of the town at the next session against the newfangled ideas which Governor Oliver Wolcott, Jr., of Litchfield had been trying to enact since the new constitution went into effect after 1818. This was a veiled slap at Orange Merwin, who had shown himself as a proponent of reforms already adopted in some of the frontier states, such as tax reform, annual bank reports to the Assembly, and suffrage for all adult males. He said how proud he was to have an associate as distinguished as Samuel Canfield in the Assembly. He paid tribute to the retiring legislators, Daniel Pickett and Eli Todd, who had not run again. He got a big hand from the crowd.

Perry invited Brendan to the house. He was exultant as he walked up the east side of the common toward his house.

Not bad for a couple of non-natives, eh?

Brendan appreciated the tacit recognition of his role in the victory. He had helped sound sentiment on several issues and brought back reports of how some of the crucial individuals were lining up. But he didn't fool himself. He knew Perry himself circulated widely and ingratiated himself energetically in key circles.

You ran a smart campaign and you won because you said the right things to the right people, he said.

In one of the front rooms of the brick house, Anne had directed the setting up of an elaborate buffet. There were chafing dishes for turkey, chicken, duck, geese, veal, red beef and spare ribs. There were pastries, sweet and hearty, whole cakes of different flavors and textures, cookies,and fruits. There were also decanters of hard cider, rum and rye whiskey.

Perry greeted his wife exuberantly. She looked flushed and happy. Brendan thought he had never seen her so pretty before. At her side little Elvira seemed bewildered by all the fuss and the turmoil as Perry's partisans arrived for the celebration. Young John, the Smith son whom Perry had never seen before, sullenly eyed the tables of food, impatient to snatch some of the pastries.

When I go down to New Haven next month, I'm going to miss you two. Perry hugged Anne and picked up Elvira to kiss her. But it will only be for a couple of months. I've told Brendan to stop by every day. If you need anything, just tell him what you want done. I know he will be ready to get a tradesman if you need one, or see to it that you get whatever you need from any of the stores.

That's right, I'll be available, Brendan said.

The crowd swelled and Perry welcomed the guests as they came up the stone steps, some puffing a bit from the steep ascent from the end of the common. He urged them to eat and drink at the tables as the hired girls endeavored to keep up with the demand by bringing more food from the kitchen down the hall. Brendan's job was to divert some of the less socially acceptable arrivals to the barn in the rear where some of the meats and a keg of hard cider were set up. He was used to this; during the campaign one of his missions was to provide a jug of cider now and then in somebody's horse barn to the elements more interested in this diversion than in any of the issues Perry addressed. Earlier in the day his job was to make sure that the chronic tipplers voted before accepting his hospitality in the back of the United States Hotel. Fortunately, most of this ilk were now too drunk to provide any threat to the social conventions at Perry's home.

When Perry set off for New Haven early in May, Brendan was there to see him off, along with Anne and Elvira. As usual, John was not to be seen. Perry was going to drive all the way in his own buggy, so he would have some means of getting around New Haven during the next two months. Perry was not given to the exercise travelling by horseback provided and the roads were now good enough to permit travel in a light vehicle. He would stay overnight in Oxford and push on to the coast the next day.

It's a bit closer than Hartford and the hills aren't so steep, Perry said. This is just practice for getting to Hartford in the next term, he joked.

The legislature alternated sessions in Hartford and New Haven for half a century after the adoption of the 1818 constitution.

You don't need to be so elated over leaving us, Anne said. It seemed to Brendan that she was speaking with some bite to her tone, in contrast with Perry's jovial tone.

No tears, no sorrow. It's just a few weeks. Perry continued in the same light tone. Then he kissed his wife and daughter, vaulted into the buggy and set the horse into a trot down the street. They waved to him, but he was busy nodding to townspeople until he was out of sight.

This is the first time he's left us for so long since we were married, Anne said.

It's only a few weeks. It's a great honor for him to be serving the town in this way.

Anne said nothing and hugged Elvira who was silently weeping.

Is there anything you want me to do today? I'll have a lot of free time now that the campaign is over and Perry isn't here to assign tasks for me. Please tell me if there's anything at all. I'll come around about nine in the morning if that's satisfactory to you.

No, nothing now. That will be fine.

Brendan headed toward the center, wondering how he would pass the days during this period. Not for the first time, he silently lamented the lack of a library in the town. There was just no way he could read to continue his education.

The next morning, once in the back office in the Smith house, Brendan determined to clean up the copying chores that had accumulated in recent weeks. He had a neat, legible hand that his primary school teachers in New York had instilled in him by dint of much practice. Perry's handwriting was execrable, so bad that Brendan had to puzzle often over the notes he had left. He liquidated the backlog of correspondence by mid-morning and began on some briefs for civil cases that Perry would need when he returned from New Haven. They mostly involved suits over land boundaries and were so uninteresting that his mind frequently wandered and he caught himself several times on the verge of committing errors. Perry would not tolerate words scratched out, so errors meant a new start on another sheet of paper.

A few minutes before eleven, there was a light knock on the opened door. Anne stood in the opening holding a tray with a glass of home-made root beer and some cookies

I thought you might like some refreshment, she said.

Good morning, Mrs. Smith. Brendan rose respectfully.

Please sit down. There is no need to stand on ceremony. She put the tray on his work table, but made no move to leave.

How is Mrs. Gunn?

She's fine. She's always very active. But of course I only see her for brief periods in the morning and the evening.

The truth is that he had never thought much about how Mrs. Gunn was. She always treated him with considerable kindness, but they didn't share thoughts with each other very often. Then he saw Anne slide into another chair. She seemed to want to chat.

I know she is a pleasant woman, but it's not like your own family. You must miss your mother and sister.

Yes, I do. But I've gotten used to it. He had never spoken with Anne about his family. In fact he had had only brief contacts with her as he carried out various chores Perry had asked him to do for her. Perry must have told her that his mother and sister were his only close relatives.

I'm sure it's very hard for you. My mother and father live in Park Lane, but I would be very lonely if I couldn't see them now and then. You know, I'm only six years older than you.

You do look young, Mrs. Smith, but with the children and all your social responsibilities, you seem more mature. Brendan hoped that was the right thing to say.

You must't call me Mrs. Smith. That's horribly formal. Everyone calls me Anne.

Brendan knew that everyone didn't call her Anne. New Milford was a small town, but there were distinctions. The youths in town didn't call married women by their first names unless they were family or had grown up together as neighbors.

Yes, Anne. Of course. It was hard to get it out.

She laughed. You'll get used to it. I do hope we can be friends. I have to get back and see what Elvira's doing.

Is there anything I can do for you today?

No, thank you. We'll see tomorrow.

Brendan was vaguely puzzled and certainly pleased by her overtures, but gave it no further thought as he resumed his work. He left at noon and during the afternoon he made his usual rounds of the center even though there was no reason for him to do so. In fact, he enjoyed his contacts with the people he met, especially the conversations which gave him insights into the relationships that tied all the residents into a community. These still surprised him, and delighted him, too. In spite of the reserved nature of most people, there was much more communication among them and a greater interest and awareness of what was happening to others, than in Five Points, for example.

Over the weeks, the daily visits from Anne continued each morning. As Brendan completed the tasks pending when Perry left, there was less and less for him to do in the office, although he sought to arrange papers and books more neatly. Anne gave him two old pieces of furniture from the cellar so he could better dispose of some of the books and files that had been stacked on the floor.

Anne went into the cellar with him to indicate the pieces he was to use. There was little light entering through the small panes of the narrow cellar windows, so Anne brought a lighted candle the better to see around the place. Brendan was surprised at the size of the cellar, but even more struck at the cut stone construction. Unlike other cellars he had been in in New Milford, there was no dirt floor but an even stone surface composed of cut squares of stone, some four to six feet in length. It was subdivided into sections and rooms.

This looks more like a medieval castle than a cellar, Brendan said in wonder.

Yes, it has always fascinated me, too. It took several yokes of oxen weeks to bring these huge stones from Mine Hill over in Roxbury, to say nothing of the time it took the stone masons to cut them and fit them into place. She held the candle high and moved it around to show various features of the workmanship.

Brendan disassembled the furniture as much as possible to get it up the stairway. He made several trips with the drawers, shelves and parts he had removed. Anne remained with the candle, looking around at items that interested her. When he had carried up all the elements, she seemed reluctant to leave the place, but finally led the way up, holding the candle to illuminate the stairs. Brendan had the opportunity to see how well shaped her ankles and lower calves were, and the thrust of her buttocks through her skirt as she ascended. Anne was strongly built, although her waist was slender, and she was supple in her movements.

As the days passed, Brendan came to look forward to Anne's visits each morning, and they now talked without constraint. Sometimes they discussed town affairs or talked about national figures they had read about, but as time went on, they talked more about their own interests, what they liked and what they didn't like, what their hopes were for the future. Brendan had never in his life had the opportunity to talk at such length with a woman, even his own sister or his mother. He found it exhilarating. He discovered that Anne had only an elementary school education, but that she liked to read, and had, in fact, read books, including novels. Moreover, she was shrewd and perceptive and had a sense of humor that surprised him. She told droll stories about members of the Boardman family, especially young George, who, it seems was frail and "peculiar." There was some question about his manhood, although Anne was most discreet about this. She knew all about the Bostwicks, the Taylors, the Canfields, the Todds, the Merwins, the Treats, in fact, not just about the "first families", but about all the people in town. Brendan reflected ruefully how superficial his sounding had been when compared with the wealth of information Anne could dispense concerning almost anyone in the town. He was fascinated.

As the weeks passed into June, Brendan realized that Perry would be returning, probably before the end of the month. The thought depressed him. His return would certainly mean the end of his pleasant sessions with Anne.

That morning he told her he would miss his talks with her.

I have never been able to talk to any woman as I have to you. I know that when Perry comes back, our time together will end. That makes me very sad.

Anne looked at him for some seconds steadily. Come with me, she said finally. She led the way out of the office toward the front of the house, but turned and at the wide stairway with the mahogany bannister and started up. He was baffled, but continued behind her.

On the second floor, she turned into a small bedroom at the rear of the house. After they both had entered, she firmly closed the door. She stood before him and again stared at him very intently. Then suddenly she advanced a couple of steps, deliberately put her arms around his neck, pulled his face down to her own and kissed him on the lips. Despite his astonishment, Brendan put his arms tightly around her and returned the kiss. After a moment, she pulled her face away and smiled at him.

I've been wanting to do that for a long time. I'm going to do it again.

Brendan never relaxed his grasp but pulled her tighter as they kissed again. Suddenly she amazed him again, by opening her mouth and trying to force her tongue between his lips. He didn't know what to do.

Anne pulled her head back and smiled at him.

I bet you never French-kissed before. I see I have a lot to teach you. Open your mouth a little.

Brendan did as he was told as she wiggled closer to him. He thrust his tongue against her's and closed his eyes to savor the pleasure of it. He could feel the pressure of her breasts against him, and her pelvis as he pulled her tightly. After a time he held her with his left arm and stroked her back with his right. He could tell she liked it. He moved his right hand to her left buttock and pulled it toward him. He could hear her gasp slightly. They continued to kiss until she pulled away. Brendan felt like he was on fire.

You're learning fast. This is warm work for June.

Ann took a step back and unbuttoned the front of her dress so that she could slide it off her shoulders and pull her arms free of it. The dress fell over her hips to the floor. Then she pulled up a shift over her head and dropped it to the floor. Then she shook herself free from her embroidered drawers and kicked off her shoes. A flash of fire passed through Brendan's guts. He stood mesmerized, motionless.

Again she approached him and clasped him in her arms. He

returned her kisses passionately, blindly, pulling her to him. After a moment her hands sought the buttons on his shirt. One by one she undid them as he hardly noticed. Then her hands dropped to his belt buckle and undid it, she fumbled with the buttons of his pants, frustrated by the pressure they were bringing against each other. Finally his brain functioned and he released her. He threw off the shirt, ripped off the pants, then his underclothes.

Please take off your shoes, she whispered.

He did. She led him to the bed.

Now you be gentle with me. Kiss me. Touch me lightly. Do you like the feel of my skin?

You're so wonderful. You're so beautiful. His words were muffled by her kisses. She steered his mouth to her breasts, her body arched and tense. Then she showed him how to rub her breasts, and she moaned softly. After a time she steered his hand to her pubic area and showed him how to stroke her. He felt her hand squeeze him. It drove him even more wild. After a long while, she pulled him on top of her, raised her knees on each side of his hips and guided him inside her.

Softly, easy. Do it slowly. I want to feel it for a hundred years.

Brendan tried to obey, but this was beyond him. He thrust deeply, quickly, only a few times. The semen spurted into her for what seemed minutes. He had never felt anything so wonderful in his life. He continued to pump for a long time and Anne groaned with ecstasy.

Finally, he stopped but continued to kiss her passionately. After a time they just lay still in the bed clasped tightly to each other. Minutes later she stirred.

Let me breathe. A gentleman doesn't rest all his weight on the lady.

He lay at her side still clasping her to him. He was still breathing deeply.

Poor Brendan. I didn't know it was the first time for you. I shouldn't have done it. But I wanted to badly. You were so good. I'm so glad we did. Don't be angry with me.

Angry? This is the most wonderful thing that ever happened to me in my whole life. I don't know how to tell you the feelings for you that are making me almost burst.

Almost burst? I think you did. It was like a spring freshet.

Don't laugh at me, Anne. I'm still trying to figure out what has happened to me and how I could be so lucky.

Don't bother, my love. Just touch me. I love to feel you against me. Just lie quiet against me.

They did lie quietly for a long while. Finally Brendan began to stir again. This time he didn't need Anne to tell him what to do.

Finally they were quiet again.

Please go now, Anne said. We'll talk about this tomorrow when you arrive. I think I can trust you not to talk about this. If you have to tell someone, write your mother.

CHAPTER ELEVEN

June 1822

THAT NIGHT IN HIS BED in Mrs. Gunn's loft, Brendan was feverish as again and again he relived the experience of the morning with Anne. He had known about sex in a theoretical fashion, without any conception of how it actually transpired or of its shattering psychological implications. The delight and the wonder of it harrowed his consciousness; he couldn't stop running it through his brain, some of it fast, some of it slowly, lovingly, concentrated.

In time though, his thoughts passed to other associations. What was to be his relationship with Anne henceforth? How could he look at her without wanting to feel her, smell her, taste her? How could he be in her presence without others knowing the overpowering attraction she held for him? He doubted that he could be near her and not show in his face how much he wanted her. How could he face Perry when he returned? These were all questions he would have to face, perhaps within days. He didn't have any idea how or where he was going to get the answers.

When was Perry coming back? No one knew. By the time the news came about the end of the session, Perry might well already be here. In spite of the deception over his education and legal training, he owed a great deal to Perry. Without the job

Perry had given him, he might well have been, indeed probably would have been, a day laborer. Brendan had done enough heavy labor to know that it was fine exercise in small doses but a grinding, hopeless existence when it occupied all a lifetime. The farmers here worked terribly hard, all year round, but at least they were the masters of their own destiny within their own domain. They could look forward to the prospect of becoming well-to-do if not wealthy. Even now, what could he do if Perry showed him the door? The answer was not very much. He has no skill, no profession, nor the prospect of either. He had been a youth when he arrived in New Milford, but now he was a man and four years were gone.

He finally slept, but when he awoke in the morning, his delemmas were waiting for him. His first decision was to accept Anne's advise. Perhaps it had been merely a quip, not advise, but it now seemed a wise step to take. Even before he descended for breakfast, he took up a pencil and wrote to his mother.

Dearest Mother,

Usually I call you Mom, but today I have something vital to tell you, so it seems appropriate to be more formal.

Yesterday for the first time in my life I had a woman. I have thought of nothing else since. It was the most wonderful thing that ever happened to me. I can hear you saying that is certainly a good thing and that you are happy for me and that now we should plan for the wedding. This I would like to do, but I can't. The woman is already married and she has two children. Her husband is the Perry Smith who, as I wrote you before, is the man who gave me a good job when I arrived here and who has been very kind to me. I owe him a great deal.

Perry is a legislator in the state government. He has been in New Haven for a legislative session and will return in a few days. It will be difficult for me to face him but I must. Clearly I must put an end to my liaison with his wife. This will be wrenching because I like her very much, I respect her and it is devastating to think that I can no longer be near her.

I know there is nothing you can do in this case, but it makes me feel better to tell you about it. In thinking back on it, I feel I was far too hasty to judge you before I left Five Points. Although our situations are not comparable, far from it, in fact, I can see now that it is not as easy as I previously conceived it to be to act responsibly in the face of terrible dilemmas.

I hope you will be understanding with me and pray that God will give me strength. I hope also that you and Agnes are well; I think of you often. Please write to me at Mrs. Abner Gunn's house on Grove Street.

Your loving son,
Brendan

For some reason, he didn't understand why, Brendan felt better after finishing the letter and addressing the envelope. He descended to the kitchen where Mrs. Gunn was waiting for him so she could cook his breakfast.

You're late today Brendan. Are you feeling all right? She hovered around him like an anxious grandmother.

I'm just fine. I just decided to write my mother. I haven't done it for quite a while.

Such a good boy! Some day you will make some girl a fine husband.

It was not a consoling thought under the circumstances, but he knew he couldn't wince every time someone made a remark that recalled Anne to him.

Later at the post office, he chatted with the Postmaster, Philo Noble. Philo had been in the job a long time and certainly knew everyone in town. Not much escaped him, but he was always discreet.

Good morning, Brendan. When is Perry getting back?

Any day now. The session must be almost over, but I don't know the exact date.

I can imagine that Perry is making quite an impression with the leaders. It's good for the town to have two men so well thought of in the legislature. But he's got to get back and tend to his business.

That's right. You can't eat off what the legislature pays you.

And a good thing, too, or more fellows would want to go up there.

Brendan chuckled appreciatively and headed up the street. In one sense he dreaded going up to the brick house, but in another the prospect filled him with excitement. How do you act with a woman you have lain with and who is the wife of your boss? He found it wildly comic, but then immediately was contrite. He marched on.

He entered the office as usual, but then remembered he had nothing to do. He rearranged the books and papers for a while, then gave up and idly picked up a copy of *The Connecticut Courant* lying on the table. He passed over the first page, which was almost always filled with advertisements. The second page normally contained accounts of events all over the world, most of them reprinted, with credit, from other American newspapers or from European papers, usually English or French. On the third page, devoted to state affairs, was an account of the opening of the General Assembly in New Haven on May 1.

The article listed Perry and Samuel Canfield as the representatives from New Milford. On May 2, Samuel Beers, the new Speaker of the House from Litchfield, appointed Perry to the committee on steamboats, an important designation for Perry because of the lively ongoing controversy with other states, but mainly New York, over docking privileges for the shipping lines of each state in the ports of the others. The *Courant* also reported on Perry's attempt to remove Litchfield County Sheriff Albert Sedgwick from office, but gave no account of the debate on the matter or an explanation of Perry's reasons. Perry's resolution was rejected, 98 to 100 and barely carried with Litchfield County legislators, 19 to 18. Perry's motion did carry among the legislators from New London, Middlesex and Tolland counties, but there was a tie vote in the delegation from Hartford County.

Brendan had never heard Perry mention the matter before the session; he sat speculating what Perry's motives might have been when, just before ten, he heard the little rap on the open door.

Good morning, Brendan. Anne walked to his chair, forced him to stay in the seat, and kissed him on the forehead.

No, sit still. I want to talk to you.

She was even more beautiful than he remembered, Brendan thought. Her eyes sparkled and her wide mouth was inviting. He noted more than he would have before yesterday the tautness her swelling breasts produced in the bodice of her dress. She began to speak.

I am Perry Smith's wife and I want to stay married to him. I don't love him nor have I ever but he has been a good husband to me. My parents wanted me to marry him because he was a rising young man with good prospects. He hasn't disappointed them, nor me either, really. I didn't resist marrying him. We have gotten along well, in the main. There was the affair of John's birth, but women expect that. John, you see, is not my son. He was the result of an affair Perry had with an old girlfriend after we were married. We adopted the boy and I try to give him the same love that I give to Elvira. Some people in town know about this, and I'm afraid John has some inkling of this because he is a strange and difficult boy. But Perry, I believe, has been faithful to me since then. His only mistress now is politics, for which he has more passion than he'll ever have for any woman.

That brings me to us. I have felt a great love develop in me for you since I first saw you in this office four years ago. You are not only handsome and manly but I feel you are sensitive and compassionate as well. I would probably love you even though you were not, but I am glad that is not the case. Since we have been here together in the mornings, I have felt an overpowering desire for you. You were all I ever hoped for in a man yesterday. I was absolutely transported. It is not good form to confess these things, but I want to tell you anyhow.

Finally, I feel guilty because I seduced you. Yes, don't protest; I know I did. I never dreamed that at the age of twenty you were still a virgin. The sexes are kept very strictly apart around here, but even so I doubt that there are many men your age who have preserved their chastity. I think this is a wonderful thing and I admire you for it. And even though I am guilty I must tell you that every second of that experience is a precious memory to me.

To conclude, I hope you will agree that this is something that neither one of us will ever mention to anyone. It would destroy me in every sense of the word if it should ever come out. You must know it would have very serious consequences for you as well. When Perry returns, we must continue as we did before, with only the most distant of relationships.

Brendan responded slowly and soberly.

You are kind and generous and wise in everything you say. Certainly I will be bound by your wishes, and I accept that this is not only the best but the only course for us to follow. But I shall never put aside the love and admiration I feel for you. I have written my mother and told her that.

Anne rose, walked to Brendan's chair and threw herself in his lap. She put her arms around him and kissed him violently.

Now that we have an understanding, I'm not going to give

you up until I have to. This morning I received a letter from Perry that he will return next Tuesday. I want you every single morning through Friday. That will give me three days to get over the excitement and make myself a dutiful wife again. Do you agree?

Any reprieve is welcome. He kissed her with ardor.

I should tell you that John and Elvira are with the Smiths in Judea Parish until Saturday. I have given the help a few days off as well. But this office is not a prudent location for us. We will be more comfortable upstairs.

He picked her up and carried her up the stairs.

You are the most special woman in the world, he told her.

CHAPTER TWELVE

June–August 1822

BRENDAN GREETED PERRY with every appearance of warmth. He asked about the session and Perry was only too glad to oblige with an exhaustive description of what had transpired as well as an analysis of the struggle between Governor Oliver Wolcott and the Assembly.

In principle, the Governor and a majority of the legislators were Jeffersonian Republicans, or as some styled themselves, Democratic Republicans. But they couldn't have been further apart. The Governor, a Litchfield aristocrat, advocated a program which he felt would extricate Connecticut from the dead-end of subsistence farming. He wanted to build roads that would sustain industrial traffic, not just paths for wagons and a few coaches. He was interested in providing access to present markets and developing new ones. He had a program for standardizing and improving education across the state so that people moving into the cities from the farms would be equipped to hold down jobs in a new industrial economy.

The legislators weren't buying any of this. Now that the reforms of 1818 had been enacted, there was a strong conservative reaction. In a sense, the Democratic Republicans, in destroying the Federalist Party, had eliminated their own *raison d'être.* They had no real program and they couldn't accept the

Governor's. Almost all rural conservatives, they were only interested in preserving the rural hegemony and cutting expenditures, no matter what. Orange Merwin and a handful of others supported the Governor, but they were heavily outnumbered. As one writer put it, "An undistinguished crowd of unknown men, representing citizens of many small towns, would set the tone of Connecticut politics." Set it for generations, as it turned out.

In listening to Perry's account, it was clear to Brendan that while Perry admired Governor Wolcott and envied him his high social station, he saw the road to success lay with going along with the rural legislators. Perry was not one to carry on a crusade or support someone else's, particularly if it might interfere with his own advancement. Frugality was not a strong personal quality in him, but he wouldn't obstruct frugality in government even if it degenerated into parsimony.

Brendan listened intently because he was genuinely absorbed in the subject. Occasionally he threw out a question, which Perry would seize on eagerly as an aid in fleshing out his presentation. Brendan asked him about his narrowly unsuccessful attempt to remove from office High Sheriff Albert Sedgwick. Perry brushed aside the query and made it plain he didn't want to talk about it.

It struck Brendan: it was easy to dissemble. Perry, in dissembling about his role in the Sedgwick affair, didn't realize his questioner was doing the same thing concerning his relationship with Perry's wife. All that was required was audacity and shamelessness. In this instance, he saw through Perry's maneuver, but did anyone see through his own? This led him again to think of Anne. It was wrenching to think she was right in this building, yet he couldn't even get to see her, let alone feel her skin. All the rest of his life he could not touch her hair, touch her life. He inwardly resisted these bonds; it just couldn't be.

After an hour of exposition, Perry realized that he had other obligations, such as catching up with his law practice. He looked at his gold watch.

I'm much obliged to you for the helping hand you gave Anne in my absence.

Glad to. Brendan was overly conscious of the irony inherent in the wording of both the question and the answer.

Perry left him some copying work, picked up his accumulated correspondence, and left.

As Brendan settled down to his new tasks, he couldn't but help think of his future. He had reluctantly come to realize that he couldn't continue indefinitely as Perry's employee. And not just because of his relationship with Perry's wife. With Perry so strongly involved in politics and correspondingly less so in the law, he really had no need for anyone to be doing much of the work that had been occupying Brendan. Before long Perry would realize this. More basically, Brendan himself was at a dead end. What had been suitable employment for a sixteen year-old was rather demeaning for a young man on the threshold of what should be his career. Brendan had given up any hope of studying for the law. Perry had made it clear that whatever Brendan's educational qualifications, Perry had no intention of having him read law in his office.

Lately, in talking with tavern keepers such as Eli Todd, John Hull and Amassa Ferriss, it had occurred to him that this was an occupation which he would enjoy. But these men all owned substantial establishments which he was as far from being able to afford as going to law school. He observed, however, that big as these taverns were, with their commodious accommodations, kitchens, pantries, dining rooms, and hostler services, in all cases it was just the bar which brought in most of the income. Why not set up just a bar business? He recalled that Five Points and the rest of New York had had hundreds of such bars or saloons. More soberly, he also remembered that many of these saloons had also offered back rooms for prostitutes. This train of thought always brought him back to the life style of his mother and sister. He deliberately put the memory aside. In New Milford up to this point there was not a single bar; he concentrated on this fact.

In looking into the temperance movement with Perry, one fact had become abundantly clear to Brendan: liquor establishments, even those rather sloppily run, were great money earners. He had no illusions about the social status of bar owners, but then what status did he have now? Even as a lawyer, no Irish Catholic would be socially acceptable in rural New England. On the other hand, he had noted that an adequate income went a long way toward assuring social acceptance, even if the possessor was not a member of the founding families. He had been told about Angus Nickelson who came to New Milford as a poor immigrant Scot and by 1790 had one of the highest tax assessments in town. The same portrait artist who had done paintings of the Boardmans and the Taylors had painted the rather graceless Nickelson family as well.

In succeeding weeks, as he continued to work for Perry, Brendan continued to ponder the venture. He figured he could rent a small house, even a barn, on the outskirts of town and set up such a business. He had heard that there were some two-hundred and thirty distilleries in Connecticut. It was not hard to imagine that he could settle on one or two out of that number who would stake him to the capital he would need to set up and stock the business. As he mulled the matter over time, he finally decided to go ahead with the project.

By fall, he had located a good, tight, horse barn a half mile north of the village on the west side of Aspetuck hill, just up from the Merryall road. The barn had been part of the Cogswell farm, but the house had burned down one winter night. The disaster drove the family to move west; the place appeared to be abandoned. Elisha Cogswell, a kin of the departed, claimed to represent the family, so Brendan made a deal with him. He would rent the barn for five dollars a month, beginning the first of November, and would have the right to alter it and run a business in it. He and Elisha drew up the agreement together without benefit of any outside consultation.

Brendan was elated at the prospect. He didn't have much experience with tools, but he figured he could make the second floor, which had served as a hay mow, into adequate living quarters. He would set up a bar on the ground floor, laying it out on the model of the public rooms in the local taverns. The area already had a rough plank floor; he would keep the barn doors closed and install a smaller doorway for the customers. He had to admit to himself that the accommodations would be fairly crude, but the saloons he remembered in Five Points had not been distinguished by their comforts. He looked around for a source of water; he knew the Cogswells would have had a supply. He discovered a barrel sunk in the ground no more than a hundred feet from the remains of the house. He cleaned it out; the bottom half of it filled with water. He bailed it with a pail and found that the water level remained constant, which was a good sign at the end of the hot summer. A spring flowed from the ground underneath the barrel. Now he had all the essentials.

In the following weeks, he used his free hours to canvass some of the distillers on the outskirts of the town. These were all farmers who were trying to convert their grain crops and fruit harvests into cash. They were all sceptical that Brendan could establish a business that would have a regular need for their products, but they didn't have so many outlets that they could afford to overlook a possibility. He didn't make any deals at first, but he was able to see which farmers were the best prospects and determine what the costs would be. He knew that these contacts meant the word would spread about his plans, but that was inevitable.

Brendan was confident he could conclude all the physical arrangements but there were other aspects of his project that made him uneasy. He was not sure that Elisha actually had the right to bargain for the departed Cogswells, but he reasoned if someone turned up with a better title, he would bargain with that person. He had some doubts about the source of his supplies; hardly any of the farmers he talked to had more than a dozen barrels of any of their specialties; he might have to go further afield to guarantee a reliable source. The other side of the coin was how many customers he would have. The town was small, most householders put in their own supply. His obvious market were young farm workers and clerks in the stores who had not yet set up homes. This was not a sector with a lot of cash. His most sensitive problem is how the town would look upon his enterprise. Would the established forces regard him as a threat to good order and stability? This was an imponderable he would have to chance. He was prepared for opposition from the temperance group, but he knew their ranks were sparse. His major challenge would be to show the town that he ran a decent house that was not a stain on its social fabric, that was not a focus of dissipation. Balancing his need for income against potential abuses which could generate powerful opposition to him would test his acumen and character.

During one of his morning sessions with Perry, in the week following his talks with the farmers, Perry abruptly switched from a political discussion to a question.

When do you plan to open your fabulous drinking emporium?

Brendan was flustered. He had hoped to put off mentioning it until he was closer to beginning the business.

I don't have a fixed date yet. There are many things I have to do yet.

I'm relieved to know that. You know, of course that you will need a license to operate from the Board of Selectmen. I presume you are planning on a tavern since no other drinking establishment can legally serve intoxicating beverages on the premises.

Perry did not mention that many such establishment did precisely this quite comfortably outside the law, a law more widely observed in the breach than in the observance. But the point had scored with Brendan; he had a sinking sensation in his belly.

No, I didn't know that.

Brendan, you are an individual of more than average intelligence. I am utterly confounded that you would initiate such an enterprise without consulting someone who knows something about the legal requirements. I thought I was your friend. I could have advised you.

Brendan reddened with embarrassment.

I could not have lived in this town the past four years without you. You have been very good to me. You have taught me many things. I owe you everything I have. It's just that I thought it was time for me to start on my own. I didn't want to bother you with my concerns when you are busy with important matters, town and state affairs.

Do you know your agreement with Elisha Cogswell has no legal validity whatsoever?

I reckoned that was the case. I though it probably wouldn't be challenged, since his family moved away.

Perry regarded him seriously for a long moment. Finally he leaned toward Brendan and spoke very deliberately.

Since you have chosen not to confide in me as a friend, I will make you a business deal. I accept that you want to launch out on your own and that is a good thing. But if you continue on your present course you are almost certain to get in serious difficulties. I think there are legal ways in which your business might be started and these pitfalls avoided. I propose to help you if you are willing. I will undertake to secure the license for your establishment, conclude a legal and binding agreement for your use of the Cogswell property, and attend to any other legal problems which might present themselve. I will also attempt to counsel you in business matters, in which I have had no little experience as you are well aware. In exchange for this, I will ask that you pay me either a fee of two hundred dollars, or agree to pay me five per cent of your gross income for the next ten years.

Brendan was flabbergasted by the offer. Two hundred dollars was almost as much as he earned a year with Perry now. Ten years seemed like an extraordinarily long time, much more drastic than the five per cent in his young perception. Even so, he knew Perry was right, he had blundered badly in attempting to enter a field he knew nothing about without securing competent advise. He felt foolish and immature. Once more Perry had demonstrated his dominance; now he would be able to do this for another decade. It was galling, but it occurred to him that the long term obligation would, in effect, make Perry his legal protector, not a bad thing in a business likely to encounter problems with the law. He swallowed his pride and resentment.

You are very patient with me, very good to make such an offer. I prefer the ten year arrangement.

I think you have made a wise decision. I will draw up papers in which you will agree to designate me as your counselor in return for the percentage. I think you will realize that I am confident of your honesty for otherwise I would have little recourse in determining what the volume of your business will be.

I'm not so sure of that. You seem to know exactly what's going on all the time.

Perry ignored the dubious compliment and continued on in a business-like tone.

If you like, you can continue in your present employment until your new responsibilities make it impossible. We might even work out a part-time arrangement after that. In your new capacity, I'm sure you will learn of many interesting developments. I will have the paper for you to sign later in the week.

Brendan could not help but reflect that the part-time arrangement would continue to give him access to Anne at least to a limited extent. In spite of what he had written his mother and agreed with Anne, he still longed to be with her again.

CHAPTER THIRTEEN

February–May 1823

By late winter Perry had concluded a legally binding agreement between Elisha Cogswell and Brendan for the use of the property on the west slope of Aspetuck Hill. More importantly, he secured a license from the Selectmen for Brendan to operate a tavern on that site. Brendan had to show up with Perry before the three members of the board; Perry had paved the way and there were no hostile questions. First Selectman Elihu Marsh did express some puzzlement why the site had been chosen, but on the whole they seemed as pleased as Brendan that it was remote from the center of the town. Second Selectman Absalom Welles, whose wife was a member of the temperance group, warned Brendan that public drunkeness would not be permitted and that the three could void his license as easily as they were awarding it.

Brendan responded on a lofty tone. Drunkeness would be as offensive to me, he said, as to the members of this board and the townspeople. I want to run a place that will be a credit to the town and which honorable citizens can visit without being exposed to a scandalous atmosphere.

Marsh and the other selectmen nodded approvingly and the session was over once Brendan had paid the five dollar license fee. Outside the house, Perry complimented Brendan.

That was a sensible tack you took about drunkeness. I hope you meant it because any problems could reflect on me as well as yourself. Neither one of us needs any more headaches, right?

Right. I'm serious about it. I may have laid it on a bit thick, but I really think it's the best way to make money in the place. That's the goal.

Even before the weather got warmer, Brendan did as much work around the site as he could afford. He continued his daily work for Perry for a time, but by late February he gave it up and started full-time on the renovations. Before long the money was so tight he reluctantly told Mrs. Gunn he would have to leave her lodging. The widow felt badly, not only about losing the small extra income, but because she had become genuinely fond of him.

Brendan, you'll freeze up there on that west slope when the wind sweeps in. Stay until April anyways when the weather won't be so severe.

I wish I could. I'll miss the good cooking and your nice warm house. But all apart from the money, I'll save a lot of time in walking back and forth. There's so many things I have to do to get the place ready that sometimes it scares me. But I'll come by and see you and do some chores for you. I have to have somebody I can share a few words with now and then because nobody lives nearby up there.

Brendan carried his few possessions up to the barn. He bought a second hand hammer, a saw, a chisel, a square, a carpenter's rule, and some eight and ten-penny nails. Since he had never done any carpentry work, he decided to start on the second floor where his initial errors would not be visible to the public. He set to work to partition off a small room for himself so he would be snug against the cold. His first attempts were ludicrous, but the fear of failure drove him to keep trying until he could cut a board squarely and accurately. Over the weeks he gained in competence. The results were not professional but they were adequate. He soon realized that the planning of the work was crucial, so he began to examine every building he went in to see how it was organized and how the construction was designed to carry out the builder's objective. He found that he enjoyed the work and the honing of his new skill. By March he had a room for himself that was passably comfortable.

Next he cut a door for customers to enter and nailed shut the big barn door. He constructed a bar at one end, made some crude tables and benches. He realized fine furniture, or even the rough furnishings found in most farm houses, was beyond him, so he concentrated on making his pieces deliberately rustic, but massive and strong. The effect was not unpleasant. He decided to obtain whatever else was needed from the estate sales of deceased townspeople and those who were moving elsewhere.

Brendan determined to start business in early April, without any announcement, so that he could feel his way and learn as the business developed. Perry visited the site and approved of what he had done. He agreed it was wise to start modestly and with no fanfare.

You will need a fireplace before very long to give the place some heat and a welcoming air. But that can wait. When you get cash flowing in you can make a deal with a mason. If there's liquor handy, it shouldn't be hard to find one.

Perry reminded Brendan that he would be going to Hartford for the next session of the Legislature in early May.

I haven't seen much of you the last few months. Please come around as soon as you can because there are some things I would like to have you do before I leave and during the time I'm gone.

Brendan's blood surged to his temples as he realized that Perry's departure could mean that he would see Anne again. He had been so busy with his project that he had not given a thought to the opportunity. He tried to put it out of his mind so that Perry would not notice.

Fine, he said. I'll come around the next few days in the morning so I can get at whatever you have in mind. I'd like to get this operation going in a week or two.

The next day Brendan decided not to keep Perry waiting; he needed time off from his solitary labors anyhow. He crossed over the hill to the brick house in mid-morning. He missed the five dollars a week; he had been forced to go more often than he expected to Mrs. Gunn's because she was generous with her cooking any time he split some wood or helped her out in other ways. Now that he was almost ready to open for business, he could spare some time for Perry's affairs.

Perry's requirements were routine, mainly involving copying briefs and other documents. There was a backlog because of Brendan's absence for nearly two months, but Brendan was confident he could get through it in a few days.

As before, Perry said, please look in on Anne as often as you can to see if she needs anything. That's what I don't like about this legislative business, giving up family life for two months. This will be the second year in a row that I will miss Elvira's birthday. She's getting to be enough of a young lady so that she lets me know she doesn't like that. And John, well John is a little hard to handle and he needs a father's firm hand. I don't believe I will run again next time. It's entertaining to be in New Haven or Hartford for a few weeks, but after a while I miss the home cooking.

I'll be glad to look in on them every day. As you know, I'm going to open next week but I don't expect many customers at first. There are additional improvements I want to make in the building, but they will have to wait until the business starts generating some income. In any event there won't be much doing in the morning and I'll be happy to come over.

Brendan was interested to hear that the only contribution of his wife that Perry mentioned that he missed was her cooking. He also mentally speculated whether Perry saw that Orange Merwin was the New Milford Democrat the state party saw as their best hope and realized there wasn't room for another ambitious hopeful from the same town.

Perry said he intended to leave a few days early so as to make contacts with the leadership before the start of the session. Even if I don't continue, he said, you never know when being on good terms with these fellows might be useful. I try to be helpful so they know they can count on me. The temperance people are putting in bills in every session. I'll keep an eye on them for you.

Much obliged to you. It's going to be tough enough getting started without any additional handicaps. Eli Todd told me the Whigs try at every session to enact more stringent controls of one kind or another.

That's right. We Democrats believe any problems that may exist with the liquor trade should be kept out of politics. If people want to inculcate temperance notions in their young ones that's their business. If the churches want to make it a part of their educational or religious training, fine and dandy. I believe public opinion by and large does not hold moderate drinking to be evil. People just don't accept that the Prince of Darkness is running the liquor business.

Will you be going in the buggy to Hartford?

Oh land, yes. I was so glad I had it in New Haven last year. There's no other good way to get around. If there were some kind of decent public conveyance such as they have in the large cities, it would be different. Lots of the other fellows said I'd done the right thing. I've read that in England engineers are tinkering with the idea of having carriages run on iron rails fixed in the right-of-way with some kind of engine powered by steam. Now that's the way I would like to go to Hartford, but I don't expect that will happen in my time.

Nor in Eunice's either, I should say.

Can't ever be sure. Who'd ever think that they would run boats by steam power? But they have a few now on Long Island Sound. Some say they might even be practical for rivers and short coastal runs.

For me the best use of a good fire is to cook a meal or distill liquor.

You tavern keepers think of nothing but the creature comforts. I've got to see some folks down the street now. I appreciate you giving me the time on these tasks.

In the days that followed, Brendan worked mornings in Perry's office. In the afternoons he spread the word about the village that his tavern would be open the following week. He invited people to come around and pass some time with him, and if they cared to, to have a drink on the house. The remainder of the time he dedicated to tidying the surroundings and putting finishing touches on the bar room. He ordered barrels of gin, whiskey, brandy and wine from dealers who were willing to take a chance on him and wait for their payment. Most of all, he resolutely maintained an air of confidence.

On the following Monday, opening day, he prepared a small wooden sign, McCauley's Tavern, and hung it on a post in front so it could be seen on the road to town. He decided not to mention hours or anything else about the facility because he wasn't sure what he could safely include. He was fairly certain no one would come in the morning so he went about his duties at Perry's office as usual.

In the afternoon he determined to read a book to curb his eagerness to receive the first customer. Hours passed and he began to think that no one would come. Shortly after four o'clock he saw a group approach. In it were Sam and Charley Bostwick, David Brownson, Harmon Buckingham, Seymour

Buck, David Ferriss and Elisha Cogswell. They trooped in, somewhat boisterous but with a measure of deference as well.

Where are the girls? Sam asked.

There are no girls, you reprobate. This is a decent establishment. Don't you know this is the old Cogswell place?

Sure, but Elisha thought you would run it on different principles than his uncle did.

David examined the stairs leading to the former haymow. You got a lot of room here, Brendan. If you don't make good as a tavern keeper you can start a whore house upstairs.

Yeah, I know. And run it by hand until I can afford the girls. If you would all like to sit down at one of these sumptuous banquet tables, I invite you to be my guest for a drink. What kind of champagne do you want? Whatever kind you want, it all comes out of the same barrel.

Draw it out of the barrel marked whiskey, Harmon said.

Brendan drew eight shots of whiskey and carried them to the table. He drank with his seven friends after they had clinked glasses and wished him luck.

I appreciate your coming very much. You're my first customers. If I had more friends I could probably make a living at this.

They laughed. Then they each bought a drink.

Now you really have customers. No more guests, Elisha said.

God grant you be right if your family wants the rent each month.

They left shortly afterward. Three other men from the village came later in the evening. By ten all had gone. Brendan checked his cash box, formerly a cigar box, and counted seventy cents for the day's receipts. Even though it was little, he was elated. He had gotten started.

As he planned, Brendan spent the remaining mornings in April working in Perry's office. From noon until ten at night he tended bar for the few customers who found their way to the new establishment. Some came out of curiosity, others looking for a new scene. Most were older men who no longer worked full time and were looking for someone to talk to. They were not disappointed, because Bendan truly enjoyed exploring what people had on their minds. His work along these lines for Perry had only sharpened what was a natural bent. The men returned in succeeding days; before long others joined them. Within days, he found he was grossing two or three dollars a day. He felt this was encouraging in view of the short time he had been open and the primitive facilities he offered.

On May 1 Brendan saw Perry off to Hartford in his buggy. Anne and the two children were there to bid him goodbye. This time Perry headed toward the cemetery and up Park Lane, or Pug Lane as some called it, on the way to Litchfield. He would see Governor Wolcott if he were at home there, then push on to Farmington where he would spent the night before going to Hartford the next day.

As the buggy disappeared in the east, Brendan looked at Anne. It's good to see you, he said. I've missed you.

Anne regarded the children for a moment. I've missed you, too. If you're not to busy with your new venture, perhaps we'll see each other more often when you come to do your office work. She smiled, then went off with the children.

Brendan returned to the tavern and occupied himself with calculating the costs of opening a kitchen. He refused to think what the next morning would be like; instead he furiously estimated the cost of a stove, an icebox, a pantry and a cook.

The results didn't look like anything that would fit within current income, but he kept reworking the figures anyhow. He knew he could not be considered a real tavern until people could eat a meal there. This would be his next objective. In the afternoon he worked hard, as hard as he could drive himself, in improving the yard and other suroundings outside. He knew he wouldn't sleep that night unless he exhausted himself.

The next morning he carefully washed himself in an improvised tub, dressed himself in the best clothes he owned, and cooked himself some ham and eggs on a makeshift grill he had set up outside the building. Thus fortified, he headed over the hill to Perry's office.

As he unlocked the door and entered, he found it irresistible to recall how he had been drawn to Anne last year in this very room. How kind she had been and how much he had enjoyed talking with her. How could he have gone all these months since then with only the most minimal contact with her? He decided that being mentally and physically occupied with the tavern project was the only way he could have done it. Since he had no reason to believe Anne would want to continue as before, he prodded himself to get to work on some of the copying tasks.

He worked conscientiously until a knock on the door shortly after ten. Anne entered, opened the door timidly.

Can I come in or will I disturb your progress?

Brendan smiled. How can I keep you out of your own house? Not that I would wish to. I have two months to do only a few assignments, so don't worry about my progress.

Anne entered, as the year before, with cold root beer and some cookies. She set it down before him.

You're very thoughtful to do this, he said. Then he raised his eyes to her. You're even more radiant than I remember.

The children are playing down the hall, Anne said. The servants are still working. Next week the children will go to their grandparents in Judea Parish for a few weeks and the staff will take some time off. Please don't be too ardent now. Do you remember the good times we had last year before I took you upstairs? Let's talk like that now. I need it badly. I haven't had anyone to talk to in that way since then.

You're right. Of course we can talk to each other again. I bet you know all about me, so tell me about yourself. I literally don't know one thing about your life during all this time. Perry can tell you about me because I work for him, but he can't appropriately tell me anything about you.

So she did, and the time went by very rapidly as he listened to her. It was like last year; she enthralled him with her descriptions of activities in which she had been involved. He had forgotten how keen her insights were, and how little that happened in the town escaped her.

Finally she paused. It's almost noon. You must go to make sure you don't miss any customers at your tavern. Next time you must tell me about your adventures with other women since last June.

That won't take long at all because there have been none. None at all. I didn't even come close to having any. I apologize for being so dull.

Don't. I am really happy to hear it. I don't know how the girls can keep away from you. She rose, quickly kissed him on the lips and was out the door before he could move.

See you tomorrow, she called back over her shoulder.

CHAPTER FOURTEEN

August 1823

BRENDAN WAS TALKING with Sam Bostwick and his cousin Charley in front of the United States Hotel on August 22 when the bell of the Congregational Church began to toll, followed a few minutes later by the bell of the nearby Episcopal Church. Since it was a weekday in mid-morning, no one at first understood the reason for the tolling.

What in tarnation is going on? Sam asked.

Other townspeople who rushed into the street from the homes and businesses were equally curious—and worried. Aside from calling worshippers to services, the bells rarely tolled. Sometimes years passed between such occasions and the tolling usually signalled a tragedy. After several minutes, however, the word passed quickly among the gathering crowd: Elijah Boardman was dead.

Sam, Charley, and Brendan walked up the street to the Boardman home. One of the servants was standing at the front door. He was instructed to respond to queries. The family had received word this morning. The Senator had died suddenly in Boardman, Ohio on August 18. Normally it took a man travelling flat out a week to reach Ohio but such news travels much faster than any man, just as the news of great battles is passed from town to town with astonishing rapidity. The servant said the widow, the daughters, and George were in seclusion and would not meet people until William, the son from New Haven arrived, either late today or tomorrow. There would be no further information until that time.

As the small crowd in front of the house drifted away, soon everyone in town knew of Elijah's death. People knew that he was frequently on trips, usually to Washington since 1821, or to Ohio where he had spent several months each year since the last century. He was by any measure the most outstanding man the town had yet produced. He, as well as the rest of his family since his grandfather came here as the first Congregational pastor in 1712, had devoted most of his adult life to public service. No other family had contributed so much. And as the Puritan philosophy in which he believed taught, his virtues and his efforts had been rewarded from on High. He was certainly the wealthiest man in New Milford.

Neither Elijah nor his family had flaunted their wealth. It was part of the code they lived by not to. True, they had a manorial home in the Palladian style with first class fireplaces, they had their gold watches, but they respected the code of gentility which decreed that the privileged elite were to avoid any appearance of aristocratic pretense. When the artist Ralph Earl had painted Elijah's portrait in 1789, he was pictured standing at his counting desk in his store, plainly identified as a merchant with his wares. He was hailed as a symbol of the entrepreneurial spirit of the fledgling republic.

Brendan well remembered how kindly he had been received by the family on that memorable Fourth of July when he, an impoverished son of immigrant parents, had only been in town a few days. Granted that nothing had come of his infatuation with Caroline Maria, but how could any reasonable person expect anything else?

Now as they walked back toward the hotel, the three young

men discussed Elijah's political career.

Sam told them that Elijah had first served in the General Assembly in 1803 and had served several terms in the House before winning election to the upper chamber. After 1818 he was elected to the new State Senate. That's when the Washington bug bit him. After his initial unsuccessful try for the U.S. Senate, the leaders remembered him two year later and he was elected.

What did Elijah do down in Washington? Brendan asked.

Not a helluva lot, Sam said. He showed up down there December 3 in 1821 when they commenced to do business in the first session of the seventeenth Congress. He was in a lot faster company down there than he was out in Hartford all those years. In Hartford he may have stood out but everyone knows he was amongst an undistinguished crowd of unknown men. But in Washington there were fellows like Rufus King and Martin Van Buren who'd been in this league for years and know a thing or two about getting things done, or seeing to it that they don't get done. The Senators put Elijah on the Claims Committee where they figure new boys can't do too much harm. Van Buren was new in the Senate, but he landed on the Judiciary Committee, and Finance as well, first whack. The seasoned fellows recognize one of their own when they see him.

Sam got all this from his father, Brendan knew, but he was still impressed with Sam's command of the facts.

Sounds like he aint done shit so far.

Well, listen to this. It might have been better if he had done nothing. But the only bill he introduced, right in January when they were just rolling up their sleeves, was one to benefit his brother, Daniel. Daniel is Elijah's older brother and a very slick fellow. He went to Yale, then stayed on after he graduated to get a Master's degree. He was partners with Elijah in the dry goods line until 1793, then struck out on his own and became partners with Henry Hunt in New York City in wholesale dry goods. He married a New York girl, Hetty More in September of 1797 and we never saw much of him after that. He had a lot of real estate in the city and speculated in new lands from Georgia to Mississippi. He was involved in Washington in straightening out claims in Georgia, mainly his own, I'll wager. It isn't hard to see that he put Elijah up to filing that bill.

What did his bill provide for?

It would have validated titles to land Daniel held in Georgia which had been approved by the British before independence. Apparently, in succeeding decades, settlers had moved into the area between the Altamaha and Oconee rivers, squatted there, and messed up Daniel's title.

Did Elijah's bill fix things?

Naw, it was referred to the Committee on Public Lands and was never heard from again.

Didn't he do anything else?

Nope. In the whole of the first session of the 17th Congress his name only appears once more in the proceedings. He voted for a motion which would have transferred land in Louisiana from the Federal Government to the state, while preserving private land claims. The motion was defeated.

How about in the second session when he had a better feel for what was going on? Did he do any better.

Naw. He put in the same bill again on Daniel's behalf and that was the end of it. He seems, though, to have prevailed upon the other Senator from Connecticut, James Lanman, to petition the Committee on Claims for a settlement of an account of a Captain Elijah Boardman in the second regiment of United States' Infantry.

I didn't know that Elijah was ever a captain, Charley said.

Neither did anybody else. He served in the war as an enlisted man when he was only sixteen and came home seriously ill before a year was up. He served a few months again in 1777 in the militia stationed on the Hudson. It wasn't likely that a boy of 17 would have been a captain. Maybe there was another Elijah Boardman who lived somewhere else. In any event, his death probably puts an end to the claim.

Charley summed up. Sam's better'n a historian, isn't he?

Brendan laughed. Where'd you get all those facts, Sam?

The Angel Gabriel.

That's good. Maybe he can fix you up like he did Jemima Wilkinson when she was here.

Sam punched Brendan hard in the arm.

Looks like we got his ass out, Brendan said to Charley.

The following week a service for Elijah was held at the Congregational Church. The body would not arrive from Ohio for months, but this was the farewell the town was giving to the man. Virtually every one in the center of town attended. For Brendan it was the first time he had ever been in the Congregational Church. As he reflected on this fact, it dawned on him that it was the first time he had been in any church in more than five years. He who had rarely missed Sunday Mass from the time he was old enough to walk when he lived in New York.

As the service ended and the crowd moved slowly out, Brendan observed that dozens of people outside had not been able to fit inside. The Boardman family took up a position in front of the church and the crowd shaped itself into a long file and slowly passed by, each mourner shaking the hand of each family member successively and softly murmuring words of sympathy. Brendan was in the line with Sam and Harmon Buckingham; they chatted in low voices as the file moved forward.

In time Brendan reached Mrs.Boardman, shook her hand and told her he was sorry to hear of Mr. Boardman's death. She smiled sweetly and thanked him. Brendan was surprised at her calm; he remembered Irish funerals in New York where mourners and family members were either dissolved in paroxysms of tears or laughing hysterically at the recollection of some pecadillo of the deceased. He shook hands with William, already self-consciously magnificent as befitted a rising lawyer, politician, and businessman; Henry, worn and haggard after his trip back from Ohio; George, fey and fragile. Then there was Caroline Maria looking him directly in the eye, Caroline Maria now betrothed to a New York City minister that fancied himself a writer and a linguist. Caroline Maria, near tears, squeezed his hand and introduced him to the Reverend Doctor John Schroeder, who even exceeded William in pomposity. Caroline Maria no longer looked girlish and spirited, but how could she? He shook the hand of Dr. Schroeder, softly expressed his sympathy, and passed on to Cornelia. He didn't remember her nor she him. Then it was over.

He said goodbye to his friends and went back to his business. He had never met Elijah personally, but the funeral drained him for reasons he couldn't fathom at the moment. He went dully about his work.

CHAPTER FIFTEEN

November 1824

BRENDAN FIRST BEGAN TO HEAR townspeople talking about Elijah Boardman's will in the fall of 1823. Since Boardman was such a wealthy man, it was natural that people would wonder who would benefit from his fortune. Most people weren't barefaced enough to troop into the Probate hearings or even make an appointment with the clerk to read the documents, but plenty of lawyers and officials had regular access to the records so that it didn't take the word long to get out. The witnesses to the signing of the will on June 9, 1823 had been Orange Merwin, now being mentioned for Congress in the next election, Anan Hine and Stanley Lockwood, three of the town's leading citizens. While they were not ones to babble about such affairs, once Elijah had departed the scene they were under no obligation to maintain secrecy. At least a couple of dozen other people had read the will.

The document was pretty much what people who knew Elijah would have expected; it was meticulously crafted, full of precise legal phraseology intended to permit not the slightest doubt to arise over his intentions in the distribution of his considerable worldly goods. For example, he did not want his stocks sold, but rather divided among the inheritors in the proportion that he specified. The widow received the use of a third of the real estate and personal property. Henry's reward for moving to Ohio to administer the former Western Reserve lands his father had bought was a bequest of $1,500. The youngest daughter, Cornelia, received $500 to continue her education. After the widow's death, the real estate was to be divided among the five children according to a formula under which each of the three sons was to receive double the amount allotted to each of the two daughters. Each heir was to have subtracted from his or her shares any debts which had been entered in Elijah's ledgers before his death.

All of this was standard practice; people saw it as another example of Elijah's acumen and precise ways. Now they would wait for the inventory which would reveal the size of the inheritance. The wait was to extend more than a year, until November 3, 1824. The executors, the sons, William and George, had offered reasons satisfactory to Probate Judge Jehiel Williams for not presenting the inventory within the usual time prescribed by law. The reasons essentially were that the properties involved were not only in Connecticut but also in Vermont, Massachusetts, New York and Ohio.

Within a few days of Judge Williams' approval of the inventory, it was a subject of intense gossip in New Milford. Most of this centered around the homely touches the document painted of the Boardman's domestic life. There was considerable hilarity over the fact that the Boardmans owned a total of thirty-five barrels, broken down into sixteen varieties. There were barrels for whiskey, barrels for brandy, barrels for wine, barrels of methylin, and at least thirteen for hard cider. Of course not all of them were full. There were also barrels for beef, pork, other meats, shad, pickles, sugar, vinegar, and other commodities. They were of oak or chestnut in sizes ranging from kegs to hogsheads. The temperance advocates were disconcerted at the amounts of alcoholic beverages involved; Brendan and his customers laughed approvingly at the revelation.

Sure, they enjoyed a glass now and then, but they had the pots to piss in, Brendan said.

He was referring to the fact that the Boardmans had at least nine utensils inventoried as "underbeds," or in one instance, "underbed WC."

Apart from the real estate and securities, consisting of eight bank stocks, stocks of two insurance companies, and shares in the Litchfield and New Milford Turnpike Company, the appraisers had made no attempt to group articles by categories, so there had been some droll juxtapositions. One line in the record (the scrivener had used a cramped hand to get as many articles on one line as possible and thereby economize on paper) included a dust pan and brush, 34 cents; 20 brown twirls, $2; gold watch, chain and fob, $100. Kitchenware was sometimes lumped together with livestock or stable equipment, pigs with loads of hay. Naturally there were a great many yard goods left over from Elijah's dry goods operation. One also somehow got the impression that they never threw anything out, since numerous broken or defective articles were listed.

There were interesting revelations of the reading habits of the Boardmans. Their reading ranged from six-cent pamphlets on obscure themes to volumes and volumes of a publication called the *British Theatre* to Adam Smith's *Wealth of Nations.* They also read, or at least possessed, Gibbons' *The Decline and Fall of the Roman Empire,* Vattel's *Law of Nations,* and the works of Shakespeare. There were also works by Hume, three copies of Dr. Johnson's Dictionary, and lectures by Priestley.

If they had let me read all their books I probably could have gone to law school, Brendan joked with Sam Bostwick.

For the more serious observers, the size of the estate, a stunning $94,263.62, was the most impressive aspect of the inventory. People still remembered that when Benjamin Bostwick, a leading member of a prominent family, died in earlier times, he left his family twenty-eight pounds. His wife got some linen cloths and half of his personal effects, which consisted largely of farm implements and worn out clothes and utensils.

Only a few persons noticed that the estate included nearly 1,300 acres of land in New Milford, but no where else. There was no mention of the lands that Elijah had enumerated in his will only four months before his death that he owned in Vermont, Massachusetts, New York and Ohio. Aside from several lawyers, no one realized that these properties were handled by ancillary courts in the other states where the lands lay. Thus the Boardman estate was far larger than almost anyone realized. With the increase in the value of western lands as settlers trooped westward, the total value of the estate may have been double the amount registered in New Milford. Probably no one but the Boardmans and their closest associates knew the full extent of their enormous riches.

Brendan asked several persons he thought might have the key to the mystery of the missing lands. Town Clerk Elisha Bostwick refused to even talk about it. Later Sam said his father figured he had enough to do being town clerk without trying to guess what went on in other offices. No one else, including Sam, had a clue. They all agreed that it was highly unlikely that Elijah could have disposed of all this real estate before his death. In any event, hadn't Judge Williams given the executors permission to exceed the time set by the statutes for the preparation of the inventory? Where were the properties that had consumed the extra months of the valuable time of the two sons? There were many whispers, but nothing came of the matter.

It's best not to bother your head over it, Sam said. It doesn't affect you one way or the other. If we can leave that subject, I've got an idea for your tavern, though.

What's that?

If you want to start serving meals, I know a young girl who is a good cook and she wants to work to earn money so she can get married. You interested?

Sure am. What's her name and how do I get ahold of her?

Her name is Chloe Jacklin. Her boy friend is Orman Wilson. He's the son of Javan Wilson, a Revolutionary War veteran. Javan married Dora, the daughter of Patience who has worked for years and years as a cook for my father. I've got to tell you that they're all colored folks. If you don't mind that, I can tell you Patience and Dora are really great cooks but I can't speak for Chloe.

I don't care if she's black or green or red, if she can cook. Where can I find her?

She lives with a bunch of her folks over on Nigger Hill if you know where that is. It's over east of the cemetery across the brook on the slope of Second Hill Road. You can find her there or I can tell Patience you'd like to see Chloe.

Before Brendan had an opportunity to look for Chloe, she showed up the next morning at the tavern. He saw her coming as he worked to clean up the bar area. He opened the door and called to her. She was tall and willowy, with a coat over her house dress and a bonnet on her head to protect her from the autumn frost. She moved with grace; her dignity was only surpassed by her beauty.

I'm Brendan McCauley. You must be Chloe Jacklin. Sam Bostwick told me you might be interested in a job as cook here.

That's right. She looked around doubtfully at the rough interior of the tavern. Where's your kitchen?

I don't have one yet. I haven't been open long and I'm just getting started. We can talk afterward about what you will need. Where did you learn to cook?

I've been cooking almost as long as I can remember. Lately Dora—that's the mother of my boy friend, Orman Wilson—has been teaching me how to make a lot of things that I never did before.

I have to tell you that I know very little about cooking, so you would have to be on your own, including the shopping. It looks like we will have to take a chance on each other, if you're interested. I hope we can work things out as we go along. What wages are you asking?

What are you offering?

If you can handle the job, I'll pay you five dollars a week.

Chloe looked startled, then wary. The wage far exceeded even the wage for a male laborer, let alone a black woman.

Let's get one thing straight. No funny business, right?

Don't worry. I don't know anything more about women than I do about cooking. You will be safe.

She put her head back and laughed.

You got yourself a cook, Mr. McCauley.

CHAPTER SIXTEEN

February 1825

THE McCAULEY TAVERN was doing so well at the turn of the year that Brendan had a hard time believing his good fortune. The addition of the kitchen and the hiring of Chloe Jacklin as cook had been a turning point. The dishes she turned out were so good that some men now came at noon to eat although they drank nothing alcoholic. His weekly take now usually exceeded twenty dollars and sometimes went as high as thirty. He himself lived frugally, but he continued to put money into the business. He had taken Perry's advise and had hired a mason to build a large fireplace and chimney from Mine Hill cut stone at the end of the bar. Brendan was very proud of the fireplace and he gradually bought new chairs and a settle to range around it.

As the tavern and Brendan began to look prosperous, he noted that people began to treat him with more deference. Not only did he meet the leading merchants and professional men on terms of mutual respect, but he noted with some amusement that the mothers of marriageable daughters began to pay a good deal of attention to him. Sometimes he was tempted to play their game just to get near a daughter, but it was not so much that he resisted the temptation as that he was usually too busy. He had not been near a woman since his two-month idyl with

Anne the year before. When he occasionally thought of her with longing, he straightaway turned his head to other matters.

Sam Bostwick approached him in February in the center of the village. After inquiring about business in the tavern and other pleasantries, he invited Brendan to a spinning bee for the next Saturday night.

A spinning bee, what the hell is that? An invernal insect?

It's time you learned about the local customs. A spinning bee or a spinning frolic is an affair in someone's home at this time of year where the women spin flax for next summer's clothing. Each male is expected to bring a pound of flax and give it to some woman to spin. It's just an excuse for a sociable evening.

Samuel, what are you trying to get me into? I don't have any flax, I'm not a farmer, I don't even know what it looks like. I wouldn't know where to find any.

Don't be so negative. You're gregarious; you would have a good time. I'll get the flax for you and you can carry it to some woman.

Some woman! What woman? Whom do you have in mind?

How about Julia Booth? You must know Gerardus. Julia is his daughter.

I know Gerardus and I've seen Julia. A generously formed young creature as I remember. This isn't some native rite that signifies we're engaged to be married if I give her a pound of flax, is it?

Brendan, you're so suspicious. No, of course not. It's just a chance for the young folks to get together. You're still young, aren't you? Do you want to turn into one of those dessicated Irish bachelors I've read about?

This Irish bachelor isn't likely to be dessicated with several barrels of beverages at his disposal. But I'll take some flax to Julia if you guide me through the ritual. I hope you realize this will cost me the Saturday night receipts, the largest of the week.

Brendan asked Chloe to keep the tavern open for him and she willingly assented. He was prepared to miss some of the income but felt it was important to keep the place open so patrons would not feel he kept the hours erratically. On Saturday night he went with Sam in the Bostwick buggy to Julia Booth's home near Gerardus' father's house on the southern end of the village. There were already a dozen young people there and Brendan threaded his way through them to present his bundle of flax to Julia. She gave him a curtsy in mock formality and thanked him. He decided she was an acceptably attractive young woman; he was pleased that she filled out her bodice so well.

You'll have to explain the rules of this activity to me, he said to Julia. From the little I know about it, it appears that the women do all the work. I've tried to relate it to what I know about bees, but in a hive I've always understood that the males do all the work and are discarded by the queen bee at her pleasure.

After her pleasure. But we don't play by those rules here. The women do the spinning and the male drones just watch and drink cider. Except for one. The woman who first finishes spinning her pound of flax requires a kiss from the man who brought it to her.

What a splendid competition. I hope you spin marvelously swift.

Time will tell. Just keep yourself available.

She flounced off to her spinning wheel with Brendan's flax. The other women were doing the same and the men congregated around a table which held cakes and cookies and various jugs of cider, divided between hard and soft. Brendan helped himself to a glass of the soft, but he noticed most of his companions preferred the hard cider. He chatted with the men, all of whom he knew. Several commented that they had heard the quality of the meals he served spoken highly of. He responded that Chloe was a natural-born cook who God in His goodness had brought to him.

After a time the attention shifted to the women who were working furiously at their wheels. The onlookers cheered as the hanks of flax began to dwindle and called out the names of the women who appeared to be in the lead. As the minutes passed it became clear that the contest was between Julia and another girl. Finally, Julia's hank disappeared and her spindle slowed. She had won.

Brendan approached her. Congratulations. You were wonderfully swift, just as I hoped. And I kept myself available.

Julia laughed with pleasure and rose from her stool. Brendan took her in his arms and kissed her firmly on her upturned lips.

That was exquisite. But that was just the first heat wasn't it? You will have to win the other competitions just as convincingly.

This is not a race track. We're not a brood of mares running for lumps of sugar. The men have to prove themselves as well.

Even though Julia had spoken archly, Brendan was taken aback. He managed to respond: *Touché.* I stand ready to enter the lists.

Actually there were no further contests; the remainder of the evening was spent in conversation and songs. Without abandoning Julia's company completely, Brendan managed to spend a lot of time talking animatedly with other flax spinners and their consorts. He was not sorry when Sam said it was time to get the buggy home. He was careful to thank Julia for the evening's entertainment and he didn't let on to Sam that the spinning frolic had ended on a sour note for him.

Less than two months later Brendan learned that Julia was engaged to marry a hatter from Westport. He reflected ruefully that he had not competed successfully in Julia's tournament. Only a few months later he heard of the marriage of Caroline

Maria Boardman to Reverend John Schroeder. He accepted that he had never been a serious suitor for the hand of Caroline Maria, but nevertheless he felt another pang of regret. He had never met the hatter and knew nothing about him, but he had seen enough of the Reverend John to judge him a pretentious sobersides.

Now that he was in the liquor business, Brendan took more interest in the temperance movement than when it was a subject of discussion with Perry. People all over the state listened more carefully during the year as Lyman Beecher, who was soon to leave his church in Litchfield to work within the Unitarian movement in Boston, delivered six sermons designed to generate emotional fervor for the temperance cause. As far as Brendan was aware, no one from New Milford went to Litchfield to hear the sermons in person, but many people learned of them from the Litchfield newspaper, which had subscribers all over Litchfield County.

Beecher warned in the first sermon that drunkeness was the end stage of a rake's progress which began with taking a drink in a spirit of fellowship. Therefore everyone should guard against even occasional drinking because God's wrath would strike those who put themselves in danger of proceeding along the path of evil. To take a drink was a presumption, a dare of a mortal to God. In subsequent sermons Beecher thundered that drinking "obliterates fear of the Lord and a sense of accountability, paralyzes the power of conscience, hardens the heart, and turns out upon society a sordid, selfish, ferocious animal." In his final thunderbolt, in which he invoked "the ghastly skulls and bones" of the victims of strong drink, Beecher said individual efforts were not enough. Instead all society must rise up in a crusade to enact laws to ban the distillation and sale of alcoholic beverages.

Temperance was widely discussed in New Milford as

elsewhere. Militants sprang up and societies were formed, some under the sponsorship of churches, others of young people, and the African-American residents. There was a "Band of Hope" and a "Citizen's Club." Most evidence indicated that the majority of townspeople were unimpressed and some who signed up in temperance organizations reverted to their old ways within a short time. After all, in New Milford the average annual consumption of distilled spirits was more than two gallons per person. A few score temperance militants were not likely to change long established habits so easily.

Brendan subscribed to the Litchfield newspaper for a time to keep abreast of the activities of the temperance movement. He left the copies around for patrons to read and there were usually paragraphs read aloud by a a man with a glass at hand to improve his delivery. A chorus of guffaws rewarded the reader. Brendan was careful never to say anything against the movement but he was not averse to making a joke about some of the more earnest pronouncements of its leaders which found their way into print.

Chloe continued to surprise him. He had long since come to believe she was the best cook in New Milford. In time he realized that Chloe's food was the best he had ever tasted anywhere. It dawned on him that his mother was not as gifted a cook as he had thought at the time; all that boiled meat and potatoes, boiled cabbage, more boiled cabbage, boiled everything was rather repulsive in retrospect. But Chloe just seemed to know not only how to cook superbly, but to do a lot of other things well, things she seemingly could have had no experience in doing. She had a flair for decoration, something, he realized now, that the tavern had needed badly. Deft and fast with a needle, she had made attractive curtains which added a touch of color to otherwise rather drab surroundings. She made napkins and tablecloths for the dining area, something no other tavern in town could boast of. She did all of this without consulting or mentioning them to Brendan beforehand. She bought the material out of her grocery money without him giving her anything extra. She used initiative and good sense, almost as if she were a partner.

Whereas Brendan had been accustomed to doing the cleaning by sweeping the floor and wiping the bar and table tops, Chloe dusted the entire interior thoroughly, thereby demolishing spider webs that Brendan and the male patrons had never noticed. She even invaded Brendan's own precinct, his second story room he had carpentered the first spring in the place, and cleaned and set it in order. Before long he found new curtains there as well as a rug she had somehow found time to hook. He was embarrassed that she had found the room in such a messy condition; thereafter he took more pains to at least keep the room orderly.

All this produced unexpected results. A few of the men who regularly ate their noon meal there, in time ventured to bring their wives and even their children for an occasional meal. The tavern ceased to be an exclusively male dominion. As the word spread, couples showed up for the evening meal, which was called supper in New Milford, just as the noon meal was called dinner. Naturally, all of this increased the weekly income substantially.

Brendan thought he should recognize Chloe's diligence. One evening after they had had a particularly busy time, he tried.

Chloe, I have to tell you what an excellent job you are doing. When I hired you I wanted somebody who could prepare the food and cook. You have done so much more than that I am continually astonished with all the valuable contributions you have made to the running of this place. You have done many things that I would never even have thought to ask you. You do everything well.

Chloe regarded him a moment before she answered. Finally she responded.

It pleases me that you are content with my work. I have tried to do the best I can. My folks always taught me that when I worked for somebody, to really work for them. Besides I should tell you, as I think you know, that I am planning to be married to Orman Wilson next spring. Orman is a mason like his father and we want to get enough money together so we can build a little house for ourselves. Working for you, I make more money than Orman, so I feel I am doing my part. You are a good person to work for and I'm glad to have this job. You treat me with respect, which many white folks in town don't, and I appreciate that. I hope my work continues to please you; I would like to continue here after I am married.

After she was gone, Brendan asked himself why he had felt some disappointment with Chloe's words. He certainly knew when he hired her that she was Orman's fiancee. She had responded soberly and responsibly to his compliments. It had never occurred to him that she might leave the tavern when she married. Her departure would be a major blow to him; he could never find as good a cook nor anyone who would take such an interest in the place. But she said she wanted to keep working, so why did he feel uneasy? He didn't know. But as with other other thoughts that disturbed him, he worked to put it out of his mind and went to bed.

CHAPTER SEVENTEEN

February 1826

Although Perry, curiously enough, had never specified in their oral agreement how the payments were to be made for his legal services, Brendan had thought it best to pay each month, rather than quarterly or yearly. It would be easier to keep track of what he owed on a monthly basis and the payments shouldn't hurt as much as they would for the longer term. It also gave him an opportunity to maintain regular contact with Perry since he had discontinued working for him. Perry, as he had previously indicated he would, had decided not to run again for the General Assembly after the session in 1823.

At first the payments were derisory and Perry pocketed the small change with a joke. Once the fame of Chloe Jacklin's cooking began to spread, however, the payments became significant in the context of the New Milford economy if not in terms of Perry's overall income, which now benefitted from the earnings from his more active law practice and his continual dealing in farms and other land. In January of 1826, for example, the tavern grossed $45.26, so that Brendan owed Perry $2.26. This was more than some workers in the town earned in a week.

The first day in February when it didn't snow, Perry trudged over the hill through the snowfall of recent days to Perry's house. He entered the office in the rear after giving a little knock but Perry was not there. He waited a few minutes, then went around the corner to the kitchen. He knocked again and Mrs. Townsend, the Smith's cook, rose from the kitchen table where she had been preparing bread dough.

Brendan, how are you? Can I help you?

I just wanted to see Perry for a minute. Is he in?

Yes, but he's with Mrs. Smith. She's dreadfully ill. We're expecting Doctor Williams any minute.

I'm really awfully sorry to hear it. Of course I won't bother him then. Perhaps I can leave the money I owe him with you. What's the matter with Mrs. Smith?

I don't know that anyone knows. She hasn't been feeling herself for some months. Recently she's come down with a fever and is very weak. She's lost a lot of flesh and is off her feed.

She approached Brendan more closely, cupped her hand alongside her mouth and whispered. I think it's some kind of female trouble.

Oh, that's terrible. Brendan didn't have any real conception of what female trouble could be, but coupled with the symptoms that Mrs. Townsend had enumerated, it sounded as if it were something internal and serious. Something that Dr. Williams or any other doctor in New Milford would not be capable of coping with. That's why so many young women lay in cemetery plots and so many men had two or more wives.

If you see her, please tell her I hope she gets well soon. Also please tell Perry if I can help out in any way, to just let me know. I'll be back tomorrow morning just in case I can do something.

As he plodded back through the snow, a sense of foreboding grew in Brendan's mind. Anne was the only woman after his mother that he had ever been close to. She was the only woman with whom he had ever made love. He admired her greatly, but more than that, he felt a great tenderness for her that was not diminished by the fact that he has seen her only rarely and for only brief moments during the past two and a half years. He knew they would have married if she had been free, but they both knew from the beginning that this would never happen, nor could it. Brendan always resisted speculating on what might have been, because he judged it a form of self torture, something unhealthy and to be avoided. Yet it was hard not to dwell on the loveliness of Anne and how much he wanted her. And now wanted her to recover, to live.

The next morning, and many mornings after that, Brendan made the trek over the hill to get the news of Anne's condition from Mrs. Townsend. She had little to tell him; each day she simply repeated that the fever was still with her and that no measures Dr. Williams took produced beneficial results. Mrs. Townsend said she had passed on his good wishes.

It had been years since Brendan had prayed, but these nights he tried to recall the prayers he had learned as a small boy. He repeated them fervently, asking for Anne's recovery. As he recalled, the applicable phrase in these straits was to pray for "the speedy recovery or the happy death" of the afflicted one, but he could not bring himself to ask for the happy death of Anne. The prayers only consoled him to the extent that he was taking the only measure he knew to keep her on earth.

On February 25, Mrs. Townsend told Brendan that Anne's death was imminent. Dr. Williams had said he doubted she would live more than another day. Brendan went back in the afternoon, but nothing was changed.

The following morning there were several strangers in the kitchen with Mrs. Townsend. Anne had died a few hours before. Neighbors were already showing up to offer their condolences and were bringing food for the family, the normal custom but hardly necessary with a hired cook in this family. Brendan, feeling terribly bereaved, waited with some of the neighbors until he could see Perry.

When Perry at last came down from upstairs, he received the condolences of the neighbors and other townspeople in the front living room. He was composed and calm, but he showed the strain he had been under in recent weeks. Brendan moved along in the line until he reached Perry, then grasped his hand.

I'm terribly sorry for your loss. That was all he could get out. He gave Perry's hand another wring and moved on. It seemed completely inadequate, but he feared the tears would flow if he tried to say more. He envied the composure of these Yankees; they met death as flinty and unflinching as they did a hard day in the fields, or in Perry's case, a losing battle in the court. Don't expect much, keep what you get, don't give an inch, and don't show your feelings. That seemed to be their code. Yet Anne grew out of this soil and came from this stock. That had not been her way. She was as honest in expressing what she felt as anybody he had ever known. He felt privileged to have known her.

The next day Brendan attended the funeral in the Congregational Church. Mr. Elliot, the pastor, officiated. The simple ceremony, spare and dignified as the architecture of the denomination's churches, moved Brendan. Mr. Elliot, who came to New Milford in this same month of February in 1808, knew the town well and worked hard at his ministry. Even with the church now disestablished in Connecticut for eight years, a Congregational pastor was still a leading man in town, and Mr. Elliot was the dean of the town's clergy. He was impressive in his role today as he recalled Anne, a mother and a wife who had given of herself freely in helping those less fortunate than herself. She gave the gift of love, he concluded.

Brendan took a deep breath and tried to think of nothing. But he could feel the tears well out of his eyes. He held himself motionless and hoped they would evaporate before anyone noticed. Later as the congregation bowed in prayer, he furtively swiped at his cheeks.

When the service ended and the people slowly left the church, Brendan noted that there was a large crowd. He knew many came because of the prominence of Perry in the community, but he also realized that many were there because they had great regard for Anne.

Because he knew he was unstable emotionally, he drifted away up the common as the crowd dispersed. Even if he were missed, an unlikely eventuality with this crowd, it was better to go silently than to reveal his feelings too transparently.

Back at the tavern, he asked Chloe to tend to things. He said he would be occupied for the rest of the day. He went to his own room on the second floor and wrote his mother a letter of many pages. He told her of the death of the woman he loved and of the funeral. Then he backtracked and wrote of the success he was having with the tavern and his growing affluence. The law as a career was out of the question for him, he explained, but he felt his father would still be able to be proud of what he had achieved. He noted that it was eight years since he had left Five Points and he was contented with his life in New Milford, but missed his mother and his sister. He again asked forgiveness for his desertion of them and implored his mother to write him with news of how they were getting on. He concluded by saying that he hoped in the not too distant future to travel to New York to see them once again.

When he posted the letter the following morning, he still felt a great sadness at Anne's death but he also felt at peace with himself.

CHAPTER EIGHTEEN

1827

ON GEORGE WASHINGTON'S BIRTHDAY in 1827 Javan Wilson, the father of Chloe's boyfriend, Orman, died. He was one of the few remaining Revolutionary War veterans in New Milford. Needless to say, he had been rarely included in any of the periodic celebrations of independence because he was an African-American. Javan seemed not to care.

As long as they keep sending me that check every month from Washington, that's what counts, he would say.

When Javan was born in 1757, nearly all the African-Americans in New Milford were slaves. When he died, all but two were nominally free. Actually, their mode of life had changed little. They were still the lowest caste on the town's social scale. In an economy where most of the white farmers were very poor, the blacks were poorer still. Only the small upper class received an adequate education, but blacks usually received none; in the rare instances when they attended school, the school marm would largely ignore them or actively mistreat such children. For the most part, they lived together in execrable housing, segregated in all but name. Javan was an exception in one regard; in an era when most blacks performed the most menial of work, usually as farm hands, Javan was a stone mason.

Javan was, in fact, the best stone mason in New Milford. He

was not a large man, but his slender, almost delicate, frame, was impressively muscled. In a town where, when he was young, virtually every farmer, that is, nearly everybody, built their own homes and barns with the assistance of neighbors, Javan plied his craft with the few wealthy or well-to-do, such as the Boardmans, the Lees or the Smiths. He not only built the foundations to their new homes of Mine Hill granite, but their fireplaces, their door-steps, decorative gateways to their estates, and stone pillars for custom made oil lamps. Because the work was slow and painstaking and the imagination of the rich fruitful in generating ideas for such projects, he worked almost constantly during good weather and earned more than most white farmers, to say nothing of the poor males of his own race. The rich who employed him made much of him in their condescending way; he was shrewd enough to assure that he was paid what his work was worth and never accepted false solicitude as a substitute for pounds, or later dollars.

Javan's moral code was that of the slave he had been before he was freed. With whites he was outwardly deferential, consistently polite, flattering when it suited his purposes, and always sly or devious enough to guard his own interests. As with other African-Americans, the animist faith of his forefathers had been transmuted into a curious Christianity. No blacks in New Milford were accepted as members of any church, but they were permitted to attend services if they sat in the gallery or in the rear of the congregation. After they were emancipated, some ministers would consent to marry them or conduct a burial service, but rarely in church. Javan cared not one whit for any of this, and over a nearly half a century, he sired a succession of children, some of whom bore his name and others who didn't. Because the black community was small in the town, there were lots of cases where some of his latest children were half brother or sisters of other individuals who were already grandparents.

The whites thought this was comical; the blacks didn't think it was as morally reprehensible as white slave owners who had mulatto or quadroon house slaves who bore a remarkable likeness to Old Master.

When Javan died, there was widespread mourning among New Milford blacks, most of whom sincerely loved him as a friend or relative. Whites also expressed sorrow, for they knew of no one around who could replace him as a skilled artisan. Many came to his little home to express their condolences.

Chloe had advised Brendan of his imminent death and told him she would be unavailable for work for several days before and after the burial.

Chloe, take whatever time you need. Don't worry about things here. We'll make out somehow, Brendan said.

Actually, he was concerned. Chloe had become almost indispensable. He, and everyone who ate her cooking, was aware that she was a talented cook, but only Brendan knew what she contributed to the business in other ways. Because she had proved to be scrupulously honest, he found he could entrust the bar to her when he was called away. As he had hoped, she was immensely capable in purchasing food and did it far more economically than he himself could. She had uncanny judgment in buying the right quantities of meat and other foods; she utilized leftovers so subtly, that there was little waste in the kitchen. She knew everyone in town better than Brendan, who had worked hard at it now for nearly a decade. She was cordial and courteous with customers, whether serving meals or working at the bar, yet maintained a reserve that warned tipplers not to take advantage. After a year, Brendan raised her wage to six dollars a week, a sum that put her among the economic elite of working people in the town. Two years later, he gave her another pay increase to seven dollars a week.

Brendan had grown very fond of her, but he was careful to

give her no cause to fear an advance from him. This is not to say that he had not thought of it. He found her tall, lithe body not only beautiful but enormously tempting. Whenever he found himself watching her too intently, particularly in the morning when usually only the two of them were working to clean and put the public room in order, he resolutely set himself a task apart to remove the temptation.

Brendan walked across town to the Wilson home the evening of Javan's death to express his condolences. He embraced Dora, Javan's widow, who was still a lively looking forty-five. He shook hands with Orman and Dora's other children, and others present, some of whom looked enough like Javan to validate a suspicion that they also might share his genes. He attended the funeral the next day, also held in the home, and at which Mr. Elliot of the Congregational Church officiated. Brendan followed the procession in which the bearers, all sons of Javan, carried the pine coffin to a rear section of the cemetery where the grave markers were either of wood or small stones with little or no carving on them. He thought how ironic it was that a master stonemason such as Javan would probably have a grave marked with some insignificant token rather than an elegant monument such as graced the graves of the people for whom he worked for so many years.

When Chloe returned to work a few days later, she immediately went up to Brendan.

I want to thank you, and all of Javan's friends and relatives want to thank you, for coming around to both the house and the burying. We all appreciated it.

Only then did Brendan realize that Mr. Elliot and himself were the only whites in attendance both days.

It was the least I could do. I would have liked to have brought something to the house, but without you around to prepare it, I didn't know what to bring.

They both laughed and she turned and went to work. There was plenty to do after her absence.

Later in 1827 another, and as it turned out the last, of the canal projects stirred New Milford. Although the westward movement was draining both manpower and money from the east, including Connecticut and New Milford, the old dream of improving navigation on the Housatonic died hard. Merchants and farmers were still seeking vainly for improved transportation to take materials to market and bring manufactured goods into the inland towns and villages more easily and economically.

The new project called for the construction of a canal from the mouth of the Saugatuck in the town of Westport to New Milford. After tidewater, both the Saugatuck and the Housatonic travel roughly parallel courses northwesterly. In its simplest terms, the plan would have connected the two streams either by utilizing a section of Still River which runs northward from Danbury into the Housatonic at New Milford, or a more direct and more easterly connection using more canal mileage. A survey of the possible routes and cost estimates for the work were made by Alfred Cruger, an engineer for the committee pushing for the project, and published in the form of a pamphlet. The route was subdivided in several segments; the final two crossed land in New Milford.

Subdivision Number II, North Section, extended five miles from Meeker's Mill outside of Danbury to the Housatonic at the Great Falls. The plan provided for the location of the canal largely on a side hill and would have necessitated cutting through rock and soil. Four culverts would be required to raise the bed of the canal. The cost for this section was estimated at $10,741.

Subdivision Number III, North Section, would have brought the canal from Great Falls to above New Milford village just north of the point where the West Aspetuck River flows into the Housatonic. The route would have been parallel to the Housatonic and would have crossed the river with an aqueduct of one arch with a hundred-foot span. The crown of the arch would have been ninety feet above the bed of the river. As in the other subdivision, a considerable quantity of rock would have to be removed. Cruger thought this would be useful in construction, both of the canal and for other purposes. The two-mile section was costly, an estimated $40,648, including $35,000 for the arch.

Using the Still River route would have eliminated the need for the aqueduct, but would have required several sets of locks.

The Saugatuck and New Milford Canal Company sought and received a charter from the General Assembly but during the legislative process railroads began to be discussed as a possibility for relieving Connecticut's transportation needs. As a result, when the company issued circulars for subscriptions to its stock, the language in them provided that the company could, as an alternaticve to the canal, ask the legislature for a railroad charter and permission to use the money raised to build it.

In New Milford the project was viewed with faint hope and considerable scepticism. As it turned out the latter was more justified than the former. Now that a rairoad was a possibility, no one wanted to hear any more about a canal. The project died, but the idea of a railroad became more and more discussed.

Brendan's tavern was the scene of many discussions about the impact that rail service could have on the town. Men standing at the bar were eloquent in painting a picture of the transformation of the town into an industrial center.

Daniel Minor, one of Brendan's regular patrons, saw the town as a future hub where limestone from the quarries, produce from the farms, timber from the forests could all be shipped to points all over the east coast. With our water power, he said, we can saw and mill lumber, convert our clay into wares.

We will be a major manufacturing center on the line between New York City and Montreal.

Others nodded solemnly in agreement.

Gilbert Crosby looked forward to the day when he could go to New York in half a day.

Can you imagine? All dressed up in my best duds, sitting back and wheeling along at thirty miles an hour. I could find me one of those city tarts and have a great time and still be back for work on Monday morning.

Gil Whitely snorted. Have you figgered out where you're going to get the cash for such an expedition? Those girls aren't going along with you because you're so handsome. And you'll never be hanged for what you know, either.

Brendan rarely participated in such discussions except to throw in a word now and then to show he was listening. Sometimes he did serve as a provocateur to get men talking on a theme in which he was interested or to entice them into conversation. Most of the time he listened, even if the talk was mere drivel. Even when nothing but nonsense emerged, which was much of the time, he was attentive because of the insights it gave him into the thoughts and dreams of the men on the other side of the bar. If the discussions were pertinent to local life or if facts emerged that were not generally known, Brendan filed them away in his memory. In time he came to have very broad knowledge of what was going on in and around town, from local and state affairs down to the lowliest household in remote areas.

Later when the drinkers were gone, he sorted out the talk he had heard in recent weeks about improvements to the town's access to the outside world. Clearly the Saugatuck Canal was little more than a chimera. But it struck him that the railroad was something else. The tavern now subscribed to all the regional newspapers available, including *The Connecticut Courant.* From these he knew there was widespread interest in rail transportation, and not just in Connecticut. He was intrigued by the manner in which the canal backers had left the door open to using the money they were raising for a railroad. Construction of a railroad was one of the few projects on which both rural and urban interests, often at loggerheads on many other issues, agreed. Within a few years it was highly possible, even probable, that a rail line would be built to New Milford. If it came to town it would in all likelihood closely follow the route of the proposed canal. This would mean it would enter the village between the river and the center but high enough on the slope to avoid the flood plain and the freshets which had washed away so many of the town's bridges. The trains would need to stop in town; some kind of station or depot would be needed to service the engines and to arrange for freight and passengers. Passengers would need food and drink, as well as shops in which to meet other needs. He must ponder this development more. It would be necessary to keep abreast of planning in the town for the arrival of the railroad, even though it was years away.

As he closed the bar and went up the stairs to his room, it occurred to him that some day he might be able to take a train to see his mother. That fool Crosby and his talk of tarts! He had received a letter from his mother in response to the one he sent her after the death of Anne. Although she had sent him short messages on his birthday in recent years, this was the first letter in which she had attempted to reach out to him in something like a conversation. But in spite of all the details of the changes in New York, she said nothing about how she and Agnes were making a living. It was frustrating not to know if his mother and his sister were tarts such as Crosby might find in the unlikely event he ever reached the city. The only way he could ascertain what their situation was, was to travel back to New York.

CHAPTER NINETEEN

April 1828

RIDING THE STAGE from New Milford to Danbury, Brendan found it hard to believe he had not left the town for ten years. In retrospect he wondered what had kept him in this insular environment for a decade, more than a third of his young life. He felt as if a conjurer had spun an invisible cocoon around him, kept him fed and happy for all this time, and had now suddenly let him out. Now that he was released, he didn't really know what he would do. His only plan was to see his uncle on Stony Hill and then proceed to New York to look for his mother and sister. As the team of horses trotted along, the heavy leather traces connected to the collars around their necks dragged the light vehicle along at a steady pace. But the minor uneveness in the gravel roadbed which gave the horses not a whit of difficulty bounced the cab of the lightly built stage in a continuous, jolting motion. The five other passengers swayed and bumped together in an erratic movement that became increasingly irritating as the miles passed. It was too early in the day for sustained conversation; they made only cursory and brief comments as they rumbled along.

Brendan was aware that the route was not the same as he had taken years back. Instead of passing along the ridge line as he had done before, the stage travelled first along the

Housatonic Valley and passed, imperceptibly, into the wide alluvial valley of the meandering Still River, through the tiny Brookfield settlement clustered around the mill on the river, and onward toward Danbury. A few miles further, the stage came to Huckleberry Hill, the first major elevation since New Milford; the horses slowed to a walk until they reached the summit. Then Brendan heard the stage driver on his elevated seat in front of the cab crack his whip and urge the team into a trot again down the slope. The fields on each side of the road were so strewn with rocks that hardly a tuft of grass was visible. No wonder farmers were heading to the prairies where the topsoil was forty feet deep, Brendan mused.

Three hours out of New Milford, the stage reached Germantown, a village on the outskirts of Danbury. The driver did not stop, but in his erratic chant, urged the team onward. A man in the seat facing Brendan took out his watch, nodded approvingly, and put it back in his vest pocket.

We're making good time. There will be a chance to get something done in the forenoon.

He didn't say what he intended to do in this time and none of the other passengers, dulled and lethargic from the constant shaking, cared to ask him. By turns they looked at the floor or out the windows.

A half hour later they arrived at a livery stable on Main Street in Danbury. The passengers stiffly alighted and looked around to get their bearings. The driver announced that the stage for South Norwalk would depart in half an hour. In response to a question from Brendan, he confirmed that the Norwalk stage would leave at the same time the next day.

Brendan realized now that the stage had passed through White Street to get to the center. He had not recognized it. Not only White Street, but the entire town appeared different than he had remembered it. There were many more commercial buildings and they were being erected on lots that had been part of the dooryards of some of the original farmhouses. The hatting business was flourishing, to judge from the number of small businesses engaged in it. Brendan bought a bottle of brandy for his Uncle Peter and some fruit for Thankful, wrapped them both in a sachel, and headed out White Street on foot. He was surprised to encounter a hack stand, since there was none in New Milford.

How much do you get to go to Stony Hill? he asked. One way.

Fifty cents should cover it. Where are you going out there?

To the crazy house that wild Irishman has on the hill. Peter O'Brien is his name.

The hack driver chuckled. I know where it is. I go out there all the time. On Sunday lots of folks like to go out there just to see it and have a good laugh. He's a pisser. Do you know him?

I met him once about ten years ago.

Get in. We should be there in half an hour.

During most of the trip, the driver tirelessly recounted tales of the people who had visited the O'Brien home. Uniformly they depicted Peter as the butt for the visitors' wit and sophistication or, rarely, allowed him a mild triumph through his native slyness. The stories sounded very much like the ones told in New Milford by white Yankees about blacks, especially, before his death, about Javan Wilson, who had been resented by some people because he had a certain status as a veteran of the War for Independence.

When the barrel chimney became visible, the driver indicated it with his whip. Here we are. By the way, why are you interested in Peter?

Because he's my uncle. Brendan jumped from the hack, gave the driver half a dollar and waved him off. He enjoyed the look on the man's face.

As he approached the house, Thankful's face appeared, just as it had ten years earlier. Only now, he observed, she had aged considerably.

Remember me? I'm Peter's nephew. You put me up here when I came from New York years ago.

Brendan! She caressed the name, and her creased toothless face broke into a homely, warm smile. She ran from the house and hugged him.

Here's a little something for you. He gave her the package. Careful. There's a bottle in there for Peter. Where is he?
He'll be nooning here directly. There he is. He's been working in our north lot. We own our own land now.

Peter whooped and ran toward him. Praise God and all his works. I was afraid I'd never see you again. He embraced him, then held him by the arms as he stood back and regarded Brendan.

You're no lad any more. You must weigh more than 16 stone. What a great ohmadon you've turned in to, he said admiringly. Where are you coming from? Where have you been the last ten years?

I never got beyond New Milford. The first morning I was there, a man offered me a job. I worked for him for five years, then I started a small tavern. I'm making enough money now to come to see you and to go back to New York to see my mother and my sister. I'm taking the stage to South Norwalk tomorrow. So how are you and Thankful doing?

Still grubbing a living out of this hard soil. Just barely. We finally did get our own land but its a small parcel and it's tough going. Thankful's made me into a Yankee. My soul is just as rocky as the land, I measure out my life in meager portions, begrudging everything I don't have and other people do. Sometimes I marvel that I'm the same lad that laughed and smiled in County Mayo a lifetime ago. How could I have turned into the me of today?

The desolation implicit in Peter's words, the hopelessness in his eyes made Brendan acutely uncomfortable. Clearly, the move from Ireland to America had had harsh consequences for both his parents and his uncle. It's hard to be transplanted and to sustain one's self, or a family, in one generation, *Qui transtulit sustinet* to the contrary.

It's what the Americans call the immigrant experience, Brendan said. You're working too hard. I brought you a little something to lighten the burden for a short time.

Thankful passed him the bottle Brendan had brought.

I'm most grateful to you, Peter said. It's been a long time since I've seen a bottle of brandy. You're a real Irishman even though you have been brought up in this heathen country. I declare a holiday for the rest of the day.

The next morning as he walked back to the center of Danbury, Brendan was relieved to get away from the O'Brien home. The despondency of his uncle had begun to affect him. Physically, the man was wearing himself out wresting a living from the miserable acres he owned. Thankful was a good woman who helped with the work on the small farm, but her handicap prevented her from reaching and soothing her husband's anguished mind. Now he wondered what an equally devastating urban environment had done to his mother and sister. He would find out in a couple of days.

As he waited for the departure of the stage to Norwalk, Brendan idly thought of Chloe Jacklin back in his tavern. He knew he was leaving her with a major responsibility, but she had shown herself to be capable and resourceful beyond expectation. She had never managed anything in her life before, yet she took control of the kitchen and ran it as her own. She was tough, too. Any patrons that tried to take liberties with her were soon put in their place by a haughty glance or cutting words. Although

Brendan had never seen an instance, he knew from friendly patrons that in his absence she had floored a customer, advanced in his cups, who had dared to fondle her. With Brendan, she was friendly and cheerful, but somehow maintained a certain dignity. When he had first left her alone to mind the tavern when he had gone to the Booth spinning frolic, he had felt some concern, but the next day he found that she had carried on the business without a hitch and the take she left was higher than normal. He had been concerned at first that customers might object to her race, but despite the racism which he knew existed in the town, he was not aware of any adverse reaction from customers to date. Before leaving, he had instructed Chloe to consult with Perry if she had any problems and had so informed Perry. He doubted that she would find the need to do so. If she was paid more than most workers in New Milford, male or female, she was clearly worth the seven dollars a week and probably more.

As he sat, Brendan saw the stage come in from New Milford and the fresh horses and driver coming out of the livery stable. The switch was quickly made, and Brendan climbed into the cab. He should be in Norwalk before evening. He would stay overnight there at a hotel and catch a ship to New York the next day. He had been astonished to find out that steamers relying solely on the power they generated in their boilers, now plied Long Island Sound regularly between Connecticut ports and the city. He was tired from sitting up late with Peter and tried to doze in the stage, but the rough motion would not permit it. This time the route seemed to coincide more with the one he had taken ten years before; he thought he recognized some of the buildings along the way.

The run was considerably longer than the one the day before but it was still daylight when he reached Norwalk, or more specifically, South Norwalk, which was directly on the

Sound. Brendan was struck by the smell of the salt air, which he had forgotten during him time inland. Of course it wasn't just saline, but also mixed with the odors of myriad marine life, alive and dead, large and microscopic. It reinvigorated him. After he checked into the small tavern, he went out again before eating to roam the wharves and docks and just nose around. He slept very soundly that night.

Once on the steamer the next day, Brendan realized it was the first time in his life that he was on a craft larger than a rowboat. Even though he had grown up in a major port a few hundred yards from the sea, he had never been on a ship. Hearing his parents tell of the discomforts of crossing the Atlantic on a sailing ship had given him a negative feeling toward ships, but now he found being on the deck of a ship to be completely engrossing and entirely pleasant. He liked the motion the waves gave the ship, he liked to see the seamen at work as the captain moved it away from the wharf, using the steam engine fueled by huge piles of wood. He stood at the rail and watched the shore recede, fascinated by the new perspective of land from out on the water..

One of the officers told Brendan that the first steamer had entered Sound waters little more than a dozen years before. It had been the Fulton, named after the inventor and founder of the company that owned her. For the past three years the Fulton had ever increasing competition. The operators were already making arrangements for docking facilities in ports along the Connecticut and Long Island shores. The officer said they were paying particular attention to towns and cities that gave promise of developing as major depots for the new railroads.

Brendan was dazzled by the magnificence of the appointments in the public rooms. The decks were richly carpeted, there were damask hangings, crystal chandeliers that swung gently with the motion of the vessel, large mirrors and gilt everywhere, and inlays of rare woods. Although he had no need for a cabin for such a short run, the officer showed him one that was vacant and it was indeed impressive. He had never been exposed to such luxury, even in the finest homes in New Milford.

Later he observed that there were those on board who intended to take advantage of the lavish atmosphere created by new money. Several times he received overtures from bold young women whom he knew immediately must be prostitutes. The officer had also warned him confidentially that there were pickpockets on board; the officers found it impossible to control their activities.

During the entire voyage the captain, resplendent in a beaver hat, never once used the auxiliary sail because the wind was constantly out of the west or northwest. So reliable was steam power, an officer told him, the newer vessels were not even fitted out for sail. Unlike in the stage, a passenger could move about, choose the persons he chose to engage in conversation, and even eat or drink in a small shipboard restaurant. He was stirred to see other paddle steamers pass them from time to time, some headed east or others going either to New York or other ports along the way. They were a stimulating sight with the flags and signals flying. In his enthusiasm he wished the trip were longer than just a few hours. A few days, even a week would be ideal.

None the less, he became a little excited when the ship sailed out of the Sound into the East River in early afternoon. Manhattan Island looked much more interesting from the deck of the ship than it ever had from its streets. He watched, fascinated, as the steamer cruised down the wooded shore on the east side, rounded Corlear's Hook and made for a pier that Brendan realized must be on Water Street. The fact that the vessel was steam powered allowed it to maneuver alongside the pier far more readily than the sailing ships he had watched as a boy. In a relatively short time, the steamer docked and passengers began to disembark. It occurred to Brendan that he was home; he faced the fact with some anxiety.

Once on shore, he decided to walk to his mother's home. She had written in her last letter that she now lived on Greene Street, some blocks above Canal. He had been heartened by this because he remembered this area as rather quiet, almost bucolic. It had to be an improvement over Five Points. It dawned on him that he had taken gifts to Peter and Thankful, but he had nothing for his mother and Agnes. He couldn't think of anything that would be appropriate. He walked up Water Street, turned on to Walnut and then on to East Broadway. This way he would miss Five Points, but he could go back later to see the old house. Then he followed East Broadway until it intersected with Canal and walked crosstown for several blocks. He crossed the Bowery, finally Broadway, and then he came to Greene, which he thought must be an extension of Church. He turned right and walked north several blocks until he came to number 277. He walked up the steps to the door and rang the bell. He wondered what to expect.

A pre-pubescent girl answered the door timidly.

Is Mrs. McCauley in please?

Please step in and have a seat. I'll see if she's in. Who shall I say wants to see her?

Her son.

The girl looked at him wide-eyed, but didn't falter. Just one moment, please.

As he sat, Brendan had to admit that the girl was well trained. The room, too, was impressive. The furniture was luxurious but subdued, in perfect taste. He had thought that Perry's house was well furnished, but it couldn't compare with this room.

Within a few moments he heard the faint sound of steps

approaching rapidly on the thick carpet. His mother burst into the room and into his arms as he rose from the chair. She embraced him tightly and buried her face on his chest.

Oh Brendan, she said. She sobbed softly.

Mom. His eyes were wet, too.

After a few moments she pulled away slightly and looked up at him. I was afraid I would never see you again. Her voice was still tremulous.

What a handsome man you've become. You were tall before but now you're grand. She emphasized the last word.

You look well, too Mom.

She did, too. Brendan knew she was forty-eight, but there was no sag to her tall, full figure. Her face was still unlined and only a few gray hairs among the chestnut. A handsome dress, obviously sewn specially for her, accented her strong points.

How is Agnes?

She's fine. I'm sorry she's not here to see you but we didn't know when you would come after your last letter. Of course you don't know that she is married.

Really? He didn't mean to sound so dubious.

Oh yes indeed. She's married to a merchant, an importer. His name is John Malone; his family is from Clare so you can be sure he has a way with the dollar. They have a lovely house way up in the country beyond Washington Square. They will be overjoyed to see you.

After a pause, she continued. It's best that I be honest with you, although it's difficult. Otherwise you will be wondering. Agnes left the life several years ago. She was highly successful and made enough money so that one day she just left it all behind. She invested her money in real estate and moved into a little house uptown. Malone is much older than she, and has no idea of her previous life. I hope it can remain that way. I'm sure he knows about me, but doesn't make an issue of it. He thinks

I sent Agnes to the best schools with my earnings and kept her away from this life. Agnes carries it off very well. I own this house; in fact, I run this house. I also own three others in this area that I run. I am no longer a practitioner, if that's the correct word. I'm sure you were wondering. If it were not such a horrid pun, I could say that I make a respectable living.

She laughed and Brendan smiled.

Oh Brendan, don't hate me for what I've done. I don't know how we could have survived if we didn't. I don't suppose it will change your opinion, but I'm sure you have heard of Aaron Burr. Mr. Burr is sweet on a a very wealthy woman, probably the richest woman in America. Her name is Elizabeth Jumel, nee Brown. She came here at age nineteen from Providence, Rhode Island, when she was already an experienced prostitute. Everyone in New York knew her. In 1804 she married Mr. Jumel, a French-born wine merchant. He bought the old Roger Morris mansion up above Harlem and conveniently died a short time later. Now Mr. Burr courts her there and there is talk that they will be married. At this point, of course, her pocketbook is more attractive than her original charms.

Catherine threw up her hands. Oh, why am I keeping you here like this. Are you hungry? When did you get in? How did you get here? I have so many things to ask you. You must be tired. Do you want to lie down and rest?

I'm fine. I slept well last night in South Norwalk. I came here by steamer from there and haven't done a thing all day except walk here from Water Street. I'd love to catch up on things with you but I know you must have obligations. I don't want to be in the way.

In the way after ten years? Don't be a silly boy. You mustn't mind if I call you a boy even though you are such an enormous fellow. You're still my little boy. The first thing I am going to do is send a message to Agnes to meet us tonight at the Astor

House. She will bring John to meet you. It wouldn't do for them to come here, of course. After I send off the note, why don't we go for a ride around New York? I'll show you how the city has grown and changed. I have my own carriage and a driver so it will be no trouble. Also, since I haven't done anything for you all these years, please let me take you to a good tailor. Don't misunderstand me, you are dressed perfectly decently, but the mode here is a bit different than New Milford. We will get you some clothes to make you even more distinguished than you are now. Nothing garish, but like a young banker. Meanwhile you can tell me about your tavern business.

That night Brendan was astonished to see Agnes. She was indeed a beautiful woman, dressed fashionably, but conservatively. John Malone was a man in his fifties, obviously prosperous but rather dull. It was clear that he was devoted to Agnes, and a pillar of uprightness. His trade was largely with London merchants; his conversation dealt exclusively with England, where he went every two years, or of the continent where he would not dream of going. He never mentioned Ireland. If he had heard of Connecticut, he knew absolutely nothing else about it and obviously had no intention of burdening his mind with such trivia. An anglicized Irishman, Brendan thought. But then he reflected how lucky his sister had been to capture this paragon of respectability. Since brother and sister could not speak candidly in his presence, Brendan felt he had not really bridged the decade long gap in his relationship with Agnes.

After leaving the Astor House, Catherine informed Brendan that she had arranged for a room in the back of her house for him to stay.

It will be quiet there and no one will bother you, she assured him.

He smiled to himself as he mentally compared the beautifully appointed bedroom with his home-made quarters over the tavern. He slept soundly, contented that his family had emerged from poverty with as few scars as could be expected. The city struck him as more barbarous, more raucous than he remembered, but it was stimulating after the peaceful years in New Milford.

The succeeding days passed quickly. The tailor had a new outfit ready for him in three days; Brendan was rather pleased with the new clothes, including the first dress shoes he had ever owned. His mother devoted as much time as possible to him and he was grateful for the opportunity to grow close to her again. They had long conversations each day in which they brought each other up to date with the details of their lives. He told her about his visits to her brother, Peter, in Danbury, and she was saddened to learn of the rigors and hopelessness of his life.

I wonder if I could do something for him in some way, she mused almost to herself.

He went with Catherine in the carriage to see Agnes several times, but in spite of John Malone's absence, he never felt that he had achieved real rapport with her. However, they were at least on cordial terms once more.

His mother never discussed the details of her own business, but Brendan gathered she was discreet in her operations and had no trouble with the law. She did not seek notoriety as some madames did and paid the police what was required, or a bit more. However, she took pleasure in describing the system of houses of tolerance in general, including the lives of the women who worked there and the popular misconceptions about them. The case of Agnes was not at all unusual, she pointed out. Few women worked as prostitutes more than four years and generally withdrew from the life into perceived respectability. It was clear from the case histories that most women prostituted themselves only to maintain themselves and left the life when they were no longer forced by circumstances to follow it. The madames generally continued for years and many became wealthy. Catherine knew of one who quietly funded the education of her son as a Catholic priest. Although some women ended in degradation, disease and an early death, far many more escaped the life once they had reestablished themselves economically.

During the week in the city, Brendan found he enjoyed being with his mother; in effect he not only loved and admired her as a dutiful son, but he found her witty and entertaining. For someone who had no responsibility but her own home when he last knew her, she had developed managerial skills that she honed not only on the thirty or forty prostitutes, themselves notoriously difficult to control, but the maids, housekeepers, maintenance men and stable hands sufficient to keep four houses in prime condition. He observed that no detail escaped her, but she was firm not picky. She had cultivated political skills in dealing not only with the ward politicians and police, but also in maintaining good relations with businessmen and civic leaders to the extent that was possible. She had a light touch, and a ready smile. Most people, he found, liked and respected her. Within a few days of his arrival, he realized it was going to be wrenching to return to Connecticut. He mentally resolved to get to see her at least once a year.

Catherine questioned him closely about his tavern. She was impressed that he had started the operation from scratch in an old horse barn. She was especially interested in the food service and wanted to know all about Chloe. When he described her in glowing terms, she looked at him intently.

You're not falling in love with that colored girl are you? I don't know anything about New Milford, but I should imagine that such a liaison would thoroughly discredit you in the town.

Don't worry, she already has a boyfriend. She made it clear on her first day that our relationship was to be strictly business. I have always maintained that kind of relationship with her. She does a good job, takes responsibility and exercises a lot of initiative. I'm very contented with her work but I have no designs on her.

I hope she has none on you. I'll have to find a wife for you. You are twenty-six now and it's time you got married. You had an unfortunate experience with the death of Anne, but that doesn't mean you have to remain celibate for the rest of your life. It's not natural for a big, strong boy like you. I don't want you to turn into one of these perverts or fetishists that I see occasionally.

Brendan laughed. Don't worry, Mom. I have normal appetites; it's just that I don't have much chance to prove it.

That's exactly what does worry me. Look at the horrible step Peter took. I would die if you ended up like that. Making a living is fine, but there are other things in life, particularly when you're young.

After a pause, she followed another thought.

Sometimes I'm happy you're living out in the country. New York has changed so much since I arrived here with your father almost thirty years ago. There are so many strangers now. And so many hotels. I happen to know that some fifty-thousand hotel guests were here last year. That may be good for business, she smiled, but it's not a healthy social atmosphere. Because of this it's difficult for a decent young man to meet nice girls. You may not believe it, but some young men even advertise in the personal sections of the newspapers. We even have matchmakers who earn their living bringing decent young people together in marriage. They advertise, too. There is greater disparity between the rich and poor so that young men starting out in life on low salaries find it difficult to marry. I see all this from my vantage point. Lack of resources should not be a problem with you, though. You're doing well in your business and I am in a position to help you, if necessary.

But all their time was not spent in serious conversations.

Several evenings Catherine took him in her carriage, once to the Park Theater, sponsored by John Jacob Astor and John Beekman, to see a play by Shakespeare, to an Italian opera at Palmo's Opera House on Church Street, and to a contemporary American play at the Chatham Theater. It was the first time that Brendan had seen a play or an opera and he was enthusiastic over both. For the first time, too, he became aware of the cultural poverty of New Milford, where there was no theater at all. Not even a travelling company could be accommodated there. He also became aware that New Milford was more fortunate to lack other facilities. In the theaters, his mother pointed out to him the prostitutes working the raucus third tiers. She also told him that the six major theaters then operating in New York were located within two blocks of bordellos and in fact in some cases shared the same city block with one.

The time went too fast. On the following Monday, Brendan prepared to take the steamer back to Norwalk. His mother took the carriage to the Water Street pier. She also had the coachman load a large crate on board for him.

This is a surprise for you when you get back, she told him.

Mom, this has been wonderful for me. I was looking forward to seeing you again for a long time, but I never dreamed that I would enjoy it in so many other ways as well. Just being able to talk to you has been a genuine pleasure for me. I'm happy you and Agnes have done so well. I go back with the blinders off my eyes in some ways I never expected. Thank you so much for being so good to me.

As Brendan walked up the gangway he saw tears in his mother's eyes. He knew his own were moist, but he walked on and waved many times from the deck before the vessel finally pulled away from the dock and headed up the East River. His last glimpse of his mother was her waving a handkerchief from the window of her carriage.

CHAPTER TWENTY

1829

CHLOE WAS MARRIED to Orman Wilson on May 18, shortly after Brendan returned from New York. The ceremony took place in the house which Orman had inherited from his father at the foot of Second Hill Road. The middle of May is a beautiful time in rural Connecticut; the dogwood bracts are still a creamy white, some of the late blooming apple trees bear their fragrant pink and white flowers yet. In the fields buttercups can be picked, held up to a friendly face; if the skin reflects the bright yellow tone, that person is said to like butter. Daisies are ready to dimple green fields with white. There is also baby's breath and, most fittingly for Chloe, bridal veil. Looking toward Great Brook and up Second Hill on her wedding day, the eye was gladdened by all these flowering delights.

The wedding was performed by Stephen Crane, a Justice of the Peace a little after eleven o'clock. He bustled through the ceremony in practiced tones, had Chloe and Orman sign a registration certificate which he promised to file with the Town Clerk, and hurried off.

As soon as he left, the celebration began. There was a fidler, and a couple of young men had harmonicas on which they rendered hymns and all the popular songs of the moment. Groups of young girls sang, young men sang, and their elders joined in the choruses. There was hard cider and whiskey and lots of good food contributed by nearly every African-American family in town. The guests sat on benches, a few chairs and the succulent new grass.

I wish Daddy Wilson were here to enjoy this, Chloe told Brendan. He really enjoyed a good party. We were planning to get married last year but we held off out of respect for his memory.

He would be very proud of you both if he could see you, Brendan said. In fact, he's probably beaming down on you, happy as can be, from where ever his spirit is. You make a handsome couple. I wish you both every happiness in the years ahead.

He then shook hands with Orman, kissed Chloe lightly on the cheek, and gave her a sealed envelope. I hope you can get something for your home that you need with this.

Brendan then stood aside so that others could congratulate the couple, accepted a glass with some deceptively clear liquor in it, and chatted with some of the menfolk.

This is the first wedding I've ever attended in my life, he told one man. I left home before my sister was married and we didn't have any other kin. Since I arrived in New Milford this is the first time I've been invited to one. It doesn't look to be as difficult as I've been led to believe.

The man laughed. This is the good part; good food, something to drink and friends around. It gets a little tougher when the woman starts breaking in her new husband. Orman will find out; Chloe has a mind of her own.

And a very good mind it is. I don't know what I would do without her in the tavern.

Inwardly, Brendan noted grimly that his words were literally and completely true. He hoped that this wedding would not be the instrument that would take Chloe from him. Orman was a mason like his father; although he was not as dynamic as Javan had been or as clever in handling the rich folks, there was no reason why he couldn't make a good living. Orman might not want Chloe working in the tavern. But he, Brendan, did. Now suddenly, he was aware how much he wanted her there, and he had to admit it was not just because she was indispensable to its operation. Perhaps his mother had been right after all. This is ridiculous, he told himself, and put the thought aside.

After a time he realized he had to go to work today. With Chloe absent, everything would be up to him until Chloe returned to work. She hadn't said when that would be. He supposed she would want to take some time off to initiate her new status as a married woman. He quietly paid his respects and left.

One morning a few days later, he ran into Perry in the center. It became apparent that the former legislator was in an excellent mood; in fact he could hardly contain himself. Finally he blurted it out.

Please don't tell anyone yet; it won't be official until May 9, but President Jackson has appointed me postmaster in New Milford.

Congratulations, Perry, that's great news. You've certainly deserved it after your long years serving the country and working for the party. I can't imagine a better man for the job.

You're very kind to say so. You know, there have been only two men in the position since the country's founding. First there was Daniel Everett and after him Philo Noble. Philo has served from 1805 up until the present. That's quite a stretch, isn't it?

It certainly is. I don't think you will ever serve that long.

Brendan saw Perry's face cloud immediately. Before the new postmaster could protest, Brendan hurried to finish his thought.

I mean, of course, that I think you will move on to a larger theater long before you serve the postal patrons nearly as long as Philo has. I know you're not interested in anything further in Hartford, but there's Washington. Orange has been in the

House; I think we should send you to the Senate one of these days.

Oh I couldn't aspire to anything that high. That's a big jump from postmaster or the House in Hartford.

Brendan could see Perry was pleased, though. He pushed on.

I don't know why not. You're a successful attorney, you've had a variety of political experience, and you've proved you can win at the polls. What more do you need?

Obviously Perry agreed, but political etiquette prevented him from saying so. He went away, highly content not only with the appointment but with the hope that others beside Brendan might now grasp the realization that he was fitted for higher office.

Brendan went away feeling slightly guilty for the flattery. While Perry might indeed come to be considered for a run for the House or even the Senate, his own perception was that Perry had lost much of the popularity he had enjoyed and profited from when he was first elected to the House in 1822. People felt that Perry pushed too hard to collect his fees in some cases when his clients were obviously in difficulty; they didn't like to see houses, lot and even farms going to him when the full force of the law was applied. It made him appear grasping and without compassion. The fact that he had gained considerable weight in recent years, dressed formally on all occasions, and smoked costly cigars gave him a sleek and predatory air that corresponded with the slick land deals.

Perry was even becoming the butt of humorous stories. Brendan smiled as he thought of the latest, told to him by Sam Bostwick. The tale involved Dr. Jehiel Williams, the well known and widely beloved physician who had settled in New Milford in 1815 and whose three adult sons had all moved to Illinois. It was he who had treated Anne. He was shrewd, had good judgment and his fees to the needy, if he charged them at all, might be as low as twenty-five cents.

One day a man ran up to him and reported that an irate former client had horsewhipped Perry right in the center of town. Dr. Williams considered the matter for a moment and reportedly commented: I don't know as I would want anybody to be horsewhipped, but if somebody must be, I'd as lieve it was Perry Smith as anybody.

Brendan knew perfectly well that no one had ever assaulted Perry, but the story was evidence that some people in town relished the thought of it. He also knew that such a local reputation would not bar him from consideration as a United States Senator, since senators were not elected by popular vote, but by the lower house of the legislature. This meant they were in reality picked by the party bosses.

Brendan was more concerned over the founding of the Connecticut Temperance Society. He had hoped that the departure some years before of Lyman Beecher for Boston had weakened the movement. It had for a time, but other leaders emerged, especially a Congregational minister from Fairfield named Nathaniel Hewit. Hewit, who became the first president of the new society, was a massive man that Bible readers thought looked like an Old Testament prophet. However he had an unseen weakness; he was troubled by nervous and digestive ills. The liquor lobby in Hartford let it be known that Hewit's problem would disappear if he would but take a bit of spirits for his stomach's sake.

Despite all the jokes which the movement attracted, Brendan did not take it lightly. He knew the society represented a small minority of the state's citizens, but he also knew that its leaders were skilful in manipulating the Whig Party chieftains. In the years when the Whigs were in power in Hartford, there was always the possibility of passage of annoying regulations if not an outright ban on liquor sales. The Democrats professed to believe that the liquor problem, if it existed, should be kept out of politics. They gave out that it was the responsibility of the family and the churches to instill temperance sentiments in the young. The first regulation voted in 1823 gave selectmen the power to order that topers not be served. Now the National Republicans, soon to be the Whigs, wanted to impose an experiment already tried in other states and which would limit sales to quantities of, say, ten gallons, with other consumption on the premises prohibited. This was intended to put saloons out of business, but it could also doom the McCauley Tavern. Brendan decided he would have to go to Hartford to associate himself with other tavern keepers who had been quietly working behind the scenes to defend themselves against the Temperance forces and their allies, the Whigs.

One morning before Chloe had returned to work after her marriage, Brendan was surprised to see a young lad enter the tavern. With a start, he realized it was Perry's son, John. He had grown since Brendan had last seen him; he was tall as a man and had his father's sturdy build. He did not have, though, his father's unctuous politician's face; his expression was as malevolent as ever.

Morning, John. What can I do for you?

John adopted a man-to-man tone. I have never seen your tavern so I thought I would drop around and see how you are getting along.

Brendan was immediately suspicious, but he decided to ostensibly accept John's statement at face value.

That's very good of you. Let me give you a little tour.

He put down his broom, and led John into the dining area, pointing out the accommodations, the massive stone fireplace and chimney, the tablecloths and napkins, unique among taverns in the town. He showed him the kitchen, not quite as orderly as it was when Chloe was working, the bar with the barrels supplying various kinds of beer, whiskey, hard cider and other drinks.

I suppose you know that your father has been very helpful in all of this. He has made suggestions, taken care of my legal work, and supported me with his interest.

Yeah. He's told us all about it, John said. That doesn't mean he's a friend of yours.

Brendan was struck by the comment. Why do you say that, John?

You don't know him like we do in the family. He says one thing to people to butter them up, but what he tells us in private is a different story. You wouldn't believe what he says behind your back.

Oh, every one says things from time to time that they don't really mean. Especially in private.

No, this is different, John said. He likes to tell how he fools people. He gets a kick out of telling us what he told someone, and then telling us what he really thinks about folks. You're not the only one.

Brendan realized that the boy had an axe to grind. He had come here deliberately to tell these things so he could avenge himself on his father for the continual slights he received. He clearly resented the favored treatment his sister Elvira received.

All right. What does he say about me?

He sneers at you because you are an Irish Papist. He has said many times you must be crazy if you ever thought he would take a ruffian off the streets of New York into his office to study law. He laughs that you really believed he would do this and help you with your education.

Lots of people here don't like Catholics. You get used to that.

That's not all, continued the lad. He said he was glad you

started the tavern because it got you out of his house. But that's not the worst thing.

What's the worst thing?

He says you're screwing that nigger girl that works for you and before long you will have a whole parcel of half Irish pickaninnies crawling around the tavern.

Brendan looked like he had been struck. In a lightning reflex he grabbed the boy by the front of his shirt as if to smash him against a wall.

John's eyes betrayed his fright, but he kept his head and did not struggle.

Hey, you said you wanted to know what he said. I'm not saying it myself. I wouldn't say that.

Brendan got control of himself. He released the lad.

You're right, I'm sorry. I shouldn't have done that.

He didn't say it just once, but a lot of times. Once he told my mother that and made her cry. He tells other people that sometimes, too. They laugh about it.

Brendan sat in a chair and ignored John.

What I really came for, said John, was a pint of whiskey. My father said to get it for some of the men. He said to put it on his bill.

Brendan rose and fastened his gaze on John. Deliberately and intensely he answered him.

Get out of here. Fast.

The lad scampered out the door and ran up across the hill.

CHAPTER TWENTY-ONE

1830

ORANGE MERWIN had been a man to be reckoned with in New Milford for nearly three decades. He was regarded as intelligent and enterprising. Around 1820 he and Elijah Boardman were the two most influential men in the town. Merwin first went to Hartford as one of the town's two elected representatives to the General Assembly in 1816. By the next year he was already a Democratic leader in the forefront of his party in its fight to dislodge the Federalists who had been dominant since the foundation of the republic.

In its November 17 edition in 1817, *The Connecticut Courant,* a fiercely partisan Federalist organ, attacked Merwin in a long article on the budget debates then going on. It wrote:

"Mr. Merwin and others were for passing it in the House, under the idea that it would be rejected in the Council (the legislative upper chamber before the 1818 constitution), though some of the more rational Democrats felt too much responsibility to pass it under such circumstances. On the second reading on the bill, Mr. Merwin declared exclusive approbation of its principles and provisions, and expressed the wish it might pass. He added that the few very slight amendments which might be necessary could be made at any time. But it became necessary to change the principles of the bill, and Mr. Merwin was deputed to form a system of amendments. Mr. Merwin now abandoned the principles which he had so much approved, and instead of very slight amendments, he came into the House with his pockets full and set about the entire change of the bill. Mr. M. chose rather to abandon those provisions which he so highly approved than to hazard its death in the House."

In spite of the *Courant's* fulminations, the bill passed and Merwin rose steadily in the ranks of party leaders.

The next year,on the eve of the constitutional convention, where he was one of the committee that drafted the new document, the *Courant* quoted his views on extending the suffrage during a debate on May 30 with a Federalist leader.

"I don't understand it when the opposition admits all are born free, yet some cannot vote. If there is an increase in voters, where is the difficulty? If a regiment appears at the polls on one side, it can be counterbalanced by another regiment on the other. Neither has bayonets fixed. Yet there are quibbles about military duty and taxes that are paid. It is inconsistent to call upon men to do military duty who then may not choose their own officers or highway surveyors. No one has objected to unworthy voters in the past, no one has been prevented from voting regardless of his character."

During his service in the 19th and 20th Congresses between December 5, 1825 and February 26, 1829, Merwin worked faithfully, if somewhat anonymously. He did not take the floor to speak during the entire four years and there is no record that he ever sponsored any legislation. However, he missed few votes of record and these dealt mainly with affairs having no impact on Connecticut or the region. He is on record as having voted thirty-two times, not including numerous voice votes.

For example, Merwin was involved with a bill to adjust pensions for Revolutionary War veterans during both his terms; he supported it on several votes. He backed a resolution to send envoys to a meeting in Panama to meet with representatives of newly independent Latin American countries despite jingoistic opposition. A loyal New Englander, he supported importation of brandy in small casks against western whiskey interests, passage of the woolens bill, the tariff bill, and a bill regulating tonnage duties for foreign shipping. Merwin was against a resolution which would have threatened manufacturing. He voted against a bill to sell the U. S. Bank. He favored bills for internal improvements, the Cumberland Road, and the Chesapeake and Ohio Canal. He several times voted for a measure to expand the judiciary to meet the requirements of a country vastly expanding both in population and geographically.

He also played politics in voting for a successful demand that President John Quincy Adams supply a list of all appointments by the Executive branch since the country's beginnings. He interested himself, as did other members, in such trivial matters as a pension for the indigent mother of a naval gunner who had been killed fighting pirates. He favored a treaty with the Creek Indians and a $15,533 payment to former President Monroe for expenses due him while he was Ambassador to France in 1810. He opposed a move to reimburse the French nobleman, Marigny D'Auterive, for slaves who were injured in the seizure of a ship by federal authorities. Mercifully, he voted not to commission a painting on the Battle of New Orleans.

* * *

As the stage from Danbury rounded the corner from Bridge Street and headed up the west side of Main, Brendan sprung up from a bench in front of the New England House, instantly alert. He joined several other persons who were welcoming travelers or receiving consignment for local businesses. They clustered around the side of the vehicle as it drew up in front of the hotel. A groom opened the door as the driver climbed down from his seat to tend the horses.

Brendan saw his mother immediately, and she smiled and waved to him when still in her seat. In a moment she stepped down into his arms.

Mom, it's so good to see you. How was the trip?

Brendan, you look wonderful. Her eyes filled with tears even as she kissed him, and then laughed at her own emotion. The trip? Oh yes, the trip. It was the longest one I've taken since I crossed the Atlantic Ocean. But this time I didn't get sick. It was interesting, I can say now. But Holy Mother, one certainly does get tossed about.

You look well, though. I don't know how you stay so young. Brendan was sincere; Catherine McCauley's face was still unlined and the flesh on her erect body appeared still firm under a gown that discreetly revealed its splendid contours. Brendan knew she was now fifty.

I had some bad moments in Danbury. I took a hansom cab, or whatever you call such a conveyance around here, out to see Peter. I was terribly distressed. He lives like a peasant. He works so hard and he looks so worn out. And that awful hovel he lives in with that poor, simple creature. I could hardly believe he was the same brother, so elegant and vital, I remember back in Dublin. It was a terrible shock for me. It was hard on him, too. You could tell it gave him pain for me to see him that way. Oh Brendan, sometimes I just want to howl when I think what America has done to our family.

But it has not done as badly by us as Europe did to those who weren't able to make it here. You have done well, so has Agnes. How is she?

Agnes is fine. She has everything she ever wanted. John Malone treats her like a queen. Even so, sometimes she seems restless. We all bear our scars, visible or not.

Forgive me for keeping you here in the street. Let me take your bag. I've made a reservation for you in New Milford's leading hotel. I hope you won't find it too primitive. The owner claims there is nothing better between here and New York.

He's probably right, but he might strive for a more challenging comparison. Oh, but your little village is very charming. All the green grass and the little elm saplings! I like it already.

Brendan greeted persons he knew in the lobby as he helped his mother check in. Her room gave on the green and was spacious and comfortable. A maid was available to bring her large pitchers of water and there was a basin for washing.

I'll leave you to rest a while. I have rented a carriage for the duration of your visit so I can show you something of this place. The town has only a bit more than four-thousand people, but in terms of area it's the biggest municipality in the state. So we do have some lovely natural vistas even if the town is largely undeveloped yet. Incidentally, there is talk of a railroad through here, which would make it much easier to get to and from New York. But it's still years away. I'll pick you up at four; we can eat at the McCauley Tavern this evening.

When he and his mother descended to the lobby later in the afternoon, Anan Hine and Orange Merwin were talking in the lobby. Brendan introduced his mother to them. He could see they were impressed by her good looks and fashionable attire. She did her best to flatter Anan on the quality of his hospitality.

Outside he told her that Merwin had been a leading figure in New Milford for years. There was talk that he might run on the Democratic state ticket next year, probably for Lieutenant Governor.

I'm sure he is a very excellent man, but your poor father would have the fits if he knew you were associating with a man named Orange. I know you don't know anything about it, but back in Ireland the Orange Order was anathema to the United Irishmen, the movement to which your father belonged. The Orange collaborated with the English in the war in 1798. They committed terrible atrocities against our people in the battle of Vinegar Hill. It was because of them that my brother and I had to flee to France. Your father faced a court-martial and was lucky to escape with his life. It makes me shudder just to hear the name.

I know you're right. Uncle Peter told me about it. But somehow the name doesn't have the same significance here. It has nothing to do with Ireland. There are lots of men named Orange in Connecticut and there is even a town of that name. But here the name commemorates triumph over tyranny of another sort. The people in Connecticut hated the Stuart kings because they repressed the Congregationalists, who established their faith here. They welcomed the Glorious Revolution that toppled the Stuarts and brought William of Orange to the throne of England.

Oh, I never thought I would hear my own son defending the Orangemen. Catherine pouted.

Oh mother, I'm not defending the Orangemen. I know they did evil things. But you must realize the name means another thing here. Please don't be angry with me on your first night here.

Brendan led her out to the carriage in front.

Let me take you for a ride. We will go south along the river to a gorge which they call Lovers' Leap. Probably the lovers never existed, but you will like the panorama from there.

Catherine was mollified and did enjoy the breeze as they cantered south. He walked the horse up the hill through the hemlocks when they reached the gorge and took her out on the promontory overlooking Gardiner's Island, where fur traders operated for decades before the town was founded. Then he drove down the thank-you-mams on the southeast to the cove and up the grassy valley toward Bridgewater Neck, then north up past several farms until they came to the ridge where they could look down over the Housatonic and the village with its two church spires.

Now if you're getting hungry, we can go to the tavern and eat. Like the hotel man, I enjoy saying we have the best cooking this side of New York. Don't let that discourage you beforehand.

Twenty minutes later they were at the McCauley Tavern. He helped his mother out of the carriage, gave the reins to a man he had hired recently to attend to the horses of guests, and led her to the door.

I like your situation here. The view to the west over the river valley is charming.

Chloe met them at the door; Brendan introduced her to his mother as the best cook in New Milford. Brendan was relieved to see that his mother was gracious with her.

We have three entrees this evening, Chloe said, roast duck with orange sauce, beef filets, or shad, if you like fish. We are also serving wax beans and scalloped potatoes with a green lettuce salad.

Brendan noticed that Chloe was dressed particularly elegantly this evening. Her dark purple gown fitted her beautifully and she wore a matching ribbon on her long hair stretched back from the temples.

I know the shad is something very special at this time of year so I must try that. Your menu sounds delicious. Do you always offer such variety?

When we have a particularly honored guest, yes we do, Chloe responded without expression. The shad is fresh from the river this afernoon and boned by an expert who never leaves a single one.

Boning shad is a much sought after skill at this time of year, Brendan explained. If it's not done right, the fish is inedible.

When she left to prepare the meal, the bartender brought a bottle of French champagne to the table. He extracted the cork and put the bottle under a linen napkin in a container filled with ice.

Well, I never expected to see that here, Catherine said. I'm really impressed.

I ordered a case when I knew you were coming. As a former resident of France, you can tell me how it is.

Brendan poured a little of the wine in a goblet and extended it to his mother. She gently inhaled the bouquet and took a sip which she rolled in her mouth before swallowing.

Mais, c'est magnifique. Tu es choisi très bien.

Brendan chuckled and poured the champagne into both their glasses. If you go much further into French you will lose me, but *à ta santée.* They touched glasses and tasted the vintage.

Your assistant is also *magnifique.* She is really a very beautiful woman.

I don't notice such things, Brendan deadpanned. But she does a terrific job here. She was married last year and I was afraid she might leave, then I was afraid she would soon be pregnant. But luckily neither has come to pass so far. I shake with fright at the thought of having to replace her.

I have a feeling that she would not want to be replaced.

I hope you're right. Brendan chose to ignore his mother's real implication.

The shad was tender and sweet, with nary a wisp of a bone. The potatoes and beans were done perfectly. A plate of warm rolls and dark breads were fresh and fragrant.

Your cook, or better, your chef, is as good as you said. Although the New England House is quite nice, I think your boast is more valid than that of Mr. Hine. All apart from the flourishes you would get in New York, this meal is just as well prepared as any you could get there. I must congratulate Chloe. First let us try her dessert.

After a chocolate cake, rich and light, with a frosting like nectar, Catherine took Chloe by the hand.

My dear, your meal was a revelation. I never dreamed I could encounter such cooking out here in the country. My son has been telling me how wonderful you are but I couldn't believe him until I tasted this meal. God has given you a wonderful talent. Thank you so much for this experience.

Chloe took the praise in stride. I learned how to cook and bake from my mother-in-law. She had no one to teach her; she had the gift to experiment and learn. I'm glad you enjoyed it. I will tell my mother-in-law and she will be pleased to learn that some of her teaching has borne fruit.

Later at her room in the New England House, Catherine adopted a serious air with her son.

I want to talk to you about your future, and I don't mean the tavern, where you seem to be doing very well. I am concerned about your personal life. You are now twenty eight years old, hardly a young man any more. It's time you were married and started a family.

Oh mom, don't start on that.

I am not only going to start on that subject, but I'm going to speak frankly about it at some length. I have had some experience with domestic relations, and I don't limit that to my married life with your father. I have been a whore and I am now a successful madame. However you might judge these activities, I have had a lot of experience with men. Men seek out whores because they want something that they can't get from their wives or they can't get anywhere else. When they are denied regular sex, they either channel this force into some other activity, or they generate all manner of unhealthy fantasies, or they develop perversions that maim their lives and leave them outcasts subject to public ridicule, abuse or persecution.

Mother, I am not a pervert.

Of course you aren't, and I don't want you to become one.

I know of the sexual relations you had with Anne, because you told me. It seems that you performed as a healthy young man and she needed you because this Perry thought more about politics than he did his wife. As far as I know, this is the only woman you have known in the biblical sense either before or since. Now all of New England, including Connecticut, is known to be a puritanical, sexually repressed area. I have known dozens of young women from Connecticut who have drifted to the city, half dead with fear and apprehension, because their families have turned them out of their homes when their young men friends made them pregnant. As you must know, most of these pathetic creatures have had no recourse but to sell their bodies so they can eat. But no one thinks about what happens to the young men. Many, if not all of them, became involved with the girls with no malicious intent, but merely because of bodily urges. They are not punished by society as severely as the girls, but they feel guilt and develop a furtive, unhealthy attitude toward sex that helps perpetuate and intensify the puritanical restrictions that caused the problem in the first place.

She paused and looked at Brendan, but he avoided her eyes and looked uncomfortable.

I don't want you to become like that. I would like you to find a woman toward whom you could develop love and respect, marry and have a family with. I don't see how that can happen around here. Even though you were born in this country, you are regarded as Irish and Catholic and looked down upon. I'm sure you know that better than I. You undoubtedly have a wide range of acquaintances here, but how many friends do you have who would hope that you would marry their sisters? Not many, I would wager.

Brendan thought of the spinning bee and Julia Booth. That had been his only overt opportunity. His mother continued.

I would like to make you an offer. I would like you to give me authorization to find some girls in the New York area who are attractive and well educated and who would like to get to know a handsome young man, and you are handsome, Brendan, and see enough of him so that the two of you can decide if you would like to spend the rest of your lives together.

I would hope you would agree, but if you don't, I have still another offer. Come to New York at least four or five times a year and I will arrange sessions with girls so beautiful it will take your breath away. You can give vent to your sexual needs. This, I hasten to add, would be at no cost to you although you could probably afford it. You should be able to take some advantage of your mother's connections in the skin trade. I want you to have one or the other. I don't want you to become one of these dessicated Yankees, with their emotions and normal appetites all wizzened away.

You don't have to respond now. I'm not going to say anything more about this during the rest of my time here. I want us to enjoy our few hours together after so many years apart. Think it over and tell me before I leave how you feel about my offers.

Fair enough. He smiled. I love being tempted. During the next few days as we take the carriage to Tory Cave, to Bull's Bridge, to Lake Waramaug, to Roxbury Falls, I'll savour your proposals.

Get out of here, you benighted ohmadon. I have to sleep.

Now I know how Christ felt when he was taken to the pinnacle of the temple. Good night, mother.

The night before his mother was to return to New York, Brendan told her he had made his decision about her offer.

My first choice is to look over the candidates for wifedom. With all sincerity, I will tell you that I would like to marry and establish a home. For some time I have felt this way, but as you have correctly pointed out, there are not many opportunities in New Milford for someone in my situation. What bothers me about your offer is not only how you will find these eligible young ladies, but how they, and myself, can decide in a few brief encounters, if we want to spend the rest of our lives together. Obviously, I cannot afford to spend more than a couple of weeks at a time in the city, and I wouldn't expect that they will want to move to New Milford to facilitate a courtship. But I'm willing to give your proposal a try, and perhaps I will be surprised.

I'm delighted, Brendan. Don't underestimate me because of my profession. I believe I can seek out some lovely young women of high character from whom you will be well content to pick a wife.

Fine, but if you don't succeed, or rather , if I fail, then with the utmost pleasure I will accept your alternative offer. After all, I don't want to be a dessicated old Yankee any more than you want me to be. It seems to me I have heard an expression, "Use it or lose it," and I certainly wouldn't want to lose it.

That refers to old men, silly. Casting a professional eye over you, I'd venture to predict that you will be fruitful for a good many years yet. Now, to move on to something more elevating, take me back to my hotel so I can pack. I don't want to miss the stage in the morning. I not only have a job that I must get back to, but an additional assignment to get to work on.

CHAPTER TWENTY-TWO

1831

ORANGE MERWIN ran for Lieutenant Governor on the National Republican ticket in April, 1831 as the running mate of John S. Peters, the gubernatorial candidate. Peters received 12,866 votes, two-thirds of those cast, and outstripped his nearest rival by more than eight thousand votes. Neither Merwin nor any other candidate for the second spot secured a majority of the votes cast as required under the 1818 constitution. It was not until years later that the constitution was changed so that the the Governor and Lieutenant Governor ran together on the ballot.

Former U. S. Senator Henry W. Edwards, a New Haven Democrat, polled 7,670 votes and Merwin 6,670, but neither garnered a majority because Eli Ives, candidate for Lieutenant Governor of the Anti-Masonic Party, received 3,794 votes.

The constitution made no provision in the event no candidate for Lieutenant Governor received a majority. Earlier, in the 1823 election no candidate for that office had emerged with a majority and the General Assembly had filled the office by joint voting of the House and the Senate.

With this precedent in mind, the House when it convened in May invited the Senate to jointly ballot with it to fill the office. The Senate unexpectedly refused, reportedly because some of its members thought it should have more weight in selecting the Lieutenant Governor, the presiding officer of that body. One senator was quoted in *The Connecticut Courant* as saying the state could get along without a Lieutenant Governor.

The rebuffed House proceeded to vote alone and named Merwin. The Senate also met alone and selected Edwards. Neither chamber would yield to the other's decision, so the post of Lieutenant Governor remained vacant until the next election.

As it turned out, the office was more important than the quoted senator had deemed it. Both houses got together to hire Robert Fairchild to carry out at least some of the duties of Lieutenant Governor. They saved money though; they paid him thirty dollars for his services, mainly presiding over the Senate, for the entire session.

In New Milford, Merwin received 208 votes to 110 for Edwards; Hartford gave Merwin 440 and 338 to Edwards. In addition to the principal spoiler, Ives, and the two main candidates, there were twenty-eight other candidates running for the job. It is apparent that some voters were thoroughly confused by the process. Merwin received fifty-seven votes for Governor, only one of them in New Milford. A character named Roger W. Sherman picked up eighty-five votes; could it be that some faction was trying to make ill-informed rural voters believe that Roger Sherman, the Revolutionary patriot and later Congressman and Senator, was still alive?

The election virtually ended Merwin's political career although he did serve two additional terms in the House in 1838 and 1842.

Brendan had other things on his mind, although he had voted for Orange and was disappointed he had lost. Even before the election, Catherine had written him that she had selected three nice girls whom she would like him to meet. She didn't give their names, but she indicated that they came from "good families," were attractive, and had graduated from what she described as female academies. Now that the weather was better for travelling, she suggested that he come to the city as soon as convenient. For some reason that was not clear to him, he was not anxious to meet the three, but since he had accepted his mother's proposal during her visit, he saw no way he could legitimately refuse.

He discussed the trip with Chloe, and it was agreed that a substitute bartender would be required again in his absence. In the three years since his last trip to the city, the number of customers, especially diners, had increased to the point where it was not possible for her to handle the bar along with her other work. He knew from what other tavern keepers had told him that unsupervised bartenders occasionally found the temptation to keep some of the receipts overpowering, but he had no choice. He hired a man who had worked for Eli Todd and told him the receipts each day were to be passed to Chloe. The bartender, Nathan Ward, made it plain he was not happy with turning the money over to a woman, especially a black woman. Brendan told him that's the way it had to be if he wanted the job. Nathan agreed.

It was June before Brendan, travelling by stage and sound steamer as before, arrived at his mother's house on Greene Street. Another young girl, certainly not the one he had encountered three years before, met him at the door. Again, he was ushered into the beautifully furnished parlor to await his mother. Their meeting this time was less emotional than in 1828, but more open and light-hearted.

So you've come to meet the bridal prospects I've picked out for you! she said.

It can't do any harm. I really wanted to see you again. It seemed like a big trip before, but this time I guess I took it more in stride. You will have to explain what is required of me. Do I get to try out each one?

Don't even think about it. These are all virginal young maidens who have been educated by the Sisters of Mercy. If you aren't a perfect gentleman, you will ruin my reputation. She laughed merrily.

I'll be good. Give me a day to get adjusted to the idea. How are you going to arrange these meetings? Certainly you can't do it here.

Of course not. You seemed to like the Astor House last time you were here. I will simply host a dinner there three consecutive evenings. Each night one of the young ladies and someone from her family will be there. So will I. And two or three other persons so it won't look like a slave auction. The girls will sit next to you so you will have ample time to talk with each one. The relatives will be at the other end of the table and won't be able to hear everything. You are the guest of honor and I am celebrating your return to New York from Connecticut where I said you are a successful businessman. It's up to you if you want to reveal what your business is or the name of the town. If I were you, I would, but that's your decision. Also if you are not enraptured with any of them, there should be no embarrassment; no one was promised anything.

You certainly set an attractive stage. What are the names of these young lovelies?

The first night will be Kathleen Riordan; her father is a politician. The second is Sabina Hauser; father is a wholesale butcher; and the last is Marguerite Bannon; her father is deceased, but he left money to widow Mary, who is a careful investor.

Two colleens and a valkyrie. Two brunettes and a blonde?

No, the reverse; Marguerite is also light colored.

How old are they? Do any of them work at anything?

None work. They are all in their early twenties. Virginal, as

I said, but beyond the first blush of innocence.

I'm not even going to think any more about them today. Are you free? Can we just go somewhere and just talk? I don't want to see anything and I don't want to do anything.

I have a hideaway on the top floor. It's comfortable and we won't be bothered. You can tell me how you and your Chloe are progressing—in the business, of course. And your friend, Orange. I read in the Herald that neither he nor any rival got enough votes in the election to win the job. I must tell you I'm glad; I hate to think of an Orange in high places over here.

The next night Brendan wore what he called his Dandy Suit, the outfit his mother had given him three years before. He had worn it only once in New Milford; there he couldn't stand the smirks. But it seemed appropriate at the Astor House. His mother, as usual, was faultlessly turned out in a dark green gown that made it look like she was in her late thirties.

The private dining room included a reception room where the guests gathered to meet, drink an apéritif and get to know one another before sitting down to dinner. Kathleen came with her father, Dan, and a younger sister. Kathleen wore a maroon satin gown with a deep decolletage showing much and promising more. She had dark hair and skin that couldn't be whiter without showing blue veins. Brendan immediately liked Dan Riordan who was an alderman but also deeply involved in the process of electing Tammany candidates. He knew something about Connecticut politics as well; he was familiar with the name of Perry Smith but didn't seem to know much about him. He actually knew John M. Niles, publisher of the *Hartford Times* and a prominent Democrat, whom he had met at national conventions, and thought highly of him.

At dinner, Kathleen talked a good deal of horses; she was an avid rider and liked the races. Despite her father's career, she knew nothing of politics. Her conversation corroborated the evidence of her flawless white hands; she knew nothing whatever about any kind of work and had no idea where money came from. Reading was not one of her interests; she attended the theater occasionally but it made no mark on her. Brendan concluded that she would be a marvelous lay and a prolific mother. He had been told, and believed, that horsey girls were avid for sex. It was easy to lust after Kathleen but he couldn't imagine her helping out in the McCauley Tavern.

The next night Sabina was accompanied by her mother, a woman of fearsome aspect who wore her corset stays as if they were medieval armor. Sabina was a large, healthy looking blonde whose roguish eyes belied any description of her as being just beyond the first blush of innocence. Brendan steered clear of the mother but rather enjoyed talking with Sabina. She was not intellectual, but clearly shrewd. She knew a lot about money, how it was obtained, and what it would buy. She knew she didn't have to work to get it. Sabina liked to steer the conversation into areas where *doubles entendres* could emerge. Brendan played this game with her to her huge amusement. The nuns must have had quite a challenge with this one, he reflected.

Marguerite Bannon was fascinated by religion, which to her meant the Catholic faith. She liked to talk about the Albigensian heresy and its suppresion, the role of Saint Domenick in the counter-reformation, and the need for the church to take a stand against the rising tide of liberalism in Europe and, of course, in the United States. She was an extremely pretty girl, but so intense in expressing her beliefs that she seemed a bit scary. Brendan wondered what her reaction would be if she knew he had not set foot in a Catholic Church since he was sixteen.

After the final dinner as they rolled back to Greene Street, Catherine probed Brendan for a reaction.

Well?

The meals were very good. That's one thing about the Astor

House. Flawless service and pleasant surroundings.

Don't irritate me. How about the girls?

The girls were all extremely good looking. They have obviously been brought up as very proper young ladies, with the possible exception of Sabina.

Sabina? What was wrong with her?

Nothing really, she was the one who seemed most in touch with life on earth. It's just that it struck me that she likes to play, or perhaps she's a tease.

You didn't like the other two?

Marguerite is the only one who I have to rule out immediately. I can't abide that deep vein of religiosity that keeps pouring cant out of her. Only someone radically out of touch with the world could afford to be so narrowly dogmatic. Her father must have made his money in a sinister way for her to be pointed so strongly in that direction.

And Kathleen?

Horses are her religion. I was violently attracted to her because of those wonderful breasts. I'm certain she would be a prodigiously fruitful brood mare.

Oh Brendan, I've failed. You didn't like any of them.

I'm sorry I was flip, Mom. I think you picked good prospects. If I had to, I could be content to marry either Kathleen or Sabina. I'm very grateful to you for all you have done. And I know it took a lot of arranging and a great deal of money. I thank you very much. Sincerely.

If you had to – of course you don't have to. But I don't understand the problem with Kathleen and Sabina.

The problem is that I...that one, can't just walk in the Astor House and pick out a wife. It takes time to get to know one another. Perhaps if I lived in New York, we could work it out. They could find out about me and I could find out what they are interested in besides horses and sly jokes. Find out what we have in common and if we could stand each other for the rest of our lives. What on earth would any of them do in New Milford? Is there one of them that could work with me in the tavern? If not, what would they do all day? I don't want to be a male Agnes all fixed up for the rest of my life with a nice income. Don't you see, Mom? You've had some pretty rough times. Can you imagine any of these three going through what you did and surviving? Please don't be angry with me. It's just that this isn't the way to head me toward matrimonial bliss.

It's all right, Brendan. I knew it was chancey, but I wanted so much to have you have a happy home life. It's been something too rare in our family. But we did discuss another alternative to this approach. Do you want me to get you a beautiful girl with big breasts and all the rest whom you can tumble with?

You're all right, Mom. You really are. It's a good feeling to have a mother that will really go down the line for me. I think I would like to take a rain check on your offer. I'm wrung out after these encounters to find me a wife. Next time I visit you, if I'm not too dessicated by then, I would appreciate the hospitality you're offering. But for now, I just want to go back to Connecticut and get in my own little rut again.

Catherine rumpled his hair.

I like you very much. You're honest. Go on back tomorrow. I know you'll work out your future somehow. It was fun tempting you. Get a good night's sleep and I'll see you off in the morning.

CHAPTER TWENTY-THREE

1832

THE GENERAL ASSEMBLY in its 1832 session finally enacted the experiment that Brendan and other tavern keepers in the state had dreaded for several years. The legislature, now dominated by National Republicans, some of whom were already calling themselves Whigs after the English political party of that name, voted to restrict liquor sales to quantities of ten gallons or more at a single purchase. This was an experiment, already being tried in other states, designed to abolish saloons, but it also affected taverns and other retail outlets. Brendan and other tavern keepers had fought the measure since it was first suggested by temperance leaders several years before. As long as the Democrats were in power, they had felt themselves safe, but the Whigs were committed to the experiment.

Brendan pondered a long while what to do. Before the incident with John three years before, he would have immediately consulted Perry without second thought. But since then, he could not but help consider Perry as a undercover foe. It was true that young John Smith had been speaking from malice toward his father when he passed on the alleged words of his father, but it was equally certain that they had the ring of truth. In his own mind, Brendan had no doubt that Perry had really made the remarks as his son had asserted. Brendan had seen

Perry only occasionally and briefly since then. He had continued to pay the monthly five percent of his gross income from the tavern to Perry each month, but usually left it in an envelope at the office. He had decided that any attempt to break the agreement could only work to his own prejudice. So now he finally and reluctantly resolved to have recourse to Perry's services once more. It was preferable to have Perry as a covert enemy rather than an overt one as long as he was aware of the danger from that quarter. Furthermore, Perry had been effective as his attorney and had not charged for occasional services in recognition of his obligation to render counsel under the agreement they both had signed. Finally, the agreement would expire in the following year. So, Brendan submerged his feeling and asked for Perry's advice again.

Perry was familiar with the new statute and told him there was no immediate problem.

The new act does not go into effect immediately, he said, so you have some leeway. The act also specifies that liquor dealers may obtain a special license from town authorities to sell in quantities of less than ten gallons. The selectmen won't be overcome with joy at the prospect of awarding you such a license now that the temperance people are creating such a hubub, but with the proper preparation I believe we could convince them to do it. The McCauley Tavern has a good reputation, so it shouldn't be too difficult. Meanwhile, the less you say about this new statute, the better. If anyone asks you about it, simply say it's in the hands of your attorney. I will quietly talk to the selectmen about it and I will check in Hartford to see how this will be handled in the cities. You know better than I how many liquor dealers are being affected. You can bet that every single one of them is consulting a lawyer just as you are. I am confident that we can keep you in business one way or another. I will keep you informed.

As if the quantity liquor sale regulation were not enough of a problem, Chloe began acting strangely. Up to now a model of regularity, she began arriving at work late or even missed half days. She was curiously quiet or even sullen in contrast to her usual crisp self. Brendan even fancied he caught her weeping quietly, all by her self in the kitchen, a couple of times. At first he did not think too much of these foibles, especially in view of Chloe's exemplary service over eight years and her dedication to the business.

When, after two months of this behaviour, Chloe showed up one morning with one eye almost swollen closed, Brendan decided it was time to intervene. After she had had time to get herself organized for the day, he entered the kitchen. At first she tried to avoid his gaze and then headed toward the back door. He spoke to her.

Chloe, please give me a few minutes. Come here and sit down. I want to talk to you.

Reluctantly she turned and sat in a chair twenty feet away. Brendan moved his chair so that they were facing each other some four feet apart.

Chloe, I sense you have some problem. And I don't mean just today with that gorgeous eye. For the last couple of months you haven't been yourself. I don't want to pry into your personal life, which is none of my business. But when you aren't yourself and it affects how you do your job, I think I have a right to know. Is there some problem I can help you with?

At first Chloe tried to deny she had a problem. She seemed distraught, not her usual cool self. Brendan persisted, talking softly to her until she gave way. Finally she began to sob, her entire body quivering. Between sobs, the words came fitfully.

It's Orman. I don't know what's come over him. He's taken to drinking and he hasn't had any jobs in quite a while, even during all this good weather. He just sits around the house.

When he's been drinking he's not nice with me like he used to be. He seems to be angry with me, but he doesn't say why. Last night he was drunk and talked terrible. When I tried to calm him down, he hit me.

Brendan had had an inkling of this. He had heard roundabout that several of Javan Wilson's old customers had expressed discontent with Orman. He didn't jolly them as Javan had, he was taciturn and unresponsive. The well-to-do were his only customers; if he didn't keep them contented, no one else could afford decorative masonry work. He couldn't live off building occasional chimneys and there were less and less fireplaces as ordinary people switched to the new metal stoves which were being turned out in factories.

Orman doesn't have the sunny disposition of his father, Brendan said. Perhaps he's too short with the rich folks. They like to think that their money makes people happy and spreads good feeling. They get nervous when someone reminds them that they aren't as important as they think and their money isn't producing the results they think it should. It's not Orman's fault, necessarily; not everyone has the gift for jollifying with the upper crust so they can feel munificent. He thinks that if he just turns out good work, it should be enough. But it isn't and he can't understand it. Then he gets touchy and you're the handiest person he can take it out on, especially if he's been sucking on some homebrew. Does that sound about like what's happened?

Still snuffling, she said it sounded about right. But her sobbing continued.

Brendan rose from his chair and took out a clean linen handkerchief. He knelt on one knee and dried her eyes as best he could. Chloe began to talk less spasmodically.

I thought he would be happy that I make good money here, but he seems to resent it. It sticks in his craw that I earn more than he does, even when he has jobs. If we both work we have a good income so we could take good care of our children and raise them up with educations. But we don't have any children and we've been married now three years.

At the thought, Chloe's tears once more flowed down her cheeks and Brendan had to give up his efforts with the handkerchief. At a loss what to do, he put an arm around her back, and softly patted a shoulder. She moved toward him and put her head on his chest. He was acutely uncomfortable on one knee, so he slowly rose, pulling her up with him, still holding her close. He put the other arm around her waist; she nestled closer, moaning softly. Brendan made comforting sounds as he rested his cheek in her hair. He noted her pleasing fragrance and she raised her face to him. He kissed her on the forehead and an electric charge passed through them both. He crushed her to him and his lips met hers and opened. Their tongues entwined and it was suddenly a new world. Their hands moved over each other's bodies.

Not here, she said.

With their arms around each other, they walked together, each feeling the movement of the other's hip. They slowly mounted the stairs, enjoying the feel of the other, and entered his room. He laid her gently on the bed; she pulled him down on her with surprising strength. Brendan had not been with a woman since Anne ten years before. His arousal was frenetic. He pulled off Chloe's clothes wildly as she clutched at his. Even working at cross purposes as they were, in a moment they were both nude and moving toward each other until they were tightly clasped. In an instant he entered her and within seconds climaxed. Without a pause, he resumed his powerful thrusting almost immediately. She arched her back to better meet him. They kissed as before, then turned their faces to whisper soft sounds to each other. Again he felt the fire run through him into her. She cried and moaned almost simultaneously. For a long time they just lay together and let their senses register the closeness.

Later Chloe opened her eyes.

God Almighty, she said. That was something.

Brendan kissed her tenderly and responded.

Something is not the word for it. I don't know what is.

He laid at her side for minutes, then laughed softly.

It's a good thing you cleaned this place up.

Yes, and now I will have to do it again. And mend some clothes. She joined in the laughter.

Then she turned sober.

This isn't really so funny. I'm married. I love my husband even if he is being a pain in the ass. I've never done this to him before.

I'm sorry. No I'm not. It was sensational, literally. But I understand what you're saying. You want to stay married, so you don't want this to happen again. Isn't that right?

Yes. It was a precious moment for me, too. But we will have to go back to running a tavern and act like this didn't happen. Can you do that?

I'll try. It won't be easy, but I think I can. We'll have to figure out some way so that Orman can slush up those rich folks better and get back working for them. If he's functioning properly, we won't be so apt to backslide.

You're right insofar as I'm concerned. It's at least seven weeks since he's been with me. You get pretty horny in that time.

You wouldn't believe if I told you how long it was with me.

Let's see. Does it go back as far as Anne?

Brendan was incredulous. You're a witch, he said.

You think you can get away with that stuff with nobody knowing in this town? It can't be done. But we better do it this time. Get your ass out of this bed, get dressed and get out so I can get to work.

CHAPTER TWENTY-FOUR

1833

LONG BEFORE BRENDAN HAD ARRIVED in New Milford, on December 14, 1801, a town meeting had taken the first step toward beautification of the center when it voted "that every goose that shall be found or taken in any person's enclosure may be retained and kept by the person sustaining the damage, until the owner pay to each person twelve and a half cents for every goose so taken and retained."

On his first rainy morning in town and also on the Fourth of July of that year he had had occasion to note that the center, or the common, was little more than a few farm houses in two rows facing each other over a swampy divide, interspersed by a few places of business.

The first white man to do a day's work in the center of the town was Zachariah Ferriss, who ploughed a lot just south of the future home of Roger Sherman in the spring of 1706. Ferriss was brother-in-law of Colonel John Read; his day's work was undertaken, not in any hope of raising a crop on the site, but to establish Colonel Read's title to the land. The rival New Milford Company, which had also purchased title from the Indians three years earlier, promptly sued Colonel Read, who pleaded and won the suit. When the New Milford Company laid out its settlement at the foot of Aspetuck Hill in the autumn of

1707, Read sued the company. This was the suit which was tried and decided in Read's favor fifteen times, but which he lost on the sixteenth try. Thus litigation and civilization came to New Milford.

The growth of the village was very slow, probably because few if any of the town's inhabitants considered it a village. Park Lane residents had as good cause to think of themselves as the hub. There were several cobbler shops in that area; Roger Sherman's was the only one in the putative village. A case could even be made for Lanesville, where there were several thriving mills and other enterprises. In fact, the mills, carding machines, blacksmith shops, plough makers, tanneries and coopers were scattered in all parts of the town except on the common.

Gradually this changed. William Sherman, Roger's older brother, opened the first store on the common in 1750. When he died, the premises were taken over by Roger who operated his cobbler shop there. After the Revolution, Elijah Boardman set up his store on the west side of the common. Anan Hine and Stanley Lockwood took over the Boardman store to operate as merchants. In 1823, Anan buit another store on Lyman Keeler's place on the east side of the green and another in 1825 near Roger Sherman's old home which was taken over by Royal Canfield in 1833. At some point a couple of taverns operated, but it was not until after 1800 that this settlement gradually began to emerge as the real center of the town. Even so, for many years the residents of the common differed not one whit from the rest of the townspeople in their customs or manners. They were all farmers, including the lawyers, the physicians, the store keepers, and even the ministers.

The major change in the character of the common was the removal of the churches from its south end. In 1833 a new Congregational Church was built on a slight elevation on the east side of the common. Reverend Heman Rood, who arrived in 1830, lost little time in planning the new building and the move to it. Wide cut stone steps led up to a Greek Revival portico with a pediment supported by six fluted Doric columns. The steeple was supported by a three-stage belfry. The effect was all that Sir Christopher Wren could have expected from one of his latter-day disciples. When it was completed, New Milford people rightfully considered it one of the best examples of small town church architecture in New England.

The Episcopalians would follow the example of their low church brethren and in 1837 remove their church from the common. Their new place of worship would be less grand than that of the Congregationalists. They would erect a wooden building much along the lines of a commercial warehouse, high and deep. Wide wooden steps would lead up to the meeting room on what was essentially the second floor. Their architectural challenge and triumph would have to wait.

With the removal of the church buildings from the green, the town took the obvious next step. It built a ditch through the center of the common to drain the water course, along with three small bridges for crossing points. The brush and weeds were cleared. Inasmuch as the residents on both sides were no longer farmers, one no longer saw geese, swine and cattle pasturing in the area. People took to calling the long strip the green, in tribute to its luxurious grass, rather than the common.

Brendan viewed these changes with satisfaction although they affected him little. He realized that anything that enhanced the town would eventually benefit him. He looked forward to showing off the improvements to his mother when she next visited him from New York. He would like to be able to show that his community was thriving even if the amenities she was used to in New York were still largely lacking. The town now had a volunteer fire department, but, as useful as this might be, it wouldn't put any sparkle in his mother's eyes.

For Brendan, the best news was from Hartford. The Democrats, newly restored to power, had amended the law mandating only quantity sales of liquor passed by the Whig legislature the year before. The amendment permitted any retailer who found it impossible to obtain a license under the restriction to petition the county court for relief. Following Brendan's request, Perry sought and received the relief from the court in Litchfield. But he charged Brendan twenty-five dollars for the service. Brendan paid it without complaint because he was so happy to simultaneously pay Perry the last money due him on the ten year agreement calling for five per cent of the gross take from the tavern. He quietly resolved to try another attorney next time he had a legal problem. Thus ended any formal tie with Perry as far as Brendan was concerned.

With the legal problem over liquor sales solved and his financial situation continually improving, Brendan gave more thought to his personal relationships. He and Chloe, as far as outward appearances were concerned, were once more comfortable with one another in the daily routine in the tavern. Neither one referred to their explosive contact a year earlier, although Brendan thought of it from time to time as he watched Chloe's sinuous body move gracefully as she cleaned and worked in the kitchen. It seemed that Chloe had reached a modus vivendi with Orman; at least there was no more pouting or sighing, nor did her face show any evidence of further beatings.

Brendan talked cautiously to some of the wealthier men in town about Orman's need for work. No one bore Orman any ill will, although they commented how much easier his father had been to work with.

It's just a question of personality, Brendan told them. He's not outgoing like his father. But he is an excellent mason. You just have to go more than half way with him.

Brendan went so far as to approach Perry, but the lawyer

would have none of it.

If that coon thinks I'm going to kiss his ass, he has another think coming. Down South they keep these fellows in their place and sometimes I think they have the right idea. Orman has got to learn to be properly respectful.

Brendan gritted his teeth and told himself he should have known better than to ask him. The others with whom Brendan spoke were more temperate, and a few said they had some projects in mind. They would talk to Orman. They understood that he was cut from different cloth than his father, but the family had always been decent and hardworking. Those he spoke to never failed to mention how much they admired Chloe, but he realized they had heard the rumors and were probably, to some unmeasurable extent, trying to make him feel good.

CHAPTER TWENTY-FIVE

1834

THE LITCHFIELD COUNTY TEMPERANCE SOCIETY met in New Milford in rooms of the new Congregational Church in September. The address, delivered by Reverend Hart Talcott of Warren, was judged to be so persuasive, that it was printed as a pamphlet for distribution by the society. The Warren minister went further than most temperance advocates had until that time; he called for the membership pledge to be extended to total abstinence from all intoxicating drinks. The first pledge widely circulated in the county had allowed the use of wine and beer by members. Mr. Rood, the Congregational pastor, was chairman of the committee that oversaw the production and distribution of Mr. Talcott's address.

Brendan was uneasy, even upset, by the meeting. He knew a majority of New Milford people accepted the use of spirits as normal, even desirable. Most people he knew felt is was healthy to take a glass now and then, or even regularly with meals. He had not been greatly concerned at the formation of the temperance groups or their meetings around the state. It was quite another matter when these zealots met in the center of town in its most prestigious church and attempted to change long accepted customs. He felt the need to consult someone, not over the legal ramifications or even the commercial aspects, but someone who spoke with moral authority, someone whose advise he could accept with confidence and comfort. During his boyhood in New York, this would have been the parish priest, a man usually respected as much for his wisdom as for his religious authority. He knew of no man in New Milford, even respected leaders and friends, who could fit in this role.

Then the idea hit him. He had heard recently that a Catholic priest was to visit Danbury. Getting to Danbury was no real problem. He might make the trip both ways in a day, certainly in two. He determined to make the effort.

Brendan took the stage to Danbury in the second week of October. When he arrived on Main Street, he had no idea where to go. He knew the priest's name was Father Fitton, but since there was no Catholic church in Danbury, he was at a loss as to where he could be found. As when he was looking for his uncle on his first visit, he had no recourse but to ask. In one of the nearby taverns he inquired for the priest and was surprised that his question got a civil answer. He was referred to a man named Dennis Collins, a hatter who lived on West Street.

At the Collins home, Mrs. Collins told Brendan that Father James Fitton was staying at their house during his visit, but was presently out seeing Catholic families in Danbury.

Wait a bit and you'll be sure to see him when he comes back to eat, she said. Father does a deal of walking so he has a healthy appetite. He doesn't miss many meals.

With Mrs. Collins' bemused permission, Brendan waited in a wooden garden swing, which gently rocked him as he enjoyed the sunshine, still warm on this cloudless day. Already, though, autumn was consolidating its daily gains; he noted that the leaves were already fallen from the ash and elm trees while the maples were either a deep yellow or a bright russet.

Shortly after the bell in the Congregational Church up the street struck noon, a tall, wiry man in a black suit entered the dooryard. When he saw Brendan, he walked up to the swing, and stuck out his hand.

I'm Father Fitton. Are you looking for me by any chance?

Indeed I am, Father. I am Brendan McCauley of New Milford. But how did you know?

Why else would a grown man be sitting in the Collins' swing in the middle of the day? Besides, people are waiting for me wherever I go, it seems. What can I do for you?

Mrs. Collins indicated you might be coming back to eat, but perhaps I could take some of your time this afternoon. When I was a boy in the Five Points section of New York, the Irish there took their concerns to the parish priest. I'd like to do that with you.

Father Fitton's eyes sparkled.

Mrs. Collins has had ample opportunity to know my eating habits, I'm grateful to say. How would it be if I met you in the swing at one o'clock?

Brendan returned to the tavern he had been in earlier, ate a meal and was back in the swing in the Collins' yard by one. Father Fitton emerged from the house a few minutes later.

If I have a touch of brogue, he explained, it's not because I'm Irish but because I was born and grew up in the Irish section of Boston. Actually, my parents were English and my mother was a convert to the church. Judging from the size of you, you've got to be of Irish blood. Most of the Yankees never get that big, for some reason.

He chuckled at his little joke.

You're right, Father. My parents escaped to France after 1798 and then came to New York. My father's dead, but my mother still lives there. I run a tavern in New Milford.

Father Fitton slipped on a purple stole around his neck and sat in the opposite seat in the garden swing from Brendan.

What do you want to talk to me about?

I feel I need help, or perhaps I should say guidance. As a boy I was brought up a Catholic in New York. I left home when I was sixteen. I haven't been in a Catholic church since then. Of course there is no Catholic church in New Milford, or even in Danbury, but I visited my mother twice in recent years in New York and did not avail myself of the opportunity to hear Mass during those two weeks. But as the temperance movement has grown in recent years, the Protestant churches around Connecticut have lent their support to it. Just a month ago, the Litchfield County Temperance Society met in New Milford and came out with a call for abstinence from all alcoholic drinks. People I like and respect suddenly are treating me as if I were the devil's helper because I run a tavern. This bothers me because I like the town and I try to be a responsible member of the community. Where I grew up, Catholics took things that were bothering them to the priest, so when I heard you were coming to Danbury I determined to talk with you about it.

Drinking has been a particular problem with the Irish. Not that it is confined to them, God knows, but it has often been a cross for your people. Have you enriched yourself at the expense of poor wretches who can't stay away from drink and whose families suffer as a result?

No, Father. It has been a firm rule with me since I started the business not to serve individuals who have had enough to drink or who are known not to be able to handle it. In fact, I am proud that my tavern is best known as a place where good food is emphasized. We have a fine kitchen.

That's fine. But you should know that the Protestants aren't the only ones who are militating against the abuses of alcohol. There is a Catholic temperance movement in Hartford that is beginning to be active. Since you don't have a church in your town, that's one thing you don't have to worry about. Why did you leave home?

Brendan was surprised at the question and the sudden shift in the conversation. He stuttered a bit in his answer.

Because my mother and sister didn't have enough money to support me.

You must have been a big boy then. Didn't you think you had an obligation to get a job and help support the two women?

Brendan reddened. He hadn't expected Father Fitton to take this tack. He didn't know how to answer without casting shame on his mother and sister.

Perhaps I should have.

Was there some other reason for your departure?

Yes, Father.

If my questions are bothering you, let me explain why I have to ask them. You come to me saying you were brought up a Catholic. My presumption is that you wish to restore yourself in the eyes of the church, otherwise you could have asked just about anyone else for counsel. If you wish me to help you, the first step is for you to make a good confession. That's why I put on the stole when we began talking. This may be an unorthodox way to administer the sacrament of penance, but when priests are too few to meet the needs, new departures are necessary. I want you to answer me frankly and honestly; otherwise we are both wasting our time. Now, why did you leave home?

Brendan swallowed hard. This was more than he had expected. But then he decided he did want to make himself whole within the Catholic Church. He didn't know why, he was just going to do it.

My mother and my sister had become prostitutes because they had no other way of making a living.

And you wished to show your disapproval of this conduct by leaving?

Yes, Father.

You were correct in judging this a serious sin, but you should know that the burden of the guilt in such cases may rest with the men who have forced them into this life and with those who take advantage of them by sexually using them without love or respect. Have you ever fornicated with a woman?

Yes, Father.

How many times?

With one married woman several weeks over a period of two years. The woman is now dead. With another married woman on one occasion.

Do you still have relations with the second woman?

No, Father. She wishes to remain with her husband; we agreed to terminate our affair.

With this knowledge that you have had illicit affairs with women, and with no pressing economic justification whatsoever, do you not feel remorseful for the manner in which you treated your mother and your sister?

I have, Father, and I told my mother so. I have also been reconciled with my sister, who has left the life and is now married.

Does your mother continue to prostitute herself?

No, Father, but she is still engaged in the business.

It is not our part to judge her here now. Have you broken any other of the commandments of God?

No, Father, not that I can recall.

Before I grant you absolution from your sins, I will return to your original question. In the eyes of the church there is nothing intrinsically evil about alcoholic beverages used in moderation. You must remember that wine is used as a sacramental in the Mass and through the words of the priest becomes the blood of Christ just as the unleavened bread, the host, becomes his body. Jesus drank wine and he performed his first miracle at Cana by transforming water into wine for the wedding feast. But greedy people have exploited those unfortunates who become addicted to wine or liquors, and have injured them and their families and caused many other evils in the world. In your work, you have a very grave responsibility to avoid and prevent such situations. If you are rigorous with yourself in this regard, you have no need to accept the imposition of total abstinence from alcohol on yourself or anyone else. But bear in mind the temperance movement would never have come about if people, including those in the liquor trade, had not abused this gift of God. Finally, as a condition of absolution, you will hear Mass at least four times a year henceforth. Now that priests are coming into Connecticut more frequently and establishing parishes in the larger cities like Hartford and New Haven, this is possible for a young, vigorous man like yourself. Now say an Act of Contrition as I grant you absolution from your sins.

Brendan stumbled through the unfamiliar words of the prayer, surprised that he was able to recall it at all.

When it was over, Father Fitton removed the stole, put it in a small leather bag he carried, and shook Brendan's hand.

It was a pleasure meeting you. I hope in the years to come that additional priests will be coming into Connecticut from Boston and from other points. There are many, many people like yourself, who, through no fault of their own, have not had access to the comforts of our religion. But now that that is changing, you have a responsibility to help with that missionary effort.

Brendan took two ten dollar bills from his wallet and passed them to the priest.

This is not what I meant, but God will thank you for your generosity, as I do. Try now to think what you can do, not with money alone, but with other actions, to make our church strong in this land.

Father Fitton then hurried down West Street toward the center. Brendan continued to sit in the swing for a time, preoccupied with the encounter he had just had.

Finally, he got up and headed back to the stage terminal to catch the last stage of the day to New Milford.

CHAPTER TWENTY-SIX

1835

EVER SINCE THE SAUGATUCK CANAL flurry of 1827, Brendan had kept his ears open for evidence that money raised through stock subscriptions for the canal would indeed be used to construct a railroad. His patience was rewarded in late 1835 when it was revealed that a convention of representatives from affected towns would be held in Kent to decide on a route from Danbury to Massachusetts. On December 23, the convention voted that the line would run northward from Danbury through the Housatonic Valley to Stockbridge in Massachusetts. A committee was appointed to hire an engineer to conduct a survey of the route. The committee would also superintend construction. It hired E. H. Brodhead to do the survey.

The committee conceived the project as part of a greater design for connecting New York and Albany. The further east the line connecting these two cities ran, according to this thinking, the less it would compete with river traffic on the Hudson. As the canal planners earlier, the railroaders spoke of "the extensive lime manufacturers of Canaan,the several iron establishments at Canaan Falls, at Cornwall, at Kent; the granite quarries at New Milford, and the water power that is now unoccupied at Canaan Falls, at Bull's Bridge in Kent, at the Great Falls in New Milford, and also upon the Still River in New

Milford, Brookfield and Danbury" as assets which would generate business for the line.

Brodhead did the survey during that winter and estimated the cost at $1,247,510. This included the expense of a line from Danbury through Ridgefield to the New York state line. The General Assembly in Hartford granted a charter permitting the Housatonic Railroad to build and operate the line from Danbury to Massachusetts. It compliantly also authorized the company to extend the line to Bridgeport and through the Ridgefield branch to New York state. A stock subscription the following winter in a short time raised $600,000, including $100,000 from the City of Bridgeport. The company was formally organized on April 5, 1837 and a contract concluded with the contracting firm of Bishop and Sykes.

The New Milford members of the Board of Directors were the ubiquitous Anan Hine and Asa Pickett. These were not just board room figures. They both personally participated in the surveying of the line northward from New Milford. This party included the engineer, Robert B. Mason; George Booth and Clark Hine, Anan's son, of New Milford as chain-men; the two directors and two other assistants.

The first night the party found relief from the January cold and two feet of snow at the home of Cornelius Baldwin at Boardman's Bridge, the second night at the home of Sylvanus Merwin at Gaylordsville; thereafter they made stops in each town until they reached the Massachusetts line. The farmers were generally willing to sell land because they expected to benefit from the line. But one man in Cornwall refused to let the party cross his land until Anan Hine, well known as a persuasive talker, devoted several hours to a discussion with the farmer. The man finally saw the light and brought out mince pies, doughnuts, ginger and hard cider to seal the bargain.

In New Milford the public was euphoric. Businessmen,

farmers and small investors saw the line as the best hope for bringing prosperity to the town. They foresaw extensive municipal improvements and a mushrooming of local business and industry. One optimist spoke of the "magnificent Weantinock Valley lighted as a city, as the most grand amphitheater of the State of Connecticut." People realized that some leaders in the development of railroads would make themselves rich, but they accepted this because they believed these moguls would also make the country, including themselves, richer. They foresaw the final result of this accumulation of monopoly power as an immense enrichment of the United States and an improvement to the entire country.

Perry Smith invested heavily in the railroad. Perry, in fact, was riding high. He was appointed Judge of the Probate Court after the spring election. Meanwhile he continued as postmaster. Perry never spent a full day working in either position. He hired clerks who did all of the work in both offices, subject to his occasional supervision. He paid the postal clerk about half of the salary he received from the Federal Government; he paid the probate clerk the same percentage, but in this office in most years he profited even more than in the post office because the state provided that most of the income from the fees went to the incumbent judge. Perry continued his lucrative law practice and his involvement in state politics. Brendan greeted him occasionally in the street but saw little of him otherwise.

Brendan was not untouched by the local fervor in favor of the railroad, but continued to study how he could profit from it. He said nothing to anyone about it, but he was aware that the survey route now confirmed his earlier conjecture that the line would pass through New Milford on a shoulder of land on the slope leading down to the river west of homes on Main Street. There would have to be a station in the village and it would certainly be located alongside the tracks in this area.

Furthermore, new streets would be needed to carry traffic generated by the rail service. One might run parallel to Main Street; other access ways to Main Street would also be required.

What better location for a tavern than on this new street right near the tracks and the station? If he could buy land beforehand this would put him in a good position to erect a more luxurious building than his present business before the railroad actually arrived in town. Now that he had the money for it, he decided to consult with an attorney, not Perry, who could advise him when land would become available from the division of the large tracts there at present.

In the midst of this planning, there was a distraction. Chloe diffidently informed him one morning that she was having problems with Orman again. He was not beating her as before, but instead was drinking heavily, staying away from home for days at a time and completely neglecting his business. She seemed reluctant to bother Brendan with her problem.

I know you went out of your way to talk to some of the monied people about him before and that you lined up jobs for him. I'm not asking you to do anything this time because there's not much you can do. If any of his customers ask about him, you'll just have to tell them that he's not practicing his trade anymore. It's a shame, he was making good money and was healthy and happy out in the air all the time. Now he lies around in huts and sheds with any town drunk who will help him kill a jug of white lightning. He doesn't eat right, he's lost weight and looks terrible.

I'm sorry, Chloe. I wish there was something I could do. It's a pity when a man has a good trade, a good wife and a home, then just gives it up for nothing.

Later in the year Chloe told Brendan that Orman had apparently left town. She thought he had gone to Bridgeport or possibly even New York because he thought he could get steady work building culverts and other structures for the railroads being built from New York along the Connecticut shore.

He's one crazy nigger if he thinks he can get a job with a big company as a mason, she said. They keep those jobs for whites; the black men will do all the bugger-lugging, the mason tending, carrying stones and mixing mud.

It was the first time that Brendan had heard Chloe protest the treatment of her race in any way. He knew she was right, but up to now she had always seemed to maintain the fiction that African-Americans had no intrinsic social or economic handicap if they worked hard and kept out of trouble. He reflected that it was another outgrowth of the polarization of racial attitudes since the rise of the abolitionist movement.

Brendan had rigorously governed his conduct so as not to precipitate any further sexual intimacy with Chloe. He had to admit that she, too, had avoided any provocation. They continued cordial, but guarded, contacts each day, confining their conversations to the affairs of the tavern and general topics of the day. They both seemed to preserve space between one and the other so as to avoid emotional lightning melting their reserve in too narrow a gap.

It was not that Brendan did not feel the attraction. Continually he had to patrol his thoughts when images of Chloe's nude body, richly colored, lean and yet voluptuous, laying on his own bed beside him, played through his memory. The recollections were so vivid that Brendan found it hard to believe that the event had occurred three years before. He wondered if Chloe ever thought of him in the same way. Probably not, he concluded. She was still with Orman during much of this time. He tried to resist the idea that she might welcome him in her arms once more now that Orman had gone away.

Brendan had kept to the terms of his absolution by Father

Fitton during their meeting in Danbury the year before. He had twice attended Mass in Hartford when he went there to meet with liquor forces concerning legislation. He had also gone to Derby once, just to attend Mass, and once to New Haven for the same purpose, which he combined with a lobbying effort when the General Assembly met there. He avoided immersing himself in doctrine, which, at best, he found vaguely disquieting, and at worst, wildly and literally incredible. He remembered his rote memorization of Catechism when he was a boy; the memory was unpleasant. He found other satisfaction from his churchgoing; although he was not doctrinaire, he did cherish the spiritual comforts of the church and appreciated the moral strength it provided. Furthermore, it produced a feeling of ethnic solidarity which he relished. He had been outside the main social stream for so many years since he had left New York, the contacts with other Catholics, who were largely Irish, made him feel once more an integral member of a group.

There were other less edifying developments. His mother wrote him that she had received a letter from Perry Smith in which he begged to bring to her attention the fact that her otherwise very promising son was living in open concubinage with his black cook, and urged her to put an end to the situation. Brendan supposed that Perry had persuaded the New England House to give him his mother's address from the hotel register when she had been in New Milford five years before. The hypocrisy of Perry's action revolted him. He was surprised that Perry, a major figure in the state, would bother his head about an insignificant tavern keeper to this extent. Then he remembered that if Chloe knew of his liaison with Anne years ago, there was every likelihood that Perry did too. The more he thought about it, Perry had known about it at the time and had patiently kept the matter deeply buried within himself all these years, never betraying the slightest sign in all his contacts with

Brendan. Nothing else could explain such conduct.

What hurt Brendan most was the way his mother had fallen for Perry's ploy. Of course, it coincided with her own long held belief that Chloe was trying to lure her only son into a relationship. This blinded her to the malicious self interest which had led Perry to send the letter. He only hoped Perry did not get it in his head to visit his mother; he might well since he went to New York occasionally, both for business and political reasons. Then Perry would have a choice morsel to nudge and wink about in New Milford.

He had responded to his mother's letter imploring him to end his scandalous relationship with a short note inviting her to again visit New Milford to establish that Perry was passing along false, vicious gossip, a gossip which he was also utilizing locally to turn people against her son. He went so far as to remind his mother that Perry had a long festering resentment which explained his conduct.

Actually, Perry had shifted tactics in town and no longer bothered to retail the line about Chloe which was so easily refutable to anyone who knew the routine of both Chloe and Brendan. Perry had found out about Brendan's meeting with Father Fitton and his attendance at Mass elsewhere, and now exploited the ever present anti-Catholic sentiment in New Milford. He bruited about stories that Brendan, acting as Father Fitton's agent, was spearheading a Papist infiltration of solid Calvinist institutions; if citizens were not vigilant, the Protestant heritage they had carefully brought from Old England and nourished in New England could be threatened.

Sympathetic townspeople had informed Brendan of the rumors. He made no attempt to refute them. He knew thinking people would put no credence in them and nothing he said would influence those who blindly accepted such nonsense. He knew also that time would efface the memory of such talk, but meanwhile he would be an individual to be suspected, feared or avoided by some.

CHAPTER TWENTY-SEVEN

1836

BRENDAN ENGAGED NATHANIEL PERRY as his attorney in 1836 with instructions to buy him a property on the slope of land to the west of Main Street. Nat Perry had settled in New Milford in 1823, seven years after his admission to the bar in Woodbury. He was elected to the General Assembly from New Milford in 1832 and was well enough connected to have served as clerk of the House. He was also appointed Judge of Probate in 1832 and 1834. Brendan felt he was better liked than Perry Smith and that his entre with the people that counted was at least as good and probably better.

Nat told Brendan he would determine from the land records how many parcels of land would likely be crossed by the future Railroad Street—the name seemed inevitable—how many were on the market or were deemed to be potentially available, and cautiously make discreet inquiries. He warned Brendan that other landholders were already taking steps that indicated they were aware of the importance of this land; the price would be more by far than ordinary farm land. All the feelers would be in his own name; no one would need to know as yet that Brendan was the interested party or what he intended to do with the land. Nat also advised Brendan that the town fathers were already considering laying out as a town street the lane which ran toward the west and the river across private holdings down the slope south of the New England House. He was sure the town was equally aware of the need to lay out Railroad Street. These things took time in New Milford, but they were underway.

Get me a corner lot at the bottom of that lane where it intersects with the new Railroad Street, Brendan said.

That will be a very expensive property, Nat replied. I have no firsthand knowledge but I would be surprised if the Mygatts, the Marshes, the Hines and people like that won't have those kind of locations sewed up early. Folks like Anan Hine, who is a director of the railroad, and those who have owned the pastures leading down to the river, or their heirs or successors, have the advantage. For your purpose, a lot in the middle of one of these blocks would be almost as good. The main requirement is that it be visible from, and accessible to the train station.

Brendan admitted that Nat was right. He had a little nest egg, but it was not at all comparable to the funds some of the shrewder of the old Yankee residents could put into play.

Meanwhile there was good news from Hartford. The Assembly, again in control of the Democrats, took another step toward weakening liquor regulation by repealing an earlier law barring judges and justices of the peace from operating taverns. This didn't affect Brendan directly but anything that tended to remove controls imposed earlier by the National Republicans and the Whigs was very welcome. The trend was hopeful, too, since the Assembly the year before had rejected a bill which would have given individual towns the power to adopt their own restrictions. In those communities where the temperance movement was strong, this almost certainly would have produced stringent local regulation. Brendan was not sure how sentiment was divided in New Milford. He was inclined to believe that the temperance people still lacked a majority, but after the show of strength they had put on two years before in town, it was virtually sure that they had gained adherents.

The new setback indeed stimulated additional temperance efforts statewide. The movement continued to circulate petitions ask-ing for absolute prohibition of the distillation of liquor in Connecticut. One argument advanced was that from 100,000 to 125,000 bushels of grain were converted into liquor in the state each year. This, it was alleged, raised the cost of food, diminished real wealth, and led to the imprisonment each year of more than fifty persons who were presumably led to crime by drink.

On September 12 Brendan learned of the death of Elvira Smith, Perry's daughter. She was only a couple of months past her twentieth birthday. Brendan was truly saddened.

I can't believe the beautiful little girl I knew has died just as she should have been entering the happiest time of her life, he told Chloe. When I first arrived in town and worked for Perry I can remember her coming into the office with her mother. She was a charming little girl, just a toddler. She and her mother were dressed in identical white gowns, all embroidered with little white stars. They each had a blue sash around their waists. They were so radiant with health, so alive. One the image of the other. How can they both now be dead?

Chloe didn't know what to say; Brendan was oblivious to the fact that Chloe might not be pleased to see the image of Anne so strongly imprinted in Brendan's mind. But one of the bar patrons spared her the necessity of a response. He responded gruffly.

We're all alive and healthy for a while and then we die. You know that by now, Brendan.

Another man added: The truth of the matter is that poor Elvira hasn't looked good for quite a while. She was thin and puny looking and didn't have good color. Probably the death of her mother set her going downhill. Doc Williams couldn't do a thing for her.

Listening to you two certainly makes a man want to pray for his immortal soul. Brendan wasn't altogether joking.

You take your comfort as best you can get it, the first man responded. I'd rather get mine right here on a stool rather than from some preacher.

Preachers and doctors can't do much when the crunch comes, added the second.

Brendan shrugged, but after a while he asked Chloe to take over the bar so he could visit Perry. She looked at him strangely, but again remained silent. Then she moved behind the bar.

Perry was desolate. Brendan had never seen him look so down, even when Anne had died. People were streaming in to see him; no one seemed much in charge. Scapegrace John loitered awkwardly around the edges of the group, looking even more sinister than usual. Brendan caught him looking his way with a fierce scowl. But the lad turned furtively away when he saw Brendan's eyes upon him.

Brendan finally got to Perry. I'm terribly sorry, Perry. After I heard the awful news I was thinking what a beautiful little girl she was when I first met her with her mother in your office back in 1818. She was adorable in a white dress with a little blue sash. You've been hit hard again.

Perry's mouth crinkled and his eyes filled. Brendan embraced him and moved on. He thought of the hurt that Perry had laid on him. But now he realized he had wounded Perry even more grievously, even in the recollection he had just voiced. In this moment they could both mourn sincerely.

Reverend Noah Porter, who had been the pastor only since the end of april, conducted the funeral service the next day. It was the first time Brendan had been in the church since it had been finished. As he looked around, he admired the construction, the lofty white walls, the mahogany pews, the tasteful pulpit and altar. Congregationalists certainly knew how to build lovely churches; the restraint in decor combined with the finest of materials, the skill of the architect and the workmen, all were evident in its austere beauty.

Considering that Mr. Porter had known the family such a short time, he unerringly settled on the correct observations in his remarks about the dead girl and her family. Brendan had heard that the church membership considered itself fortunate to have secured such a learned and talented man as pastor. Others said wryly that he was too good to stay very long; it would have been better to look for a less brilliant pastor who would stay longer.

Afterward Brendan chatted briefly with Perry, who seemed to have recovered his composure to some extent, but whose every lineament reflected his great sorrow.

* * *

A few weeks later, Nat told Brendan he had found him a property on what he felt sure would be the new Railroad Street. It was a lot one hundred feet wide and two hundred feet deep. It was across the street from where it was expected the new railroad station would be erected. He had found nothing else available.

How much? Brendan asked.

Five-hundred dollars. That might seem like an elevated price, but I told you it wouldn't be cheap. My fee, including the closing, if you decide to take it, will be fifty dollars.

Done.

Brendan tried to contain his elation. He finally had his own property. And a good site, too. The lot was large enough so he might even divide it and sell a portion. And he still had enough money left to erect the building.

Thank you, Nat. You've done what I hoped you would.

It was my pleasure. I enjoy pushing the town forward. By the way, have you heard that our friend Perry has been selected by the leaders in Hartford to represent us in the U. S. Senate? The legislature still has to act on the matter, but it should be a done deal.

CHAPTER TWENTY-EIGHT

1837

FOR A LONG TIME NO ONE KNEW how Orman had died. Chloe had only heard from him intermittently after he left New Milford more than a year and a half earlier. Orman could read and write; he was capable of scrawling short notes to her. First he reported that he had been hired in New York to work on construction of the railroad in northern Manhattan. The progress of the line could be measured by the postmarks on his letters. After the work crossed the East River into the Bronx, the work progressed more rapidly. Chloe had been correct about his status. He wrote that he was doing masonry work on the culverts, but was being paid as a mason tender because the contractor insisted that a white mason superintend his work. There were few days free, even when the weather was bad; dirt could be moved when it was too wet or too cold to work with mortar. The postmarks became New Rochelle, then Rye, Larchmont, Harrison, and Port Chester.

The scratched messages were not very informative about the way Orman was living. The contractor provided shacks for the workers that were moved every few miles as the work progressed. They provided only the most minimal shelter and no protection at all from the cold of winter or the heat of summer. Life became increasingly primitive for the workers; like an army, they tried to forget their hardships by gambling, drinking and whoring in their spare time. Few of them saved any money and Orman did not even make a pretense of sending anything to Chloe. Actually there was no need in any event; she was making as much as he and netting much more.

After a year the work camp moved into Fairfield County in southwestern Connecticut. The letters did not come as often and they were so repetitious in their simple phrasing that they were virtually without news. The last letter was postmarked Norwalk. In the late spring, Chloe received a form letter from the contractor informing her Orman had died a three weeks before. It gave no details how his death had occurred. It didn't even state if he died on the job or in one of the frequent fights that broke out when the men were drinking during hours after work. The letter enclosed a check for three dollars and sixty-seven cents, the amount of pay the contractor claimed was due Orman at the time of his death.

Chloe took the letter and showed it to Brendan. Her face was drawn, her eyes sad, but she was composed.

They didn't even say where he was buried or if there was a funeral for him, she said.

I'm so sorry for your loss. Orman didn't deserve to die like this. He was a fine workman who did honest work. If someone could have been his go-between with the families here who needed and appreciated his work, he would have been with us a long time. He just couldn't stand all the verbal bowing and scraping to the folks with money just to get a job.

His father was good at that. Orman was more like his mother, Dora. Dora learned to cook all by herself, trial and error. She couldn't bear to ask anyone for help. Orman was like that, just fierce to do things right without anyone else interfering.

Is there anything you would like me to do?

Do you suppose there's any way we can find out what happened to him? I would like to know where he is buried. How it was at the end for him. Details like that make a body more comfortable.

I'll try, Chloe. I think I may be able to do something through Anan Hine. He's a director of the Housatonic Railroad. If there's anything else you want or need, just tell me.

Brendan went to see Anan and asked for his help. Anan didn't hesitate to say yes. Brendan and Anan were not close friends, given their difference in age and station, but they had known each other for years and chatted together often. Anan liked people with ambition and initiative. He had seen enough of Brendan to know that he had plenty of both. He didn't even ask any questions; he already knew enough about Brendan, Chloe and Orman to get the picture. Anan, too, knew his town.

I'll be happy to look into the matter, Anan said. I'm curious myself to know exactly what happened and I think the railroad owes it to Chloe to give her as many details as possible. The trouble with these big organizations is that they have so many layers of management to go through, it's hard to get a human response. Chloe is a great girl; I know Lucius Lum in the hotel wishes he found her before you did so that she could cook for the hotel. It's too bad she couldn't get some sense into that Orman. He was such a good mason, and then to go off to the kind of life the men building that line lead, well it's unfortunate. But God made us all different, and it's a good thing he did. Anyway, I'll send word to you as soon as I find out anything. I know some of the people working on this project, so I think I can come up with something.

A week later, in response to a message from Anan, Brendan went to see him in his office in the fire brick company he had recently started. Anan passed him a letter on the railroad's stationery.

The letter, quoting the official report, stated that Orman died on the job in Westport. He was constructing a culvert of cut stone when a wagon carrying a load of such stone toppled over on him when the wet earth on a slope gave way under the wheels next to him. The coroner ruled he was crushed and death was instantaneous. The badly mutilated body was finally dug out and buried in the Congregational Cemetery in Westport. A wooden cross with his name marks the spot and a service was conducted by the minister in Westport. There are several other construction workers from the railroad buried there with him.

When Brendan finished reading the letter, Anan explained that the contracting firm was under such pressure to complete the work that more lives were lost than should have been the case. This was not right, but it was inherent in the system as it was constituted. Anan had learned less formally that Orman did not have more pay due him because he had received several advances on his pay.

There is a great deal of gambling, drinking and general hell raising when you get a tough gang of men together for a job like this, Anan added. Orman would have been no different from the rest of them if he drew down his pay in advance, whether for booze, women or to meet his losses at the table. It's too bad, but that's the way these things are. I just hope the railroad does enough good for us to balance out the evils that building it has visited on us. I must say, I think it will.

Brendan broke the news to Chloe more gently. He showed her the railroad letter Anan had given him, but he didn't pass on Anan's comments. Then he held her gently as she sobbed on his shoulder.

Some day, he told her, you probably will want to go to his grave in Westport. But it will be better to wait a time until the anguish from the news has moderated. Travelling will be easier when the dry weather comes later on.

She nodded wordlessly. She clung to him for some moments, then broke away.

You have been very good to me. I truly thank you.

* * *

In May the legislature elected Perry as U. S. Senator. Perry had been on pins and needles even though he knew the result was virtually assured; in politics it is wise never to take anything for granted. Later in the year Perry submitted his resignation as postmaster. He also announced he was terminating his law practice so he could devote all his energy to his job as U. S. Senator.

In a chance meeting on the street, he told Brendan he would go by stage to South Norwalk, would take the Sound steamer to New York and from there go by ship to Baltimore. He felt he could get a boat from there to Washington. The second session of the 25th Congress would begin on December 4.

I'm going to take the trip in easy stages. I'll spend some time in New York and have plenty of time in Washington to find a lodging for myself and get to know the town and some of my new colleagues. John Niles, the senior senator from Connecticut and an old friend of mine, can give me a hand in getting around. As you suspected, I have dreamed about serving in the Senate for some time, but now that I'm bound for there I find it absolutely incredible.

Brendan felt the old urge to flatter Perry, but this time he resisted it. He was his own man now, no longer under any compulsion to be subservient. In fact, as U. S. Senator, Perry was the servant of all the people, including himself. He determined to speak accordingly.

Perry, the nation is facing awesome problems. I don't know the answer to them, but you are a skilled lawyer with considerable experience in government, as much as most of the men in the Senate. I hope you will think of all of us when you make your key decisions.

He put the emphasis on all of us.

Very kind of you, Perry responded smoothly. I'll tell you honestly that I look forward to a change of scene. Elvira's death was a blow to me, especially after losing her mother just a few years before. I hope to immerse myself in the work of the Senate. It should be good for me and I hope for others as well.

No doubt at all. We all look forward to following your career on the national stage.

He feared that Perry had not grasped the implication of his emphasis, but even if Perry had, he knew, the new Senator was too wily to show it .

Perhaps when I come back, I can do the trip by rail. I'm sure you know they've started work on the Housatonic Railroad. I can envision making the entire trip between here and Washington by rail in just a few years. The railroads will be a great boon to the country.

Perry left in October to assume his seat.

Cynics in New Milford said the railroads would be a great boon to Perry. His investments in rail stock were well known, since he often referred to them. Now that he was a United States Senator, those who knew Perry fully expected that he would be one of the more subservient supporters of railroad interests in the upper chamber. Since nearly everybody at this juncture sincerely hoped for the success of the new lines which were so badly needed, hardly anyone could envisage how ruthless the railroads would become or what a pernicious influence for corruption they would be in the national political life.

CHAPTER TWENTY-NINE

1837

EVEN THOUGH IT WAS WINTER, Brendan decided to make the trip to New York to see his mother. He really did want to see his mother again; it was six years since his last trip, in spite of his resolve to go at least once a year. But he acknowledged to himself as well that he had another reason. He had been troubled ever since he had once more held Chloe in his arms following the death of Orman. Each day as he saw her, busy and active in the tavern, he wanted her so badly that it began to dominate his thoughts. He cursed himself for not having made love to her at the time. If that had been inappropriate, as it clearly had been, why didn't he create another opportunity? It shouldn't be difficult; they were in the same building for hours each day, alone in the building in the early morning and late evening. He was tormented constantly by his ardent thoughts of her. He began to think his mother had been right when she warned him that without a wife he would shrivel emotionally as well as physically. He also thought more and more of his mother's alternative offer after the failure of her matrimonial brokering. At the age of thirty-six he was healthy and strong, but he began to wonder about his virility. Was there something lacking in him that prevented him from marrying? He told Chloe of his travel plans and directed her to call in Nathan Ward again to handle the bar during his absence.

The weather was seasonably cold on the stage trip to South Norwalk, but there was no snow. He and the few other passengers wrapped themselves in blankets, but they still suffered from the cold, especially their feet. The driver, exposed to the full blast of the cold outside the cab, had to stop along the way to warm both himself and his passengers, thus falling behind schedule. Driver and passengers headed for a bar in Danbury and again in South Norwalk for whiskey to restore circulation to their members numbed by the cold. The passage on Long Island Sound also took longer, but the main lounge was heated by forced hot air from the boiler room. There were snow squalls on the Sound and the water was much rougher than during the warm weather. Many of the passengers were ill, but Brendan felt no queasiness. He found it exhilarating.

Once in the city, Brendan took a hansom cab to his mother's place and rejoiced to be once again in a heated building. He was surprised to see that this time his mother had aged. The wrinkles were plainly visible, the body no longer youthful, the hair very gray. She was animated but withal somewhat saddened as she greeted him.

Brendan, Brendan it's so good to see you. Why has it been so long?

They held each other tightly. She dabbed at her eyes as she finally released him enough to look up into his face.

Please don't ever stay away so long again, she said.

The years pass much faster than they used to. I think I spend my life on things that don't matter, but I wonder if I can change.

Catherine got a bottle of Bordeaux wine out of the cupboard and filled two goblets. Soon they were talking animatedly and the sadness evaporated. Brendan told her he had come to accept her offer so she wouldn't think him a dessicated Yankee. His mother laughed delightedly.

You've come to the right place, she joked. First you must have a good meal and a nap. Then you shall have a beautiful woman to warm your soul. She will stay with you tonight, and there shall be others, even more ravishing for the nights to come. They will make you forget your ebony assistant.

Brendan decided it was more prudent not to respond to the last point.

You know that I have only known one woman, speaking in the biblical sense, in my entire life. So I am relatively innocent. They must not expect too much of me. He hoped God would forgive him this lie to his own mother.

When they're alone with a woman, all men say something like that. They just brag about their conquests when men are around.

Once in Catherine's apartment, Brendan ate ravenously, downing a meal of rare roast beef, baked potatoes and several vegetables. He consumed a salad of green lettuce and fresh tomatoes, unheard of at this season in New Milford. Catherine explained that these, as well as the other vegetables, were grown in a special hothouse for luxury customers like herself. Brendan finished with a pint of chocolate ice cream, a delicacy that he had first eaten at the Astor House on his former trip to the city. Along with this, he finished the bottle of Bordeaux.

In a darkened room, he slept most of the afternoon to restore himself after the rigors of his recent trip. He awoke at seven, feeling much refreshed. He chatted with his mother. He told her about the plans for his new building, Perry going to the U.S. Senate, and his visit to Father Fitton.

Catherine was delighted when he told her about his Confession in the garden swing to Father Fitton, and how he had since attended Mass several times in various Connecticut cities and towns.

I suppose I'll have to go to Confession again after this week, he said.

Don't let it concern you unduly, she smiled. I go once a month regularly and make all the First Fridays. We are the same clay as Adam and Eve, we are all sinners. Even the priests, and I know whereof I speak. The important thing is to admit our failings and ask God's forgiveness. Meanwhile, enjoy yourself so that you don't develop any terrible perversions.

About eight o'clock Catherine took him to the large bedroom in which he had slept during his last visit.

There are drinks and snacks in the ice box. There is a maid at the end of the hall if you need anything further. Your young lady will be joining you in a few minutes. Just be courteous and natural with her and don't worry about anything. She will know what to do. Enjoy yourself. I'll see you in the morning.

When the door closed and he was alone in the room, Brendan thought how strange it was that he was about to spend a night in the closest intimacy with a woman he had never seen before in his life and probably would never see again. It was a completely unnatural episode, even bizarre, yet his mother had told him to behave naturally. He thought how his mother and his sister had earned good livelihoods doing just what this unknown woman would be doing with him. He tried to put it out of his mind; he feared if he continued in this vein he might not be able to go through with such an encounter. But he was determined to do just that.

A light knock at the door brought him out of the chair, like a runner at the starter's gun. He smiled at his own nervousness, then walked slowly to the door and deliberately opened it.

A young woman of astonishing beauty smiled timidly at him.

May I come in?

Yes, of course. I was expecting you.

They both laughed lightly at the inaneness of his comment. She passed into the room and smiled at him.

You mustn't be nervous. Just relax so we can become good friends. First, if you like I will pour you some wine or whatever else you would like to drink. I will have a little, too, if you don't mind. You sit in your chair and I will join you. Then we will talk a while. You can call me Monique. Alright?

I hadn't expected that you would be so beautiful. It is always unnerving to be in the presence of a beautiful woman, especially if one has not seen her before.

Oh, you are such a cavalier! Your mother told me you live in the country. Most country boys don't talk like that. She handed him a goblet of wine. Then she spoke again.

I didn't mean to belittle you by saying you are a country boy. I'm from the country, too, but not from Connecticut.

After a while she asked if she could remove his shoes; she knelt at his feet to do this before he could respond. Then backing away, she looked at him intently. It's quite warm in here, so why don't you let me take your suit coat? She helped him remove it, then hung it in the closet on a hanger. She returned and began to deftly remove his tie and collar. She also removed a wrap she was wearing.

Isn't that more comfortable? Let me give you more wine.

Brendan began to enter into the spirit of the occasion. When she returned with the glass, he put it down on the side table and reached out to pull her toward him. She sat in his lap and put an arm around his neck. He inhaled her marvelous fragrance and admired her decolletage, displayed admirably by her tightly fitted gown. Before long, they were kissing, at first tentatively, then with more ardor.

You are the most beautiful girl I have ever seen, he told her truthfully. She giggled.

You haven't even seen me yet.

Can I? May I?

Yes to the second question. I don't know about the first.

She rose from his lap. Standing before him, she slowly unhooked the snaps and hooks of her gown and let it fall to the floor. Brendan made a move to pull her to him, but she raised an admonitory finger before his face.

Wait.

Still standing close, she pulled down a petticoat and stepped out of it. Then she backed away, raised a shift over her head and stood nude before him except for her black net stockings, fastened by two red garters. The same electric charge went through Brendan's vitals that he had not felt since his initial experience with Anne when he was twenty. He could feel the erection strain within his garments.

Now you must help me take off my stockings.

She moved, still standing, as close to him as possible. She pulled his head toward her, so that his head was buried in her flat belly. His hands, solely by feel, found the garters, one by one, and slid them down her legs, followed by the stockings. Then he stood up and put his arms around her and kissed her lips, then thrust his tongue between her open teeth to meet hers. Finally, Monique backed away again and pushed Brendan away.

You're overdressed for the occasion, she said.

Then she unbuttoned his shirt and removed it. Next she undid his belt buckle and the buttons on his pants, which fell to the floor. Then she unfastened the vertical row of buttons on his union suit, allowing his erection to spring upright.

Get out of that, she ordered. You won't need that anymore tonight.

Then she fled to the bed, pulled down the covers, jumped in and lay demurely waiting for Brendan. She had not long to wait. He sprang in beside her.

You've gotten awfully quiet. Don't you like me?

Actions speak louder than words, he said in a muffled voice.

He fondled her wonderful breasts, kissed her fervently, then gazed at the length of her body.

You are so lovely it hurts me to look at you, but I love the pain.

It's been a long time for you since the last woman?

I don't even want to think about it. I want to live in the present. I want to live in you.

Go ahead, she said.

He did. The senses ruled. Neither one spoke. Instead their skin rubbed, heated. Breathing accelerated. There were groans, moans, frenzied movement. Time was not relevant but fifteen minutes passed. The bodies finally subsided.

That was sensational, Monique said.

Brendan looked at her, unbelieving.

No, it really was, she said. I mean it. You can tell the difference when a fellow has been a long time without it. It's much better. Then she smiled. We're off to a great start. This is going to be some night.

Catherine looked keenly at Brendan as he joined her for breakfast. He appeared neatly combed and shaven, dressed neatly for the day ahead.

Well? she asked.

I bet you know better than I. Didn't you get a report?

I always get reports. I mean did you enjoy it? Did you find Monique adequate?

You know I did. She was marvelous. I'd marry her if I knew her name.

She couldn't afford to take the pay cut. She did say that you behaved well. Performed well, too. Are you still game to be entertained by another of my beauties tonight?

Of course. How could I turn down such an offer? It would be nice to see Monique again but I don't want to get in a rut.

Who will do the honors tonight?

Her name is Alexandra and she has red hair. Unless you would prefer another color. I thought that you would want a change from the deeper hues.

Please don't talk like that mother. You know how much I depend upon Chloe in running the tavern. What's more, I respect her as a person and I like her very much.

Forgive me for being catty. All mothers want their sons to marry someone like themselves and I'm no exception. I know she is a very capable girl and cooks beautifully. Then with a rush of emotion she added: But I want you to marry a white girl. I don't want a parcel of little brown grandchildren.

Brendan was caught off guard. He retorted hotly. Wouldn't you rather have a parcel of little brown grandchildren than none at all?

Catherine wilted, tears came to her eyes.

Of course, Brendan. I would, really. Forgive me. I have no right to interfere in your life. I do so want to get along with you in the little time we have together.

You're right, Mother. I'm sorry I spoke in anger. The years rush by and it frightens me.

She rose and kissed him. I'm going to be busy most of the day but we can eat together this evening before your next tete-a-tete. Try to go out and walk around this morning. The maid will serve you lunch in the room where we ate yesterday. Take a nap this afternoon. I'll see you later on.

Brendan did walk to Five Points later in the morning. It looked even more disreputable than he remembered it. The old house on Anthony Street was almost unrecognizable as a result of the abuse it had suffered in the past two decades. The area was so filthy, the stench so overpowering, that Brendan quickly left Five Points for the old center of the city. This, too, had deteriorated, but it was still decent. Lower Broadway retained few landmarks that he remembered. It was so disheartening, that he headed for the waterfront where at least the tang of salt air was familiar. He wandered among the chandler shops and looked at the ships moored on Water Street and on the Hudson. Even the ships looked so different from his youth; now there were trans-Atlantic packets, both English and American, and many more foreign ships than before 1818. Now, too, there were special wharves for the small steamers which were beginning to take over more of the riverine and coasting trade. Not only were the streets, the buildings and the ships different; he realized suddenly that he had not maintained contact with a single individual he had known as a schoolboy and, apart from his mother and sister, knew no one in the entire city. The unfamiliarity, coupled with the biting wind, drove him back to Greene Street long before noon.

With two meals and a nap behind him, he felt much more lively by evening. After his mother left him to await Alexandra, he smiled to himself at the situation. Most of his customers at the McCauley Tavern would not believe what he was experiencing if he were rash enough to relate it to them. He was sure that very few natives of New Milford had ever resorted to a prostitute. Even if they wished too, there wasn't one in the town and very few in Danbury. To have consorted with one in these surroundings would have addled their minds, he concluded.

Alexandra, when she entered, was like apple blossoms in winter. Her hair was more mahogany than red and her skin was very white, save for some freckles. She was more slender than Monique, but her breasts were of equal splendor. As soon as she spoke, he knew she was not American. She spoke English well, but there was a trace of accent that lent piquancy to her speech.

Oh, what a big man! Your mother did not tell me that you were a giant. I hope you will not hurt me.

She giggled as if she knew very well that could not happen.

I promise to treat you very, very tenderly. Where are you from?

I am from Bretagne, which is a part of France. The Bretons are Celts, like the Irish. Your are the son of Irish, are you not? The Bretons are very poor, like the Irish. We have to work very hard.

Tonight we will work together as good Celts. I hope it will not be too hard for you.

The work is only difficult when it is not hard. She laughed softly. Please forgive my little jest. Let me get some French wine so we can toast our Celtic union.

With two flutes of Bordeaux, Brendan and Alexandra toasted their joint enterprise, arms entwined. Then seated next to each other, he moved to take off his shoes. Alexandra was horrified.

That you must not do. Let me do that. That is the role of the woman.

I was just trying to help out. Is it a house rule that a man can't take off his own shoes? I don't like to see you on your knees. You are too lovely for that kind of work.

You must not disturb the rite, or do you call it the ritual? Everything must be done at the proper time. You must not be impatient; it will be over too soon as it is. We must make love slowly and gracefully. Until everything is *à point.*

I put myself in your hands.

Alexandra rose and clasped his head in her hands and kissed him hard.

I like to use my hands, too, he said. He caressed the curve of her haunch and then moved one hand to one of her fabulous breasts.

In that case, clothes are in the way. Stand up.

He did as she ordered. She quickly unbuckled his belt, unfastened the bottons, and pushed them to the floor. He was glad now that he had dispensed with his union suit today. Next she unhooked her gown and it joined the pants in a heap on the floor. Her petticoat and shift followed, then his collar and shirt.

Now you may touch as you please. She led him to the bed.

I hear you acquitted yourself well last night, his mother said the next morning.

I'm beginning to like the work. I'm making up for lost time.

Did you like Alexandra?

She was like a dream. She is very ingenious. I never would have imagined that two people could do so many things with their bodies. I was a very attentive pupil because the teacher was so accomplished and helpful.

Catherine laughed delightedly.

My girls are professionals. I'm very proud of their ability to bring pleasure to the men who come here. But tonight I have a surprise for you. I think you will like it.

All day Brendan wondered what surprise his mother had in store for him that evening. He could think of several surprises he would not like, but none that would please him. So when he heard the knock on the door that evening, it was with redoubled expectancy that he opened the door.

A dazzlingly lovely blonde entered the room and demurely smiled at him. He was so struck by her beauty that initially he had no other reaction. As he closed the door and watched her take off and hang up her wrap, it suddenly hit him. He resolved to say nothing until she spoke, but he was sure that his face, as usual, had betrayed his recognition.

My name is Marguerite, she said. I think you recognized me, didn't you?

I can't be sure, I must be mistaken. But, yes, I thought I did. You are Marguerite Bannon.

You are very kind to remember me. In six years most people

would have forgotten.

When a woman is as beautiful as you, it would be very hard for a man to forget you.

You make me happy when you say a thing like that. When you saw me before I thought you didn't like me.

I thought you were beautiful before too, but not as much as now. You have improved with age.

Why didn't you like me?

Oh, I would have liked you well enough, but, quite frankly, you frightened me with all that talk about the Albigensians and Saint Domenick. I thought the Sisters of Mercy had done too good a job on you.

She smiled wistfully.

My mother told me to say those things. She said you and your mother were very fervent Catholics. It was years before I knew about your mother's business.

They laughed together.

How is your mother?

She died after we lost all of our money. She just couldn't tolerate being poor.

The reason for Marguerite's presence today dawned on Brendan.

Is that why you came here?

Yes. Your mother was very good to me. I don't know what would have happened to me. I had no other relatives and I'm sure you know yourself that friends disappear when you are destitute.

Marguerite, I can't go along with this affair with you tonight. It would be too awful. It would be just like taking advantage of my mother and my sister when they were in a similar situation. It would be monstrous.

Oh, don't say that. Please don't.

She flew at him and grasped him with all her strength. Her

distress, fright even, showed in her face. She continued to beseech him.

I could lose my job. We are never, never supposed to tell our clients about our problems. I did it without thinking when you began to question me. Oh, Brendan, please. I liked you immediately when I saw you before. I hoped you would pick me. Please don't turn me down again. It would be too terrible.

He put his arms around her and attempted to soothe her. She clung to him frantically, her face tense with anxiety. Another rejection, he saw, would drive her to tears, or worse.

There, there, my pretty. Don't fret. Everything will be all right.

Can I stay? Please. It's not like it was the first time for me. I've already been working here for more than a year. That did it; Brendan caved in. He kissed her forehead tenderly, then as she looked up, he kissed her on the mouth. She was wild with emotion. She clung with both hands to the back of his head and opened her mouth to his tongue. He kissed her for a long time and began to run his hands over her body. She arched toward him with all her strength. Finally, breathing heavily, they separated. She tore her clothes off wildly, clumsily ripping buttons and fasteners. When she was nude, she began to grab at his. He helped and soon he too was naked.

Oh my darling, she cried, I have always pretended it was you when I did it with others. Now it is. I wish I were a virgin again for you.

You are perfect the way you are. I want you, too, like I never did before.

Arm and arm they went to the bed. Now for the first time he noticed what a beautiful body she had. She had matured since 1831; her breasts were full and firm and the erect nipples were a deep pink in contrast to the whiteness of the rest of her body. He kissed her breasts as she closed her eyes. Then he kissed her soft belly with just the hint of a curve. Finally, overcome, he buried his face in her. The scent drove him to a passion. Marguerite gasped and moaned and twisted under the pressure. Finally, she flipped him off, and pulled him upward.

Don't. I can't stand it any more. No one has ever done that to me before. It's the most wonderful sensation I have ever felt.

She wiggled so he could kiss her face. The rest was instinctive, ferociously animal.

Finally spent, they lay still in each other's arms.

My darling, she said at last, I have never felt anything like that before. Ever.

It was a gift that God has given us, he answered.

Now who's the religious one, she asked with a smile.

At breakfast the next morning, Catherine asked him if he were ready for another session that night.

From all reports, you got along well enough with Marguerite last night. I was a bit fearful after your adverse reaction to her six years ago.

Her point of view has changed. She's much nicer than when she was rich. Anyhow, she says her mother made her say all those ridiculous things because she thought we were very pious.

They chuckled together over that.

To answer your question, no, I think I have carried your hospitality far enough. I can tell you truly that my education has been advanced more than I ever dreamed; what's more, I reassured myself, and I hope you, that the juices are still flowing. I have reason to believe I'm normal, with no discernible tendency to perversity or dessication yet.

You made quite an impression on Marguerite. She refused to accept her money. What did you do to her?

Just the usual. I liked her, too. All three were wonderful.

Brendan feared telling his mother how shaken he was after

his encounter with Marguerite. He knew Catherine was a stern taskmaster and if she knew what had really passed between them, it could affect Marguerite's tenure. Even so, he couldn't resist a question.

I don't suppose you allow any contact with any of the girls outside of work?

Absolutely not. I hope you didn't have anything like that in mind. Once they have any kind of social contact, or develop a crush on a client, it reduces their effectiveness in their job. They have to make a choice, the man or the job.

Don't worry, I won't interfere. I'm going to catch the next Sound steamer to South Norwalk. I'll pack up and say goodbye.

CHAPTER THIRTY

1838

MONTHS LATER, Brendan was still remorseful over his trip to New York the previous winter. It was a new feeling for him; he had never felt guilt after the weeks he had spent with Anne nor after the occasion with Chloe. These episodes had seemed natural and unforced, even though he had confessed them as sins to Father Fitton. But his relations with the three women in his mother's establishment were different. Even though he felt attracted to all three, and notably Marguerite, he had to admit that his basic motive was lust, not affection or love.

It bothered him to feel this way, because he had enjoyed it so much and wasn't sure he wouldn't do it again. Certainly his mother had condoned his conduct, even praised it, but as much as he admired his mother, he had to admit that her lifestyle over the years made her approbation somewhat dubious. His mother had been right about one thing; he should be married and stabilize his situation.

He thought of Marguerite as wife. The problem was, though, that when his thoughts turned to her, it was always in a situation just as the one he had passed through with her in New York. He just couldn't see her at his side in the tavern. He couldn't even imagine her in New Milford. It was such a pleasure to dwell on that wonderful body and that beautiful face, not to mention the apparently genuine crush she had for him. He just ached with longing at the memory of her.

Now that there was a priest in Danbury to say Mass occasionally, he knew he would go and confess his most recent transgressions. But what would happen after that? He didn't know why he should be so much more prone to sexual desire now that he was entering middle age than he had been as a youth, but that was the case. Probably he had worked harder then or had not encountered the same stimuli.

The stark reality of the choices open to him was obvious. He was seriously interested in only two women, Marguerite and Chloe. If he wanted to get married and end his torment over sexual desire, he had to make a decision. Still he hesitated.

* * *

Brendan developed considerable admiration for the resourcefulness of Nat Perry, and not just in the acquisition of land on Railroad Street. Nat, as a practicing politician, was an avid follower of the goings on in Congress; in conversation about developments in Washington, he revealed an almost encyclopedic knowledge of the fate of legislation. Specifically, he was completely informed how Connecticut members stood on important legislation and how they had voted. His grasp of the minutiae of bills amended, sidetracked or eventually passed far exceeded any reporting Brendan ever remembered hearing during the terms of Elijah Boardman or Orange Merwin. One day he questioned him.

Nat, where do you get your information on developments in Washington? I've never heard anyone with such a handle on things.

It's quite simple but not easy, Brendan. I read *The Congressional Globe,* which is the daily record of the debates in both houses of the Congress. I started getting it when I was the clerk of the House in Hartford. You have to wade through an awful lot of shit to extract the facts you want, but I think it's worth the effort.

Could I subscribe to it?

You could, but it would cost you more than you would probably want to pay. As a former state legislator, I get a substantial discount. If you like, you can read my copy when I'm through with it.

So Brendan read Nat's copies each week. The information was delayed because of the printing, mail holdups and Nat's schedule, but it was infinitely more complete and accurate than anything else available, including *The Connecticut Courant.* Right away he noted that Perry Smith was in his seat when the second session of the 25th Congress got underway on December 4, 1837. A few days later the record showed that Perry's committee assignments were on Agriculture and Revolutionary Claims, about all a new boy could expect in a Senate which counted among its members such luminaries as Henry Clay, Daniel Webster, John C. Calhoun, Thomas Hart Benton, Silas Wright of New York, and two future Presidents, James Buchanan and Franklin Pierce.

As he waded through the deluge of verbiage recorded on paper, Brendan concluded that Perry was a very minor player in his new league. During the session he was recognized to speak a couple of dozen times but on more than half of these occasions, his contribution was routine business connected with claims bills. His first major speech on February 14, supported the Democratic Party line on the so called Independent Treasury Bill on the issue of a national bank. Perry went back to the War of 1812 in attacking the opposition. The clerk, evidently wearying of the tedium of transcribing such a stem-winder, cut it short with the comment that Mr. Smith's speech was "able and argumentative." He said the remainder would be printed in a later edition.

He spoke against dueling twice. This was to be a regional division between northerners and southerners during most of his time in the Senate because of the death of a northern congressman who had been challenged and killed by a southern representative. On March 30, the clerk noted that Perry spoke "long and vehemently." Perry said the object of the bill against dueling "was not so much to prevent those fond of dueling from engaging in it, as to protect those coming from states where the people were not fond of murder or killing in any shape. For his own part he was not afraid of any man with pistol or sword; but he advocated the bill to protect the representatives of New England from those gentlemanly assassins who might seek to call them out for words spoken in debate."

Brendan quoted these words to some of his customers. The thought of Perry fearlessly facing pistol or sword produced loud laughter.

When Connecticut's senior Senator and state Democratic leader, John M. Niles, filled up twelve columns of *The Congressional Globe* in forwarding a resolution of the Connecticut General Assembly opposing the Sub-Treasury bill, Perry, a co-signer of Niles'response to the Assembly politicians, added four more columns of diatribe, both against the drafters of the letter from Connecticut, but also against Senators Chittenden and Clay from Kentucky, who had criticized Niles and Perry for their answer to the Connecticut letter. Smith also charged that "missionaries from Kentucky" had agitated in Connecticut to produce sentiment leading to the Assembly's resolution.

Perry took the floor on May 7 to present a petition more to his liking, one from "certain citizens of Connecticut" who proudly stated that "the best guns now in use were made of the iron of Connecticut, and praying that the contemplated national armory might be erected on the spot where the ore was procured." The petition was referred to the Military Affairs

Committee and that was the end of it.

The appendix for the session contained three of Perry's speech texts. There is reason to believe that two of them were never uttered on the Senate floor, but simply entered in the record. One registered support for giving federal land for the construction of the New Albany and Mount Carmel Railroad in the states of Illinois and Indiana.

Brendan wondered greatly at Perry's profound interest in a railroad remote from his own state. Given Perry's well known interest in improving his own financial situation, and persistent reports of widespread bribery by the railroad interests, he could not help but ask himself if Perry had given in to temptation on this stand.

The second was the full version of Perry's Valentine's Day speech on the Independent Treasury Bill. Brendan noted that it ran eight pages of small type in the appendix. No one had heard it at the time it was delivered and very few would read it in the future, he concluded after sampling a small part of it.

The third appendix speech Brendan found the most interesting of anything Perry said during the entire session. It was a reply by him to a speech by Senator John C. Calhoun on January 9 in which Calhoun had introduced five resolutions defending slavery.

Perry, the *Globe* stated, said he agreed with northern opinion opposing slavery, but admitted that, were he from a slaveholding state he would be "well enough satisfied with it." He was against slavery, not only because it was opposed by the people of his section of the country, but because it was an infringement of a natural right.

So far, so good. Then Perry began to waffle. "He did not mean to say that such natural rights could be exercised by the black population of the United States, or that they were in a condition to exercise them; but he believed that if this population was in a condition to exercise them, there would be almost a unanimous sentiment throughout the country in favor of their emancipation. We mean at present (Mr. S. said) to declare that we recognize the constitutional rights of the slave states in their slave property—that we do not have the means to infringe those rights."

Perry then said he approved Calhoun's first four resolutions because they dealt with the constitutional rights to hold slaves. But on the fifth, dealing with slavery in the District of Columbia, his twisting and dodging became almost pathetic.

First, he said that Americans had a right to discuss it, but he didn't think it would expedient to legislate on the matter because it would be unjust to the holders of slave property. On the other hand, he was unwilling to say that it was unconstitutional to abolish slavery in the District. "He opposed this resolution, not because he did not go heart and hand with the gentlemen of the South in the maintenance of their constitutional rights, but because he believed its adoption, so far from answering any good end to the people of the slave states, would have an injurious effect on their interests."

The men in the bar hooted when Brendan read them this stand of Perry's.

When Old Perry skates, he cuts some mighty fine figures, one drinker said. He seems mighty concerned over the interests of those big plantation owners. The constitutional right they are always harping on is really to keep the money and power in their hands. They say slavery is just fine in the national capitol but, just the samey, they never want to give up a slave anywhere.

Perry has skirted around the law so many years he's lost all idea of right and wrong, said another.

Brendan observed that Chloe was listening intently to the discussion from the door of the kitchen. Just then Jed Harris had his say.

Perry's right about one thing though. It's all right and proper to be agin slavery but to say that these coons have the same rights as a white man is nonsense. Ain't nobobdy I know of wants to have em around because they're lazy and shiftless, ain't got a brain in their head. They're an inferior species, and that's the way God made em, just like it says in the Bible.

Brendan glanced again at Chloe; her eyes met his for an instant. Then she turned and walked back into the kitchen.

After closing, he approached her.

I'm sorry for what that ignorant Jed Harris said. I don't believe that most of the men felt that way and you know I don't. In fact, most people in town would tell you that Jed is the one who is lazy, shiftless, and ignorant. So don't put any stock in what he said.

She shrugged. We're all used to the way certain white folks run off at the mouth. But it seems to be getting worse. I rarely heard this kind of talk when I was a girl. It seems like the more you hear of abolition, the more hatred grows against my people. Most of us work hard and behave ourselves. Why do we have to put up with this?

You shouldn't have to. I can tell you that you are respected highly in this town. I never heard anyone say anything derogatory about you. And they better not in front of me.

Go on. I don't believe you. Perry Smith would never say anything bad about me to you, but all the time he's saying right down there in Washington that we are inferior, that we're in no condition to exercize our natural rights, that most of us are just property like a horse or a goat. I've heard you talk to Perry. To speak frankly, you're always licking his ass and flattering him. Why don't you tell him he's wrong about me, because I'm one of my people?

Brendan reddened. He had never faced an onslaught like this from Chloe. After a moment he answered her.

You're right. I have flattered Perry. I started doing it when I was working for him and it became a habit. I even caught myself doing it, and I resolved to stop. I talked to Perry before he left for Washington in October and I told him he had to represent all the people. We had been talking about the railroads. You know a lot of people think he is their man. He just passed over it as if I hadn't said anything. I did go to him and to others about Orman. I can't stop people from expressing an opinion in my tavern even if it's an asshole like Jed Harris. But man to man, Perry or anyone else, I would not quietly accept abuse of your people, including you. Especially you.

Chloe said nothing more, but continued to busy herself. After a moment, Brendan spoke again.

You know that I'm figuring on building a new tavern on Railroad Street. I want to have it ready when the railroad first comes to town, which means the next year or so. I've been doing some drawings to give to the builder. They are only provisional at this point but I would like you to look them over. The building will be three stories, brick, with a flat roof. There will be a cellar. The main floor will be for the bar and the dining room, the second will be for rooms for the guests. The top floor will have two apartments, including one for me. Please give me any suggestions you may have, especially about the kitchen and dining area or the rooms. Take your time and think about it.

Brendan, forgive me for getting steamed up. I shouldn't have gone at you so after what you've done for me.

The shoe's on the other foot. I couldn't have operated this business without you. I don't blame you for resenting the constant slurs on your people. They knock the Irish around here, too, but I know it's nothing to what you have to face. It's a good thing that your people are good natured. Otherwise there would be fights all the time.

They aren't that good natured. That's only what you see. We

are just like you but we don't have the means to fight back. You see what happened to Orman. Who knows if that was an accident or some white teamster had it in for him because Orman beat him at cards or in a fight? But let's let it go. Who are you putting in the other apartment?

It will be for rent. Know anyone who needs quarters like that? Do you want it?

I've got a house, remember?

Of course. Let me know what you come up with.

After she left, Brendan thought about the apartments. He could rent one to Chloe and she could sell her house. It would be a lot more convenient for her. Then his thoughts took another direction. He could ask Chloe to live with him. He still ached with longing when he watched her some days. He had thought about Marguerite, too, but his hours with her were fading into his memory. In any event, nothing in her life had prepared her for living in the country and living two flights up over a bar.

On the other hand, Chloe and he had been working in tandem for years now. He admitted to himself that he would never find another woman who would be as dedicated to the business and, more importantly, to him, than Chloe. Besides that, she was beautiful and they appreciated each other. What more could he ask?

CHAPTER THIRTY-ONE

1839

AFTER PERRY'S EVIDENT ATTEMPT to flood *The Congressional Globe* with verbiage during his first session in the Senate, he offered a more restrained profile during the third session of the 25th Congress which ran from December 3, 1838 until March 3, 1839. Eleven of his fifteen interventions from the floor during the session dealt with petitions or other routine business of the two committees on which he served, Revolutionary Claims and Agriculture.

At the McCauley Tavern, newly supplied with copies of the *Globe* by Nat Perry, the patrons speculated why Perry Smith had become so much less voluble.

They probably told him that they had enough famous mouths without him trying to get into the act, Dan Minor said. After all, he is a new boy and the veterans don't look kindly on neophytes getting into the act until they've been there a few years.

Gil Whitely had another view. I see Perry is still sticking his hands in the candy jar when it comes to transportation improvements in other states where he can pick up a few bucks from the private interests.

Whitely may have had a point. Perry had opposed an amendment to a bill which would have permitted the Government to buy stock in the Louisville and Portland Canal. The amendment would have made the Government the de facto owner. Perry's often reiterated desire to keep the Federal Government out of enterprises could have accounted for his vote, or he could, as Whitely thought, have had his hand out for the pay-off.

It's doubtful we will ever have the evidence one way or the other, Seymour Buck said. Perry also favored an amendment to improve Florida roads. There couldn't have been any pay-off on that one.

Everyone present agreed that Perry had been right to cross swords with Henry Clay over the same dueling bill Perry had spoken to in the last session. Clay moved to strike out the fourth section which would have not only banned dueling in the District of Columbia, but also beyond its borders. He claimed it was unconstitutional. Perry, however, pointed out that if an act precipitating a challenge occurred in the District, the perpetrators could evade the will of Congress by simply crossing over the line for the duel.

"If the parties who intend to fight without the District have that understanding within it, is not this understanding the incipient step to the final consummation of the crime? Perry asked. He answered his own question. "Most certainly so." He pointed to a parallel hypothetical situation of people within the District conspiring to commit murder outside it, some going on to do this and others staying behind in the District. Could all of them be punished under the laws of the District? "Yes sir, every step, every act, and every motion tending to the perpetration of the crime is criminal."

Sometimes when I read all this hair-splitting Perry and the others are playing at down in the capitol, I just don't want to know any more, said Gil. None of it sounds like they are living in the same world. I just want to pull back into our own world that we know right here in town. I can understand paving the brook on the green, for example. It's a problem we can all see and a man with any sense knows that once the town can afford it, it should be done. We watch when it's being done. We see it's twelve feet wide, it's curved on the sides and rises twelve or fourteen inches to ground level. The stone work is nicely laid and the joints well mortared. The result is an improvement we all can appreciate; it's a credit to the town. This is the kind of thing we understand, not the constant talk we see reported in this *Congressional Globe.* It's too much.

Don't forget the elms Solomon Bostwick and other folks have planted on the west side of the green, just to the east of the wagon track, Seymour added. Now the people on the east side are doing the same thing. No talk about it, people know what to do and do it. Why can't these fellows in Washington act that way?

How can you fellows talk about elms and channelling a brook when everyone knows the greatest building project in the history of New Milford is getting underway on Railroad Street?

In posing his rhetorical question, Reggy Wildman, winked broadly at the other drinkers at the bar and all turned to see what Brendan would say.

Doing his imitation of Perry Smith, Brendan rocked back on his heels with his thumbs hooked under the armholes of his vest, and pompously intoned: I'm highly sensible of the honor which this community is tendering to me. As you know, I'm a convinced supporter of the railroads, especially the Housatonic Railroad, so when an architectural monument of the first water is constructed near its route on a vital public artery like Railroad Street, this is a development that all of our citizens should cherish and support. Anything I can do to contribute to the profitability of the railroad, feel free to call upon me.

Then he bowed and the men gave three cheers for the new project.

How's it getting along? Gil asked. Last time I was down there the horses were scooping out the cellar with those scrapers.

The masons are moving right along. The cellar walls are done and the carpenters are putting in the joists for the ground floor. Next week they will have that floor laid and the masons will start on the brick walls. Then you will begin to see some progress. They expect to have the bricks in place for all three stories by the Fourth of July. With three masons laying bricks, it goes right along. By frost the roof should be on and the building all closed in.

Some change in town recently. When you think how it looked thirty years ago, it's hard to believe. Clarence Cook, wagged his head and spat a direct hit at a spittoon.

After the men left and the bar closed, Brendan went back to the kitchen to chat with Chloe. They usually sat and talked for a few minutes before Chloe headed over the hill to her house beyond the cemetery.

The carpenters will be putting in the floor for your new dining room and the kitchen next week, Brendan told her.

It's not a room until it has a roof, as far as I'm concerned.

When the roof is on, then your bedroom will be done.

How am I going to get another husband if I'm living in your building?

Brendan and Chloe had gotten in the habit of joking about mates for each other. It was thin ice, they both realized, but they couldn't seem to stop teasing each other.

You won't need a husband–he broke off abruptly and moved toward her. Let's stop this game. Chloe, I want you, I need you. Please marry me.

That's pretty sudden. What made you think of that.

She sounded cool and unmoved. She didn't stir in her chair.

It's not sudden. I've been thinking about it ever since the

time we were together in my room upstairs. But now you're free. We get along well together.

Then he knelt at her feet and, with his head in her lap, he but his arms around her hips.

Chloe, I love you. You must know I do. We've been close so long, we know what each other is thinking.

She caressed his face and ran her fingers through his hair. For a long time she said nothing.

Finally she responded. Do you really believe white and black can make it together?

We've been doing it for fifteen years now.

But not as man and wife. There is a big difference between boss and cook and man and wife.

Probably most people that know us already think we're living together. I don't know why they wouldn't with the hours you put in here. You must be attracted to me a little, at least, the way you acted when we were in bed together.

Yes, I love you, Brendan. I have for a long time. Even when I was married to Orman, I'm ashamed to say I did. It's a feeling you can't control. I do love you, Brendan, but I'm scared. The hatred that some whites have for blacks, the contempt they show. These are hard, hard things to contend with.

Brendan stood up and pulled Chloe to her feet. Then, looking into her eyes, he deliberately pulled her close and slowly kissed her.

Stay tonight, he said.

She nodded. I will. But we've got to think how we are going to handle some of these problems.

Not now.

They headed up the stairs together.

CHAPTER THIRTY-TWO

1840

SEEN FROM THE FRONT, the new McCauley Tavern was but a mass of red, white, and blue bunting. The only part of the facade of the red brick three-story building besides the windows not covered was a horizontal strip across the middle of the structure which proclaimed in large red letters Welcome to the Railroad. If it were not for the cold on this February 11 of 1840, Brendan would have remained outside gazing at the front of his building, so proud was he of it. As it was, he darted out from time to time to enjoy the sight of it.

The tavern was not the only building decorated to welcome the first train. All up and down the new Railroad Street the new stores and other businesses were decked out in patriotic colors in honor of the occasion. Even up the hill in the center there were also decorations, but it was on Railroad Street that the most fervor was demonstrated because the merchants here hoped to benefit most from the new addition to the regional transportation system.

What time is this engine due here? David Ferriss asked Brendan.

Dan Marsh is the new station agent, and he's hedging just a bit, Brendan answered. He says it's due at noon, but I get an idea from the way he said it that it might arrive some later. Quite a bit later, in fact. You know it's an excursion train. That means it will be chock full of politicians from down the line as well as bigwigs from the railroad, the construction company, and God knows what other free loaders.

After all that talk about how these cars were going to give punctual service on a precise time schedule? Shit! Dave spat a jet of tobacco juice neatly into a shiny new brass spitoon.

They'll do better when they're at it for a while. You can't begrudge them a celebration after all the years this thing has been in the works. Remember, we first heard about a railroad coming to town when the Saugatuck Canal people covered their bets in Hartford by wording their stock subscription circulars so a railroad might be built with the same money. Do you recall that? It was in 1827.

There's people come here from all over Litchfield County to see this. Some are a little put out. They don't think it will get here today at all. You got nice heat in here from that furnace, but some of the temperance folks would rather die than come through the door.

There always welcome. They can drink a glass of water or a cup of coffee if they would rather. But I wouldn't force them to come in if they're happier out in the cold.

Most of the crowd that thronged into New Milford that day never did see the train, because, being mainly farmers, they had to leave in mid-afternoon to arrive at home in time to do chores. The train chugged into town in late afternoon. People could hear it coming even before it crossed the new iron railroad bridge to the east side of the river a mile below town. When it could actually be seen coming up the stretch, excitement was hard to restrain. Onlookers were awed by the power of the engine as it drew the three cars and a caboose. The noise was overpowering, especially as metal clanged powerfully against metal at the train came to a stop. The periodic hiss of escaping steam frightened men and women.

Brendan and the men in the tavern, and people all up and down the street, emerged from their shelter to see the new contrivance up close. Dan Marsh headed a group of railroad employees who kept the crowd from getting too near. One of these was John Riley, an Irish immigrant. Brendan was no longer the only Irishman in New Milford.

It was too cold and late for speech making, but Dan Marsh tried anyhow until he was waved away by one of the railroad officials. It was apparent that many of the guests on the ride had indulged well if unwisely in the excursion hospitality. Some tried to climb off the train, perhaps with an eye to visiting McCauley's Tavern, but they were herded back on by the trainmen, who only hoped they could get all their guests back to Danbury without incident.

The bells of the Congregational and Episcopal churches began to peal furiously and someone shot off an old cannon on the rocky promontory a quarter of a mile south of the green. From time to time the steam whistle of the engine added its shrill clamor to the din.

Sam Bostwick stopped by to congratulate Brendan on his splendid new building. He thought New Milford people had high hopes, probably too high, for the railroad.

It's the same all over the nation, he said. There are extravagant visions of a new prosperity as the lines spread into regions just opening up. People expect factories to spring up overnight to make jobs for those who have had hard going on these rocky upland farms. Even if it doesn't happen right away, people along the rail line ain't never going to stop hoping that the magic man is going to show up with a new factory and make them all rich.

There would be other disillusionments as well. The new rails were made of iron fastened to wooden beams; steel rails would not replace them until the 1870's. The iron rails sometime came loose from their fastenings, and curled upwards like an errant letter C. These sometimes caused serious accidents during the early years.

A customer told Brendan about an incident in New Milford not long after the line had been established.

Joel Bailey, my neighbor in Gaylordsville, was walking along the tracks last Sunday morning when he spotted one of the rails bent up like a copperhead ready to strike. He was afeard, and rightfully so, that it might cause an accident. He used some heavy stones he found handy to bend it back the way it orter be. He figgered he'd done the right thing and went off whistling and happy. On Monday he was arrested by one of the constables on a complaint of someone who seen him and brought before a Justice of the Peace for breaking the Sabbath. The Justice, he didn't say which one, allowed as how he had broken the law by working on Sunday and fined Joel one dollar and forty cents costs. That's nearly as much as poor Joel makes in a week. He says next time he'll let the damned train crack up and kill all hands afore he'll lift a hand to prevent it on a Sunday.

Some of those jaypees ain't got the sense God promised a jackass, Gil Whitely said. That kind of judgment makes a mockery of the law. We orter pay more attention to those names on the ballot.

By summer, folks along the railroad line had grown accustomed to the trains, the noise they made and the dangers they presented. They began to talk about the presidential campaign the long dormant Whigs were putting on with "Tippecanoe and Tyler too". They had some fodder for this from *The Congressional Globe* reporting on the First Session of the 26th Congress, which ended in July.

The *Globe* showed that Perry's major activity continued to be the work of the Revolutionary Claims Committee. Again he was suspiciously active in blocking involvement of the Federal

Government in the affairs of railroads and canals. On February 3 he promised to give his reasons for opposing purchase of stock in the Louisville and Portland Canal. Later in the session he backed authorizing Virginia to incorporate the Falmouth and Alexandria Railroad Company. Near the end of the session he favored the Government's return of stock in the Chesapeake and Ohio Canal to Maryland. As usual, he said the Government never should have owned it in the first place.

Looks like old Perry still has his hand out to collect from the railroad and canal interests whenever he can, said Dan Minor. He figures he's got to do something to make up for giving up his law practice when he went to Washington.

Perry did a couple of dances for the voters back in Connecticut. Also on February 3, with a bow to the Litchfield County iron foundries, he introduced a resolution to direct the Secretary of War to furnish information on the cost of cast iron cannon, wrought iron cannon, and brass cannon, together with an evaluation of all three. At another time he presented a petition of Connecticut citizens asking for reduction of postage on letters. The Senate understood his motivation in both cases and did nothing. This was standard log-rolling.

The *Globe* reported he "spoke at much length" in opposing a bill for benefiting the Howard Institution. The bill would have assigned lots in Washington, D.C., worth five thousand dollars to Howard. He clashed with Henry Clay again on July 3 over changing Senate rules on the eve of adjournment so as to facilitate passage of a bill Clay was interested in. Perry complained that rules were worth little if they could be changed just to please interested parties.

It sounds like Perry finally got himself on the right side of one, David Brownson commented.

Perry spoke strongly against Congress granting charters to banks in the District of Columbia or in any of the states. In his opinion, he said, before there can be such banks, there must be a great change either in the country's banking system or the government of the country.

Perry's longest speech of the session seemed to align him with the southern wing of the Democratic Party against leaders in the north who were trying to attract the rising supporters of abolition within its ranks. Largely directing his remarks at Senator Tallmadge of New York, Perry complained of the persistence of supporters of abolitionist petitions in bringing them repeatedly before the Senate after they had been killed for lack of favorable votes.

Perry claimed that Tallmadge and others like him , although sympathetic to the Abolitionists, did not dare integrate them in the Democratic Party because they realized the Abolitionist cause was viewed as unjustifiable and an unholy one.

Smarting from claims that Benjamin Franklin was an Abolitionist, Perry said "Dr. Franklin was understood to be such an Abolitionist as nearly all the Northern people are, and perhaps a great share of the Southern people. They believe slavery to be a political evil; they are willing, so far as they can constitutionally, to aid in removing it from the land. But they understand that the right to hold this species of property in the states existed at the time our Constitution was formed..."

"As much as I deprecate the existence of the evil, I believe, as it is here among us, it is much better for the slaves, and much better for the whole community, that negroes should remain slaves. So far as I am acquainted with them, either in the free or the slave states, the slaves appear the most moral, most cheerful, and most useful...

"Sir, place in juxtaposition the whites and blacks, and make them all equally eligible to high social stations. You have only to look to Mexico for the consequences, where you will find a perfect illustration of it. A people occupying the fairest portion of the globe, with all the natural advantages necessary to make one of the most powerful nations on earth, so mixed up, divided into castes, and degraded, that they are incapabable of binding themselves together, and forming such a government as to give any security to party or person."

Sounds good to me. Suits my views to a T, Jed Harris said after hearing Brendan read the paragraphs. A few other voices expressed agreement. Brendan could see that others were troubled by some of Perry's statements even though they also distrusted the abolitionists. Still they didn't know how to express themselves.

Brendan called a halt to the discussion.

That's enough for tonight.

When the crowd wandered out a little later, Brendan took *The Congressional Globe* sheet to discuss with Chloe. He knew she was greatly disturbed by Perry's stand; he wanted to talk with her about it.

When Perry was in town, I was pretty hot under the collar at all those nasty things he did to me, Brendan told her. But that was all negligible compared to the harm he's doing the whole country now.

This is a man with no vision and no compassion and I can't even vote against him, Chloe said. No woman at all can do a thing about it and no black man. How long are we going to be in bondage in Egypt?

CHAPTER THIRTY-THREE

1841

BRENDAN WAITED until he was sure that railroad service was really regular and reliable, then he wrote his mother to inform her that she could now travel to New Milford in just a few hours by making only one train change in South Norwalk. He himself had travelled to Danbury and back by train several times and had found it a fascinating experience. The trains ran more or less on schedule and sometimes attained a speed of forty miles an hour. The run to Danbury rarely took more than half an hour and, compared with the same trip by stage, was comfortable beyond belief.

Brendan took Chloe with him on one trip and the two went by horse cab out to see his Uncle Peter and Aunt Thankful. Brendan had decided that if he and Chloe were to live as man and wife, it was time to present her to his friends and relatives as such. He knew there would be adverse reactions in doing this, but he was determined to be open about his commitment to Chloe. As it turned out, the visit was not much of a test. Peter had aged terribly; he was quite feeble. His formerly tanned skin was now a wrinkled white; he hardly got outside the house of many materials now. Thankful was in good health, but very thin. It was apparent that she did all the farm work now, planting and harvesting their small fields of rye and oats, their garden, and taking care of their pigs and solitary cow. In their state they hardly noticed that Chloe was an African-American; they merely though her darker than the usual run of people. Chloe, for her part, was astonished that Brendan had relatives who lived in such poverty. Her former neighbors at the foot of Second Hill, for example, lived in much better circumstances.

Although Brendan considered Chloe his wife, they had never actually got around to getting married. From the night they had gone up the stairs together to his room in the old tavern on the side of Aspetuck Hill, they had made love and slept together. After the move to the third floor of the new tavern building on Railroad Street, they had moved into the front apartment and left the rear one unoccupied. Brendan talked of renting the rear apartment, but never took any steps to do so.

Brendan liked living with Chloe. She was warm and affectionate and even-tempered. If Brendan got excited about something, she kept her head and quieted him down. She was sensible, shrewd, and as as good a housekeeper in their own living quarters as she was in the tavern. She made the apartment into a home which was more spacious and well ordered than any he had ever lived in. If its furnishings were a far cry from the tasteful and sumptuous interiors of his mother's building in New York, they were comfortable and easy to maintain.

Once the tavern was established in the building, the volume of business soon outstripped that in the previous location. Most of the regular patrons, both from the bar and the dining room, continued to come to eat and drink as before. In addition, the railroad brought a new clientele each day, not only for food and drink, but persons in transit who stayed at the rooms on the second floor. These were mainly business people and salesmen who also used the other facilities. Before long Brendan added a fulltime bartender and a maid to the staff. The maid took care of the second floor rooms and helped Chloe care for the ground floor establishment.

But not everything was on an upward plane for the tavern. Brendan liked to joke about the temperance movement reaching its "high water mark" in New Milford in 1841, the year when more than nine-hundred persons out of a population of 4,508 were members of the newly founded New Milford Washingtonian Temperance Benevolent Society.

People can only sustain their militancy just so long, he told Gilbert Whitely. It's like a wave which gets more and more massive as it rolls toward shore. Just at the moment when it seems irresistable, it crashes on the sands, scatters and is dissipated. That's what will happen to this group.

Time proved him correct. After 1847 there is no further record of the society.

Whitely asked Brendan when he would have copies of *The Congressional Globe* for the second session of the 26th Congress, which convened in December of 1840.

Got them right here. Look them over and pass them around so the men can see how our boy Perry is getting along.

The second session of the 26th Congress was a rump session that sat in the interval after the election of the new Whig President William Henry Harrison but before his inauguration in March of 1840. Perry Smith, the *Globe* reported, was absent when it convened but showed up a few days later. In addition to his former committee postings, he was also named to the Committee on Public Buildings, not an assignment calculated to enhance his importance within the Senate or in Connecticut. Again in this session, most of the mentions of Perry in the *Globe* dealt with his routine work on the committees.

On December 30 Perry presented a petition on behalf of the heirs of Silas Deane, the Wethersfield man who served as envoy to France during the American Revolution. On February

17 Perry reported a bill out of the Revolutionary Claims Committee authorizing a settlement of the Silas Deane accounts. It was ordered for a second reading.

Along with Silas Wright and John C. Calhoun, Perry got involved in opposing temporary provisions for the mentally ill, or lunatics as they were then called, in Washington, D.C. Perry held to his normal strict constructionist position and cited the want of power under the Constitution to appropriate for local purposes. On this day, January 18, Perry opposed every motion that came to the floor except that to adjourn.

Perry also involved himself in a political skirmish over the reappointment of the printers of *The Congressional Globe,* Blair and Rivas, who were regarded as unduly favorable to the Democrats by the opposition. He defended Blair from accusations that he was of "infamous" character. He implied that Blair's critics were more involved with "entertainments" with him than any of the Democratic senators. The Senate upheld the contract with the printers. Perry's remarks provoked another dust-up with Henry Clay, who referred to Perry as "the Senator who sits in the corner yonder," and that Perry should excuse him if he found him "unworthy of notice."

Perry rose again to huff about "the acts of his (Clay's) public and private life" which reflected his character. "Humble as he (Perry) might be, he would not descend to the prominent points of the character of that honorable Senator (Clay) which gave him such fame all over the world."

Loud laughter rang out in the McCauley Tavern when Brendan read this section to the men at the bar. It had the unlikely result of generating applause and sympathy for Perry because Henry Clay was held in such low esteem in New Milford. In spite of this, some of the men present cackled pleasantly to themselves in subsequent days when they thought of Perry described as "the Senator who sits in the corner yonder."

In spite of the obvious contempt of Clay for Perry, Perry was servile enough, once back in New Milford, to claim a great friendship with the much better known Clay and to praise his intimate knowledge of Western Connecticut as manifested by his command of the facts relating to the marble quarries in nearby Marbledale.

In the first session of the 27th Congress, dominated by the Whigs, which began on May 31, Perry lost his chairmanship of the Revolutionary Claims Committee, which he had held since he started in the Senate. The Whig Senator Jabez W. Huntington, who replaced Democrat John M. Niles after the election, was named chair of the Commerce Committee, an assignment more important than any Perry had ever held. Perry continued as a member of Revolutionary Claims and Agriculture.

One of the loudest political frays of the session surrounded the voting of a pension for the widow of the late President Harrison after his untimely death. Perry, as one of the minority now, voted unsuccessfully to recommit the pension bill. He also took the floor to attack the widow's pension, complaining that the pension augmented Harrison's pay as President beyond the limit set by statute and would raise his annual pay to $372,003. Claims in some Connecticut cases were pending for more than fifty years, he said, including that of the Revolutionary hero, Nathan Hale, whose grave was located, Perry declaimed, "near the spot where the women of Connecticut donated their underwear to make wadding for the American cannon."

Of course he brought up the petition he himself had presented in Congress. "Where is there any monument of national gratitude to the memory of Silas Deane? He went on a secret mission for his country before the Declaration of Independence. His life was at stake and he sacrificed it in the service of his country—he died from grief and absolute starvation. Yet, though it has been since ascertained that $60,000 were due to him by the Government from that time to this, the sympathy of Congress has not been awakened to the just claims of his representatives.

Perry's magnum opus of the session was a speech on the bill for a United States Bank. It was so long, almost five pages, three columns to a page, that it was only printed in the appendix after the close of the session. In it Perry rehashed his stand on the bank vis-a-vis the Connecticut General Assembly petition taking the contrary position; the remainder was an involved constitutional argument designed to show that Congress had no power to charter the bank. The speech was so infinitely boring that Brendan knew of no one besides Nat Perry who had ever succeeded in reading it all without falling to sleep.

In response to the invitation to his mother, Catherine wrote that she would be delighted to try the new railroad to New Milford, but not just at present. Her letter reported that there was considerable violence in New York in recent years and that it seemed to be growing. She said groups of young men had taken to attacking "certain establishments," rioting through them, destroying furnishings and beating the women they found. The violence was random, not general, but one never knew where it would break out.

Later Brendan discovered that gangs of men, not always young, had, since the late thirties, taken to breaking into selected houses of prostitution, where they systematically destroyed the furniture and physically attacked the madame and any of the whores they could find at the time. There was no uniform pattern to these disturbances; some seemed to be directed by city officials or the police who had experienced delays in receiving payoffs from certain houses. These were well organized and usually led by bully boys such as the boxer Tom Hyers. Other attacks were led by young men motivated against vice by the religious revivalists of the time; the men who participated in these assaults were young wage earners making paltry salaries and therefore jealous of the munificent incomes of the women engaged in prostitution. Other riots were mainly occasioned by bored young hoodlums to vent their destructive urges.

Brendan knew that his mother ran a very discreet operation, but that had not spared other houses which had been overrun, some more than once. However discreet she might be, there was no doubt that people in the neighborhood knew of the existence of prostitution in the several buildings she owned. He worried that she might come under attack. He wrote her again to be careful of her own personal safety. It might be better to close down, even temporarily, rather than risk her own life and those of her girls, not to mention her substantial investment. He told her about the vacant apartment in his new building and urged her to either come for a protracted visit or to move to New Milford permanently. He knew his mother considered the town to be more than dull, but it was safe, at least.

CHAPTER THIRTY-FOUR

1842

THE DEMOCRATIC LEGISLATURE in 1842 repealed all restrictions on the sale of liquor. Despite some subsequent attempts by the Whigs to return to the local option laws, the vacillation in liquor control ended with a period of stability that was to endure for several years. People were weary of the constant bickering and even those who favored temperance began to work in arenas outside of the legislative halls. Reformers continued to exhort, but largely through religious and educational channels. Clearly there were groups in Connecticut who felt reform by statute was transitory at best and counterproductive at worst. The growing reluctance to resort to the law for social objectives was to delay in Connecticut legislative action to benefit the blind, the insane, the poor, and other disadvantaged sectors.

Brendan, however, welcomed the lull in the legislative tussle over liquor regulation. This is how he put it to Nat Perry:

We can concentrate on running our businesses and will be spared the constant harrassment. It will save me trips to Hartford to deal with lobbyists and appeasing legislators.

Now you can devote more energy to following the fortunes of your old mentor in the Senate, Nat said. From what I hear, though, next year will be his last. The powers out in Hartford aren't too happy with him. He has not grown in the job as some men do. It's not that he did anything they didn't expect, but I think there is a feeling that times have passed him by, particularly on the issue of abolition. Abolitionists are still but a minority, but it's a minority that is starting to grow more rapidly. At least in the north, all this talk about property rights when human flesh and blood is involved is no longer appropriate. People may fear and dislike blacks, but at the same time they feel a revulsion for slavery.

You're right. Perry's views on slavery go back at least to 1820. He lectured me then about property rights and the constitution. Incidentally, the men in the tavern like to read about Perry in the *Globe*. The issues are a big hit. They skip those dreadful, long speeches, but the maneuvering fascinates them and they admire anyone who gets down to basics and calls a spade a spade.

The Congressional Globe readers in the McCauley Tavern were upset that Perry had voted against a land distribution bill on April 13. Gilbert Crosby sneered.

Does he think he's the only one who ought to own land? He can get it through his legal tricks and then use it to speculate. A poor man needs it to make a living.

Perry was more in tune with the men in the tavern when, in brief remarks in a long debate, he objected to leaving coffee and tea as dutiable items in debate on a tariff bill. They were indifferent when he listed his reasons for opposing establishment of a service school, like the Army's West Point, for the Navy.

Perry strongly opposed a bill for the relief of the heirs of General William Hull, a native of Derby, Connecticut.

"I would just as soon have expected a bill introduced for the relief of the heirs of Benedict Arnold," he said.

General Hull was simultaneously the civil governor of the U.S. territory and the commannder of the American forces on the Canadian border in the War of 1812. After a disastrous campaign, he was arrested and tried by court martial on a charge of treason, cowardice and dereliction of duty. He was acquitted on the first charge, found guilty on the latter two and sentenced to be shot. President Monroe set aside the death penalty. The government refused to pay him his civil salary from the time of his arrest, from February to October, 1813. The claim was now reactivated.

Perry claimed Hull had betrayed his country. "General Hull not only did not do the service for which he was to get his salary during the time for which he claims, but did the greatest injury which a citizen could inflict upon his country and government by surrendering up his trust to its enemies."

Another Senator, Merrick, called Hull "a miserable gentleman."

Perry made another attempt to settle the claim of the heirs of Silas Deane of Wethersfield for expenditures he incurred on behalf of the United States while on a mission to France during the Revolution. After Deane's imbecile son died in 1830, accounts, vouchers and books supporting Deane's claim were found in State Department archives. The claim was referred to the Treasury Department, which after 1838 determined that $60,000 was due Deane's heirs for his expenditures. The Continental Congress, in a secret contract with Deane, had authorized him in 1776 to sell American produce and to use the proceeds to buy one hundred artillery pieces and munitions for 25,000 troops. Deane was to receive five per cent of the purchase price, but an erstwhile colleague, Arthur Lee, passed insinuations against him in congressional circles where any excuse for not paying a debt was welcomed.

In the Senate debate on May 23, several senators, including Perry, supported the claim, but others felt that Congress had had good grounds for rejecting it and moved that the accounting officer report in the next session the amount "fairly due."

Later in the year, Congress made a partial restitution to the heirs by voting them the sum of $37,000.

After Senator John C. Calhoun moved to amend a bill to regulate enlistments in the Navy so as to bar blacks from every job except as cooks, servants, and stewards, Perry uncharacteristically said Northern states, especially Connecticut and Rhode Island, which had passed laws making it a penal offense to draw distinctions between blacks and whites, would be insulted. He said Rhode Island had raised a regiment of black soldiers to protect the people against a group trying to abolish the state's colonial charter and establish universal suffrage.

Following this, for him, extraordinary statement, Perry later in the debate reverted to his usual point of view when he argued that employment of negros would tend to degrade the white sailors. He said they were "sufficiently degraded by the tendency of the laws, as now enacted and administered, without causing them to be mingled with the negro race." He wanted white sailors to be freed from "an illiberal and anti-democratic policy" so they could be promoted for meritorious conduct.

In an August 27 debate on duties, Perry traded political punches with his Whig colleague from Connecticut, Senator Jabez Huntington. Perry said he would not support a bill, the result of which "would be to build up an aristocracy of monopolists, under the pretext of protecting the laborers, whom they have reduced to the state of paupers." Huntington responded that the manufacturing laborers of Connecticut were entitled to all the constitutional protection which the government could give them. It was the want of this protection which alone could reduce them to pauperism. No law was sufficient to compensate for the destitution and misery of the industrial classes of New England.

Perry, who had ridiculed the payment to General Harrison's

widow, had no problem with a bill to refund to General Andrew Jackson the fine levied on him by Federal Judge Dominick Hall in New Orleans in 1815.

In his later years General Jackson, suffering from ill health and pains from old wounds, was further plagued by pressing personal and financial problems. His cotton crops had failed, land prices were too low to sell any of his holdings, and his incompetent son had run up debts that Jackson was called upon to honor. Supporters sponsored a bill to reimburse the General for the fine and costs imposed on him. Jackson was always sensitive about the fine and claimed it was levied by a tyrant who denied him his constitutional right of self defense. He wanted the U.S. Government to repudiate Hall's action. The bill touched off a partisan battle, with the Whigs determined to uphold the Judge's action.

Said Perry: "General Jackson's duty to his country required him to do what he did. Because he did what circumstances demanded he should do, he had the approbation and gratitude of the whole country. Had he neglected to perform that duty, he would have received universal condemnation. In the performance of such a duty, if he suffered a loss, it was unjustly, and the injustice would be heightened by any qualification of the restitution (such as an amendment proposed by the Whigs stating that Judge Hall had acted legally).

Payment of the $1,000 fine with interest was passed with the amendment but General Jackson said he would rather starve than accept the money upon these terms. The Democrats then voted down the bill.

Perry, who a few weeks before had been calling for a more open promotion policy for U.S. sailors, on August 8 opposed a new Navy pension bill which, among other things, would have curtailed pension rights for widows and children of sailors killed or injured in line of duty.

* * *

In October, Brendan received a message from his mother, via the conductor of the morning train from New York, that rioters had invaded her house on Greene Street the night before. They had done thousands of dollars worth of damage by smashing furniture, mirrors, chandeliers, and by throwing other household articles out the windows. They had also started fires in two parlors, which had been extinguished before major damage was done. They had terrorized the girls, but had not injured anyone seriously.

His mother seemingly took the attack in stride, judging by the straightforward account she gave of it, but Brendan was sure she was deeply affected. Although she was aware that such attacks were one of the hazards of her business and had mentioned them on his last visit to the city, it was a hard blow for a woman now in her sixties.

Brendan told Chloe that his mother's business had suffered damage from rioters and told her he must go to New York for two or three days to help her in any way he could. He had never confided in Chloe the nature of Catherine's business and this didn't seem the appropriate occasion to make the revelation.

He took the afternoon train and arrived in New York late in the evening. He immediately took a hansom cap to Greene Street and was relieved that, from the outside at least, the damage was not obvious. After he rang at the door, it was some time before a maid finally answered. She recognized him and took him directly to his mother. He was startled to see how old and worn she looked; she broke into tears when she saw him.

Brendan, she sobbed, they've done awful things to my beautiful house.

It was some time before he pieced together what had happened. A group of seven men had knocked at the door about eight o'clock the previous evening, and had not revealed their destructive intentions until once inside. They had raced through the house, breaking anything they found. They had yelled at the maids and the girls and threatened them with beatings and jail, but had done nothing much more than shove some of the women around who dared to talk back to them. Finally, they set the fires in the parlors and left. The entire episode had not lasted more than twenty minutes. Neither the police nor the firemen were called; the women put out the fires by themselves.

Catherine was not sure what had been the motivation for the attack. She was on good terms with the police captain in her precinct and did not believe it was instigated by officials. She leaned to the idea that the men were young fanatical followers of one of the local preachers against vice.

Given his mother's financial resources, he did not believe that the damage represented a major loss for her. Within a short time, he believed she could replace the broken items and have the destruction repaired. But it was apparent that his mother was shaken beyond any physical considerations. She had assumed so much of the responsibility for her operation personally, that, as far as he could see, she had no assistant to help her through this crisis.

After a good night's sleep, he told his mother, we can talk tomorrow about what's to be done. I think you should close down temporarily and come up to New Milford until you can get over this shock.

His mother didn't respond, but he felt he had not convinced her. At that moment a woman entered to speak to his mother and Brendan realized it was Marguerite Bannon.

Marguerite, how are you? I'm glad to see no one was injured seriously. Were you here when the rioters came?

Marguerite sadly shook hands.

Yes, we are all unhurt, but some of the women were hysterical for a while. I'm happy you could get here so soon from so far away. It's a comfort for your mother. And for the rest of us, too.

Her eyes met Brendan's as she said this, and she smiled.

I'm sure you have been much more comfort than I, having been here right through all of this.

Marguerite has been a tower of strength, his mother said. I don't know what I would have done without her. She has been my right hand for the last year or more. But Brendan is right; we better go to bed so we can do a day's work tomorrow. Marguerite, please show Brendan to that upper bedroom that wasn't damaged.

As he followed Marguerite up the stairs, he saw that she still retained all her charms, especially her wonderful body. When they arrived at the room, she bustled around to see that everything was in place; he stood awkwardly, wondering what was required of him. When she had finished, Marguerite took his hand and spoke soothingly.

It's so good to see you again, Brendan. Your mother passes on all the news she receives from you. I know you are tired tonight but I hope I can see you tomorrow.

Then she was gone. Brendan, however, thought about her for some time. Just the sight of her had ignited the same lust he had felt for her five years earlier. Guiltily he wondered why he should feel this way when he had a good woman like Chloe who was devoted to him back in New Milford. Nevertheless, images of a nude Marguerite ran through his mind before he finally drifted off to sleep.

The next morning his mother looked composed and more her usual incisive self.

Brendan, I'm grateful for your offer. But I've decided to stay here and get this mess cleaned up. When I've done that and replaced the furniture that was destroyed, I can reopen. Then, with things running normally, I would indeed like to take some time off with you. Would you mind if I brought Marguerite with me?

No, of course not, Brendan lied. Just to be perfectly open with you, I must tell you I have been living with Chloe. But there is a whole apartment vacant and you, and whomever you chose to bring, will be most welcome.

You're not married to her, are you?

No, not yet. But I've been thinking about it.

Then there's nothing that can't be changed. Please promise me you won't marry before I can get there.

I promise, but don't count on anything changing.

He took the train back to Connecticut without seeing Marguerite again.

CHAPTER THIRTY-FIVE

1843

ON THE RETURN TRAIN TRIP to New Milford, Brendan marveled at the speed and ease of the trip compared with his journey afoot in 1818. It only took slightly more hours than it had days in that long walk a quarter of a century earlier. But he spent most of the time thinking about his relationship to Chloe and to his mother.

As soon as he entered the tavern, once off the train, he found Chloe and asked her to step upstairs with him. She wondered at his look and aprehensively asked how he found his mother.

She's fine now.

He brushed aside any further discussion of Catherine's situation.

I wanted you to come up here so I could again ask you to marry me. I asked you four years ago and you never gave me a direct answer and you suggested there were too many problems for black and white to marry. We have been living together ever since then and, as far as I'm concerned, it has gone pretty well. We haven't advertised that we were together, but on the other hand I would bet that most of the people in this town know all about us. I'm sure some of them don't approve of this but they're the same people who never approved of any Irishman ever, or any black ever, so it makes little difference.

On the way back here I've though more about it and I've decided that I should marry you to show that I not only love you but that I respect you. I don't know how it is in your religion, but Catholics believe that marriage is a sacred and permanent commitment on the part of both the man and the woman. That's the kind of commitment I want to make to you and I ask you to do the same for me. It's a pledge before God and the community. Until the last few years, I hadn't paid much attention to religion since I left New York as a boy. Now I feel the need for the strength it gives. Does all this sound strange?

No, Brendan. I understand and approve of what you're saying. I'm happy you have asked me again. I've thought about it, too. So I'm going to say yes.

The kissed each other tenderly.

What happened in New York to bring this on? she asked after a moment.

Nothing so much this time as over a long period. There are things you don't know about me and my family that I should tell you.

Brendan reached back to his early life in New York, his family's poverty after his father's death, the prostitution of his mother and sister and the changes in their lives over the years. He told of his mother's efforts to have him marry as well as about the sessions with the three women at his mother's house, especially Marguerite. Then he related the details of the attack on the house on Greene Street and the emergence of Marguerite as his mother's chief assistant.

Finally, he told Chloe that his mother, and very possibly Marguerite, would probably come to stay in their spare apartment for an extended period sometime in the next few months.

When they come, even though you may not wish to have the ceremony by then, I want to be able to tell them both that we are finally and irretrievably pledged to each other. To be honest with you, my mother may not like this, but this is our decision to make, not her's. I hope by telling you all of this I have not given you cause to change your mind.

I won't change my mind, Brendan. If your mother's influence and the constant presence of a lovely woman, who, I sense from what you haven't told me, is in love with you, doesn't change your's, we can be married. But after they leave.

Fair enough. It's a deal.

* * *

David Ferriss spoke for all of Brendan's customers when he anticipated the end of Perry's Senate term in Washington.

I can't wait to see what that son of a bitch has been up to during the past year. He's been unnaturally quiet when he's around here.

Perry was unnaturally quiet in Washington, too, during the third session of the 27th Congress, which was his last. From December 20, 1842 to March 4, when it adjourned, Perry only took the floor eleven times and made no major speech. This is in contrast to the previous session when he had the floor twenty-seven times and delivered at least three major speeches.

When Nat finally passed along the copies of the *Globe*, Daniel Minor summed up Perry's performance.

I think the poor bastard just ran out of steam when he realized he wouldn't be a big shot any more.

On January 16 Perry spoke at some length in a discourse the scribe termed "a speech of much research." But it was a comparison of the distinct structures of the English and American governments. He theorized that the independence of judges in Britain was a counterpoise to the sovereign power, while in the United States, the judiciary was independent of the legislative and executive powers. Although he attempted to relate all this theory to a proposed amendment to the Constitution concerning the terms of judges, it sunk almost without a ripple. Perry was already out of touch.

There was also a brouhaha in January when Senator Thomas Hart Benton of Missouri claimed that the official record had misrepresented his remarks at a secret session on the proposed Webster-Ashburton Treaty and its handling of the disputed boundary between Canada and the United States. He said the error had been compounded when another Senator had made a policy decision based on it. Perry said on the record that he recalled hearing "here are the bloody red lines" when looking at a map with the proposed change. He said he remembered the words because they made such a strong impression on him. Obviously this recollection was not helpful in straightening out the record.

It would have been better if the poor sap had kept his mouth shut, said Harmon Buckingham. It sounds like he wasn't paying very close attention.

On February 17, Perry wanted to speak again about General Jackson's fine, but he was persuaded to yield. Then the Senate adjourned for the day before he could speak.

On February 28, Perry had his last chance to speak on the Louisville and Portland Canal, which always seemed to intrigue him. But not to vote, because the decision on Ohio River navigation and the onerous tax imposed by canal authorities was put off until the Secretary of War could render a report on the matter to the next session of Congress.

On February 24 Perry defended a pension bill for the widow of a Revolutionary War veteran. There was conflicting evidence if the soldier had deserted or not. Senator King of Alabama created an uproar later when he said he was vexed "with old women who were married over and over again to a succession of Revolutionary veterans. The women never did any service, nor did their husbands and now they all want pensions."

A great burst of laughter rung out in the McCauley Tavern when Brendan read these lines aloud.

I'm glad there's one Senator down there who can still see straight, said David Brownson. What did Perry say when his committee ran into a dose of reality?

Perry stood up for his relief bill. He said "the females of that day were more or less compelled to make sacrifices and that they rendered material assistance."

More laughter.

Perry once more objected to the existing bankruptcy act on February 24. He repeated that amendments retaining the ex post facto provisions of the law would be unconstitutional. He objected that the law favored the debtor to the disadvantage of the creditor.

Every time old Perry deals with that law, all he can visualize is himself as the creditor and some poor failed farmer from around here as the debtor. So the Constitution becomes holy writ for him in these cases.

Gilbert Crosby spoke with disgust and spat juice in one of the spitoons.

Perry finally got to speak on General Jackson's fine when he presented several resolutions passed by the Connecticut legislature. One of these called for passage of the refund to the General.

After the Judiciary Committe was not as forthcoming in reimbursing General Jackson as the Democrats wished, the Democrats backed a resolution to print ten thousand copies of the Whig majority report and twenty thousand of the Democratic minority report.

Perry defended the resolution, saying the expenditure was for the information of the people. "It is necessary to spread before the people, in an authentic form, the reports. They will be able to give expression to their opinions and to make it known to their representatives whether they approve of General Jackson's conduct at New Orleans or not. Having given the people this information, and ascertained their will, the representatives should obey their injunction."

Perry spoke for the last time on the General's refund on February 20. The clerk noted he "proceeded at considerable length," but the clerk himself quoted only a couple of paragraphs which he described as having "great force of argument." In essence, Perry said General Jackson, in imposing martial law was simply responding to natural rights of self defense.

The Whigs finally decided that it was useless to try to obliterate the hold that Old Hickory had on American imagination and affections and withdrew their objections to the bill restoring the fine, both the principal and the interest. The bill passed in the House on January 8, the anniversary of the battle, and in the Senate on February 10. After the flow of millions of words, Jackson received $2,732.90. The old hero subsequently thanked all the legislators who had supported the restitution of the fine. He singled out a few senators for special thanks, but Perry was not among them.

The Senate adjourned in some confusion at 2 p.m. on March 4 after having barred the door to the official recorders. Thus ended Perry Smith's Senate career and also his political career. When the 28th Congress convened, Huntington and John M. Niles would represent Connecticut in the Senate.

I hope the next man we send down there from New Milford will have more sense than Perry, Dan Minor commented.

We may have to wait a few years, Brendan said. It's beginning to look more and more as if the cities in Connecticut are going to call the shots on who goes, not the small towns like New Milford.

* * *

In March, Brendan received a letter from his mother saying

she and Marguerite would arrive for a stay of two weeks early in April. Brendan showed the letter to Chloe.

We'll have to buy some furniture for the apartment, since I promised them they could stay there with us.

We can afford it. We should furnish it anyhow. There's no sense in letting a good location like that stand idle. We can rent it to someone later on. You can earn more with it furnished.

Brendan inwardly admired Chloe's good judgment. He silently resolved to be faithful to her in what he knew would be a difficult time just ahead.

On April 11 Brendan and Chloe met the afternoon train from New York.

There they are, Brendan said. Come on.

He pointed to two women descending from one of the rear coaches. The conductor helped the two women down the steps. Brendan hugged his mother tightly, then kissed Marguerite on the cheek. He introduced Chloe to Marguerite; the three women shook hands. Brendan tried to keep things bright.

At least we don't need a cab here. All we have to do is cross the street and walk a few feet.

His mother saw the sign on the tavern and clapped her hands.

Brendan, what a beautiful building! It's so satisfying to see the name McCauley right up there in bright letters.

It's nothing compared with your house on Greene Street. Have you been able to get it completely repaired?

Yes. Marguerite made the arrangements with the the contractors. She did a good job and it once again looks lovely. Marguerite did all the purchasing to replace the furniture and other articles which were lost. You heard about it, my dear?

She addressed the question to Chloe, who responded:

Yes, Brendan told me. I was very sorry to hear of your loss. It must have been a great shock to have such a thing happen.

Brendan asked the obliging John Riley to help him carry the women's bags across the street to the tavern and on up to the third floor. Brendan opened the door so the women could enter the newly furnished apartment.

It's not magnificent like Greene Street, but I hope you will be comfortable here. There is some fruit on the table and a few things in the icebox, but you will probably want to take your meals downstairs. If you need anything, just speak to Chloe or myself.

Oh, what beautiful flowers! Marguerite exclaimed.

They're from our garden in back, Chloe said.

Chloe has planted a garden so we can have fresh vegetables for the dining room, Brendan said, but she also put in some daffodil bulbs last fall and they have done very well. Now we'll leave you alone to rest and wash off the grime from the railroad. We will return in half an hour, if that is all right.

Chloe and Brendan went across the hall to their own apartment. Chloe couldn't wait to speak.

Marguerite is certainly a beautiful woman. She seems very nice, too. You sure you don't want to change your mind?

You're my beauty. I only need one and you're it.

When I look at her all I can think of is you making love to her.

That's not fair. It was before we were together. How do you think my mother looks? It's a long time since you've seen her, but I can tell you she's bounced back from when I saw her the day after the riot. She showed her age that day, but she seemed spry today.

She seems healthy enough, Chloe responded.

In the succeeding days, Brendan contrived to keep Chloe at his side whenever he was with Catherine or Marguerite. The conversations were cordial but hardly intimate. When Brendan took the two guests sightseeing, Chloe went along too. All four took the train to Bull's Bridge to see the covered bridge, the gorge carved by thousands of years of Housatonic waters, and to walk on the island where the trilliums, both white and deep red, were shyly blooming along with purple lady slippers. Another day they took the train to Cornwall Bridge and Kent Falls, where they picnicked. Brendan brought along six bottles of champagne, which he had specially ordered beforehand, to the falls, so the picnic was notably convivial.

Finally one day Catherine caught Brendan when Chloe was in the kitchen.

Brendan, I want to talk to you alone. Where can we go?

Let's walk up to the green.

The two walked up Bank Street to the green, found an empty bench near the horse trough, and sat down among the budding elms.

Catherine came right to the point.

Are you really going to marry that black woman?

Yes,Mother. We love each other. We have lived together now for more than four years and we get along very well. All apart from the personal attraction, she is invaluable in the tavern. You know she is a good cook, but you have no way of knowing what a good manager she is. She has good sense and works hard. I hope she can give give me a son or a daughter.

If she hasn't done it in four years, the chances wouldn't seem too bright.

Perhaps. We're still hoping.

You must know that Marguerite is deeply in love with you. She would make you a wonderful wife. How can you turn down a girl like that, truly beautiful and well educated?

I like Marguerite very much and all you say about her is true. But she is a lot younger than I and a city girl. I don't think she could stand to live out here in the country, which I'm sure she would find very dull before long. The real reason, though, is I don't love her. Chloe and I have forged a life together and we love each other very much. The fact that she is black doesn't make one whit of difference to me.

Well, it does to me. I can't bear the thought of our Irish blood mixing with that African's. Think what your children will look like and what they will have to put up with in a white society.

I have, or we have. We don't think that's as important as living in an atmosphere of love. I should think when you see the sterile life that poor Agnes leads, you would value such a richness.

I don't know what it is about this Connecticut air. My brother marries an imbecile and you a blackamoor. It makes me woe the day we left Ireland.

Brendan said nothing.

That afternoon Catherine and Marguerite took the train to New York. Catherine was cool at the parting; Marguerite fluttered unhappily, and bid farewell to Brendan sadly. Chloe was impassive.

Brendan and Chloe walked back to the tavern, hand in hand. As they climbed the stairs to the apartment, they were very close.

Now we will get married as soon as we can, Brendan said.

Chloe kissed him fervently as soon as the door was closed.